Laura

Sarra Manning

Fashionistas

Laura

Hodder
Children's
Books

A DIVISION OF HACHETTE CHILDREN'S BOOKS

YA

Text copyright © 2007 Sarra Manning

First published in Great Britain in 2007
by Hodder Children's Books

4

A Catalogue record for this book is available from the British Library

ISBN-13: 978 0 340 93220 9

Typeset in Bembo by Avon DataSet Ltd, Bidford on Avon, Warwickshire

Printed and bound in China by Imago

The paper and board used in this paperback by Hodder Children's Books are natural recyclable products made from wood grown in sustainable forests. The manufacturing processes conform to the environmental regulations of the country of origin.

Hodder Children's Books
a division of Hachette Children's Books
338 Euston Road, London NW1 3BH
An Hachette Livre UK company

Acknowledgements

I would like to give the most extra special thanks to Jill Wanless, super-stylist and all around generally ace person. Not just for her impeccable fashion tips but for giving me so much practical help, information and secrets of the trade while I was writing this book.

Thanks also to Emily Thomas, Andrew Sharp and all at Hachette Children's Books. And my unflappable agent, Kate Jones, Laura Sampson and Karolina Sutton at ICM Books.

Finally, undying gratitude to Marc Jacobs and Miuccia Prada for inspiring me and ensuring that I'm always beautifully accessorised.

http://sarramanning.blogspot.com

BOOK ONE:
Laura

'You've got a beautiful face, it will take you places . . .'
– Dress Up In You by Belle And Sebastian

Prologue

The studio lights were hotter than a heatwave in the Sahara Desert. Despite the fine dusting of face powder, Laura was sure that she was starting to sweat. Beside her, she could feel Nemi shaking. Her hand squeezed Laura's tightly, even though last week she'd been caught on camera calling her 'a fat cow'. Nemi didn't deserve to win. Nemi wasn't going to win. She had bulgy eyes, weird thread veins on her legs and, worst of all, she was a shrieking drama queen who thought that Europe was a country 'somewhere near France, innit?'

Laura tried to concentrate as Daisy Bloom, ex-supermodel, now shiny-haired TV presenter, went into her final spiel of the night. 'The judges have deliberated, the public have voted, and soon I'll reveal the winner of *Make Me A Model 2007*. But first let me remind you of the prizes the lucky girl will receive: a contract with international model agency Fierce Management, a cover shoot with *Skirt* magazine shot by renowned photographer Gerry Valandry, and an exclusive contract with Sparkle Cosmetics worth £100,000 . . .' blah blah, for the love of God, blah blah . . .

It was too bright to see the audience as anything other

than a vague blur of faces, but Laura knew her mum and dad would be in their usual places at the left end of the third row, Tom sitting behind them. His face would be a conflicting mess of emotions, from embarrassment that he was live on ITV, to pride that he had such a gorgeous girlfriend. Aw, poor conflicted baby.

Time had become just a relative concept. Laura was standing right on the edge of her new life and it was starting to feel a lot like being trapped in purgatory, eternally condemned to wish that Daisy would just quit amping up the tension even though the studio manager was holding up a card which read: 'SPIN IT OUT FOR ANOTHER 30 SECS'. Also, she really needed to pee and the tape which was holding her dress together was itchy.

'Good luck,' Laura whispered to Nemi, who squeezed her hand even tighter. What she really meant was, 'Good luck when you find yourself asking your customers if they'd like to supersize their fries, beeyatch.'

'So I have two beautiful girls standing in front of me,' Daisy husked, gliding towards the two girls. Laura's face was shifting into a frozen grin, her lips sliding over dry teeth because all her saliva supplies had been directed down toward her bladder. *Stop thinking about peeing*, she told herself sternly.

Daisy paused yet again for dramatic emphasis. It was verging on excruciating. 'But I only have one photograph in my hand. One of these girls is undeniably beautiful but that's only one small part of being a model. We want to see if the beauty is on the inside too. Week after week, we've watched Nemi rock the cameras but we've seen an ugly side to you at the judging panel. The public love your look, Nemi, but is it enough?'

Nemi seemed to think it was, because she was crying on cue like she did every week. A single crystalline tear gently rolled down her caramel-smooth cheek, telegenically, but not enough to smudge her make-up.

'But the public also love you, Laura. You haven't had a single bad shot in this competition but we also got to see your beauty of spirit, your quirky sense of humour, and even when you fell over during the final runway test, you made it work to your advantage. But is your spark enough in the cut-throat world of modelling or will it just burn out too quickly?'

Laura was tempted to scream at the top of her lungs, 'Just announce the fricking winner!' But common sense prevailed at the last moment. It was taking all her last vestiges of strength to make her eyes Bambi-big so she wouldn't start crying. God, she wanted this more than anything. She wanted it so much that she could taste it – and it tasted exactly like the world's biggest chocolate fudge sundae with extra sprinkles.

Daisy stood there for another five seconds. She'd told Laura off-camera that she counted in her head 'One elephant, two elephant, three elephant . . .' so she got the timing exactly right. Finally, she drew herself up to her full five feet eleven inches and tossed back the platinum-blonde curls, which netted her one million pounds a year in shampoo commercials. Then she drew the photograph out from behind her back.

Laura squinted at it. For one deliciously dreadful moment she thought it was Nemi. She shut her eyes and opened them again. Had it been Nemi? It didn't look like Nemi. It looked like her in that last ridiculous shoot, where they'd had to dress up as sea creatures. Laura had been a dolphin. That grey satin dress really had done her no favours and as for—

'Congratulations, Laura, we're going to make you a model,' Daisy was saying, but her words were drowned out by Nemi noisily bursting into tears.

Chapter One

When Laura thought about it, the moment that she'd been spotted in the Trafford Centre by a *Make Me A Model* scout had simply been inevitable. And all the moments after that had been too. Without them, she wouldn't be where she was now: wedged into the back seat of her dad's Mondeo along with half her worldly possessions as he pulled up in front of a row of terraced houses in Camden, north London.

Because, secretly, Laura had always set her heart on becoming a model. She'd kept tight-lipped about it, because the minute you started telling people that you were considering modelling as a viable lifestyle choice, you might just as well have a T-shirt printed up that said: *Oh my God, I think I'm so beautiful.*

So it was just one of those little dreams that she'd entertained herself with during particularly boring study breaks or thought about with a tiny smirk while her careers teacher was banging on about UCAS forms and vocational training. OK, she might have whiled away many an afternoon in TopShop hoping that she'd get spotted by a model scout, but it wasn't like she'd ever asked her dad to take a picture of her preening in a bikini and sent it off to a modelling agency. That would have just been sad.

Laura smoothed out the crumpled letter from Fierce Management, though she'd already memorized the contents.

Dear Laura

Welcome to Fierce Model Management and your exciting career as one of our new models.

You'll be pleased to know that we have arranged accommodation for you in one of our 'model' flats. You'll be living with three other girls, all new to London, so you can help each other settle in.

Your new home is Flat 3, 47 Bayham Street, Camden, London NW1. Enclosed are your door keys and an inventory. Please check and sign this and hand it in to your booker when you come into the agency at ten a.m. on Tuesday morning.

The rent on this property is £750 per calendar month, which we will deduct from your earnings.

Contractually you are obligated to live in the accommodation provided until your 18th birthday. Alternative living arrangements will only be made on receipt of signed parental consent.

Please remember that as well as being your agency, we here at Fierce Management are also your friends.

We look forward to a long and successful friendship with you.

Best wishes
Fierce Model Management

She hadn't just dreamed it. It was real. She was a model. The letter proved it.

Inside Flat 3, 47 Bayham Street, everything was beige and white. It was where neutral shades went to die. There was a series of fleeting impressions that didn't quite make up a complete living space. A tiny entrance hall that led into a living room – big picture windows, a squashy leather sofa that made a farting noise when her dad sat on it – a tiny bathroom, a tinier kitchen and four closed doors that felt as if they should have *Do Not Enter* signs pinned on them.

If there was one teeny seed of doubt blossoming it was the unknown quantity of three other models. But had they beaten six thousand other girls to win a nationwide model search? Nuh-huh! And when it came to dealing with non-supporto girls who had their jealous on, Laura was a world champion. Besides, she was first through the door and that gave her certain rights. So while her father was dispatched to unload the car and her mum was packing a mountain of Tupperware into the fridge, she gingerly started pushing open doors.

Two of the rooms were fairly large but they looked out on to the street, complete with the sound of honking traffic and the 'beep beep' of a zebra crossing. The third room was right next to the loo so, by process of elimination, Laura picked the smallest room (it might actually have been a broom closet in another life) because it had a really big cupboard and scenic views of an overgrown wilderness of a garden.

'Oh, Laura, there isn't room to swing Colonel Meowington in here.'

Her mum was standing in the doorway with her Marigolds and second-best apron on. She'd brought along a bag of cleaning products and, by God, she was going to use them.

'This is OK,' Laura insisted, sitting on the edge of the bed and bouncing heartily. 'OK as in it would make a really good cupboard, but the view's pretty and it's quiet. I'll probably get my own place once I've got a few ad campaigns sorted out.'

'Hmmm, well, let's not get carried away,' her mother said, pulling off her gloves, all the better that she could sit down next to Laura and rub soothing circles on her back. Even though she didn't need soothing in anyway. Except . . .

'You could be a bit more positive, Mum,' Laura sighed, the note of reproach done to perfection because she must have said this once a day, every day, since she'd won *Make Me A Model*. 'I know that you didn't think I'd be leaving home at seventeen, but I'm going to be a model. I *am* a model! It's just a little bit exciting.'

Her mother didn't say anything right away. *Probably still*

stuck on the 'but what about your A levels?' meltdown, Laura thought wryly. 'Well, it's a wonderful opportunity,' her mum said finally. 'You'll do six months or so, make some money and then go to university with your tuition fees already paid.'

'So, does that make the glass half empty or half full?' Laura asked her with a grin. University didn't figure too highly in her plans to be living in New York with several multi-million-dollar contracts under her Gucci belt by the time she was nineteen, but now probably wasn't the time to get into that.

'It's half something,' she laughed and squeezed her tight enough for rib breakage. But just when Laura thought she was going to have to get medieval on the old maternal apron strings, her mother's frown turned upside down pretty sharpish as she cast a longing look at the mound of boxes and cases waiting to be unpacked. 'I'll just help you get straightened before your father starts moaning about rush-hour traffic.'

The goodbye was painful but mercifully brief.

'Don't forget to switch things off before you go out,' her mother fretted for the umpteenth time, while she was hustled into the car. 'I'll phone every night and you're to call us any time. And remember that you need to get a travelcard. I printed out the instructions and I left them in the folder in your blue bag and—'

'Goodbye, dear,' her father called, already turning the key in the ignition. 'Don't drink too much and don't go all uppity on us.'

They drove off; her mother's hand fluttering frantically out of the window until it nearly got yanked from her arm by a passing cyclist.

Reluctantly, Laura trailed back inside. The unknown horror of her three mysterious flatmates was starting to matter terribly. Hopefully they'd be more scared than her. Not that she *was* scared, because she was a fully paid-up member of the beautiful people club now, and she could show them the ropes. After twelve weeks of *Make Me A Model*, she was practically a veteran of the biz.

Her mother had filled the fridge with wall-to-wall Tupperware containers and left a list of instructions on how to heat stuff up in the microwave, because Laura didn't do cooking. Besides, she'd hate to lose her only child to salmonella. Laura munched on a flapjack and waited for the kettle to boil, then froze as she heard the sound of . . . well, it was possible that a herd of buffalo were thundering up the stairs.

'Hello! Anyone home?'

Laura knew that voice. She didn't know why but something about that transatlantic drawl was strangely familiar.

Laura took a deep breath and poked her head round the kitchen door.

'Hi, I'm . . . Oh, shit, you're Candy Careless!'

It totally was. Standing in her living room, brushing back her preternaturally black hair so Laura could see those piercing blue eyes and alabaster skin in the flesh rather than on the TV.

'You're the girl from that modelling comp.' Candy peered at a piece of paper she was clutching in a hand that was weighed down with brightly coloured plastic rings. 'Laura Parker? You're taller than you looked on the show.'

'But . . . what . . . I mean . . .' Candy waited patiently for Laura to spit out words in some semblance of order. 'But you're not a model, right?'

Candy struck a pose; one hand resting on her hip, her index finger touching her chin while she pouted. It was way bizarre, like she was performing for an audience of one: Laura. 'Yes, I know I'm too short for runway and shooting with other models and, like, I'm two inches away from being a certified dwarf, but hey that doesn't matter in the world of celebrity endorsements.'

'O . . . kaaaaayyyyyyy,' Laura mumbled, trying to resist the urge to hunch over because it was entirely possible that she was two inches away from being a certified giant. Candy was exactly like she was on television: one hundred decibels of loud – and tiny with it, but in a way that suggested that the rest of the world was just too damn big and it really wasn't her problem. With her knees bent slightly to compensate for the height difference, Laura tried desperately to think of something else to say.

'It's weird that we were both on reality shows,' was all she managed to come up with.

Candy's head whipped around so quickly it had to hurt, or maybe it was just the warm-up to a full-on 360° *Exorcist* spin. '*The Careless* isn't a reality show,' she snapped. 'It's a genre-defining, *reality-based* dramedy. I'm going to pick my room.'

Candy Careless. Known as Fearless in the papers after her family revived their flagging fortunes by starring in their own reality show. (Laura didn't care what Candy said, it *was* a reality show.) *The Careless* introduced the world to her father, David, and her mother, Bette, the patron saints of grunge and emo and just about every other musical genre of the last twenty years. Apart from maybe R 'n' B and crunk. Their band, The Careless, had come out of the New York art scene in the mid-eighties and influenced everyone from Nirvana to Deathcab, but they'd never made any money until they scored primetime glory with their decidedly wiggy antics in a small Manhattan apartment. Candy's dad was a monosyllabic stoner, her mom an elegant, edgy neurotic, and the formidable Conceptua, their housekeeper-cum-nanny-cum-business manager, held the ensemble together. But it was Candy who had stolen the show. Candy, with her spectacular shopping sprees, caustic wit and screaming rows with her

14

mother – all televised for optimum viewing pleasure – and the source of the oft-quoted line, 'My life, my business, my arse, Moth-er', after she got a tattoo of a tiger on her butt for her sixteenth birthday.

Laura sighed heavily as she heard Candy shriek something about 'this poky shithole of a flat', but was saved from having to do anything about it (like maybe knock down a few of the internal walls) by the arrival of Candy's matching set of skull-and-crossbones-adorned luggage.

Candy was so busy haranguing the hapless delivery men about a missing suitcase that she didn't notice the dark, lanky girl clutching two stuffed-full laundry bags slink in. Like a cat. A big, jungle cat with a predatory smile on her face. She raised a mocking eyebrow in Laura's direction and disappeared in the direction of the biggest room.

'Hey . . .' Laura tried to say, but no one was listening until approximately five seconds later when Candy ordered the delivery men to start moving the stuff into her room of choice.

Laura closed her hands over her ears as the inevitable 'Who the hell are you?' reverberated round the flat. It was possible that one of her eardrums had permanently perforated.

There was a muffled reply.

'But that's my room! I'd already said I was going to have that room.'

'Tough sheet.' The cat-girl followed Candy back into the lounge, folded her arms and gave Laura the mother of all dirty looks. 'You know thees girl, huh?' she enquired in a thick Eastern European accent.

There was a beautiful moment of sweet silence before Candy exploded into one of her trademark hissy fits. It was better than a *Supernatural* double bill. 'Oh. My. God,' she gritted out. 'Why am I surrounded by utter assholes? Why did no one pre-select my room? What kind of shyster agency is this? We had better sort this out right the hell now, or I'm gonna sic my manager on you – and she makes me look like a little fluffy bunny.'

It was impressive. Candy didn't pause for breath once. She finished by grabbing her smallest case and throwing it across the room, where it sent a black-and-white photograph of a snogging couple flying off their picture hook. *Our security deposit is dust*, Laura thought as the delivery men exchanged looks that said very clearly: 'Christ, we've got a live one here'.

In the three minutes it took Candy's minions to make their excuses and scramble out of the door, Laura escaped to the relative safety of the kitchen to make a recuperative cup of tea.

'Meelk, three sugars,' said a voice behind her and Laura looked up from the flapjack box to see the cat-girl leaning against the fridge.

Don't bother saying please, she thought, but got another

mug down. Tomorrow she'd establish some ground rules. 'I'm Laura.'

'Irina,' she grunted.

'So, are you from Russia or something?'

There was a diffident shrug. 'Whatever.'

Oh, whatever yourself.

Then Laura looked at her properly, *really* looked at her, and all the air was sucked from the room. For all her theatrics, Candy had nothing on this girl for sheer presence. Irina was the most freaky person Laura had ever seen in real life. But she was more than freaky, there was something shockingly surreal about her features; slanting eyes that were an extraordinary shade of almost silver-grey, slanting cheekbones and a slanting gash of a mouth that drooped downwards as if it was too much effort for her to hold it upright. Her skin was definitely at the sallow end of the colour spectrum and covered with big, blotchy freckles. And even though her hair was scraped back in a Croydon facelift, it just made the angles of her face stand out in stark relief. She looked as if she'd crash-landed from a far-away solar system. And it didn't even matter that she was wearing a dingy lilac shell suit or that she was staring down Laura's gobsmacked expression, she was still managing to work it like no one had ever worked it before. But she wasn't, like, *pretty*.

There wasn't a single thing Laura could think of to say

so she just dunked tea bags and added milk and sugar on autopilot. She didn't know why Irina was smirking so hard when she was wearing the most fashion-backwards outfit ever.

Laura pushed the mug in her direction and held out the box of flapjacks. 'Want one?'

Irina slunk forward and grabbed three (*three!*) squares of yummy, oaty, calorific goodness. 'Spasibo,' she mumbled through a mouthful of flapjack. 'Fucking starving.'

'Is that tea? God, you're so British,' Candy announced, pushing her way past Irina with a shudder. 'Be an angel and make me a cup?'

Laura sighed as she took down another mug. *Way to go, Laura. You can be the homely girl who endears herself by her willingness to make hot beverages for her flatmates.*

'What's your name?' Candy asked Irina belligerently, who gave another indifferent shrug and carried on shoving flapjack into her mouth.

'Irina, Candy. Candy, Irina,' Laura said, by way of an introduction. 'Candy is—'

'You on TV,' Irina supplied and then gestured at Laura. 'You too. Weird.'

And with that pithy remark she sauntered out, leaving Candy and Laura staring at each other in disbelief.

'She thinks *we're* weird?' Candy echoed in disbelief.

'Well, I guess we do seem a bit *Celebrity Big Brother*. Not like I'm that famous or anything but I've been on telly . . .'

Laura trailed off because she really didn't want to get told off any more about genre-breaking, reality-based whatevers.

Candy grinned. She didn't do that very often but it suited her; made her less scary. 'You were good on that model show. I mean you held your own because some of those other girls were bitches on wheels. Me and my mom kept playing back that thing you said to that stupid Noel dude.' Candy struck a pose, which was meant to be Laura standing with her arms folded looking royally unamused. 'You're a very rude man and I get that you have to critique us but . . .'

'. . . I don't understand why you have to completely destroy our self-esteem to do it. It doesn't serve any purpose, it just makes you look like a twat.' Laura knew the speech off by heart. It had appeared in enough papers. She'd even had complete strangers (well, usually gay guys) approach her on the street and shriek it in her face.

'Well, he *was* rude,' Laura muttered fiercely. 'And I'd just had to stand there, week after week, and take it. And I knew that my shoots were good but he just kept going on about how being pretty wasn't enough.'

'Well, it didn't do you any harm and I speak as someone whose temper tantrums have got me where I am today.' Candy shuddered dramatically as they walked back into the lounge. 'Figuratively speaking.'

Laura took a moment to ponder on the fact that she was bonding with Candy Careless. Maybe they'd become best friends and Candy would invite Laura round to the Careless rent-controlled apartment in the West Village so she could be filmed. Candy's dad would bang on incoherently about their dogs crapping all over the rugs. And she'd go to hip nightclubs with Candy and her occasionally glimpsed step-brother and—'

'Anyway I'd better get on with my unpacking. God, I wish Conceptua was here.' And with that, her new best friend disappeared in the direction of the second-largest room and didn't ask Laura to come with.

There was absolutely no way that Irina was going to be her new best friend so Laura went back to skulking in her room.

In the *Make Me A Model* house there was always someone to talk to. Besides, the producers would plan these special events, like having beauticians on call, so they had something to film instead of twelve girls sitting about and staring at their split ends.

After she'd finished staring at her own split ends, Laura got to work on her pinboard, which she'd made her dad nail to the wall before he left.

With careful precision, she made a display of the pictures that she'd taken at her going-away party. There was the photo of her standing with Jen, Chandra and Cath, the three of them mugging for the camera, while she posed with her chin slightly tilted down. Colonel Meowington got his own special patch, including the picture of him yawning, all whiskers and teeth. And Tom got a whole corner. There was the strip of photo-booth pictures from their day out in Blackpool. And the picture of them at his eighteenth birthday party, just after she'd won *Make Me A Model*. There were even a few action shots of him playing football, which was so she could admire his tackling prowess long distance and had absolutely nothing to do with how cute he was in his shorts.

The only regret Laura had about imminent supermodel-dom was that Tom couldn't come too. She'd had this carefully planned-out scheme that once he'd finished his A levels he could go to university in London so they could be together. But Tom had his heart set on Oxbridge and all her wheedling and pouting and even tears wouldn't change his mind.

'It doesn't work on me, Laura,' he'd sighed the night before, as he helped her pack and she'd had one last chance to bash down his defences. 'I'm immune to the trembling bottom lip. It's Oxbridge or bust. End of.'

He really was, too. Immune. Most times, his unswerving ability to not go wibbly in her presence, like the rest of boykind, was refreshing. But right then, it had been infuriating. Especially as they'd just spent an hour rolling about on her bedroom floor and banging stray limbs against half-packed suitcases. Her kisses usually made him promise all sorts of things that he'd try to retract when his blood flow went north again.

'Wish you weren't leaving,' Tom had breathed, when they'd eventually had to come up for air. He'd stroked the hair back from Laura's face. 'What am I going to do without you?'

'As long as it doesn't involve even looking at another girl, I'm sure you'll come up with something.' Laura had sat up and poked the edge of one of the cases with her foot. 'Y'know, it's so weird to have a dream and then it becomes real. It shouldn't be this easy. I mean, OK, I had to spend twelve weeks with those stupid cows in the *Make Me A Model* house and listen to them go on about how ginormous their pores were and, "Oh my God, I came into contact with a bar of chocolate" and "Actually in a certain light, you're really ugly, Laura".' Coming to the end of the longest sentence in the world she scowled because Tom was laughing at her. Again. He did that a lot. It was part of his charm, along with his big brown eyes and floppy dark hair, which she really wished that he hadn't chopped into a buzz cut. But Tom sang his own tune, even if it was five seconds behind the beat of hers.

So Laura had contented herself with wrinkling her nose, so the freckles shifted and rearranged themselves. 'Don't keep sniggering at me, laughing boy. It gives me frown lines – and I didn't win *Make Me A Model* because of my attractive wrinkles.'

'Well, having an extremely articulate temper tantrum on primetime TV may have helped just a smidge,' Tom had conceded with a shrug, laying back down on the rug and wincing as he'd caught his elbow on a vanity case. 'Beauty *and* brains. Guess it's a fatal combo, Miss Parker.'

'That's not why I won! Jeez, why does everyone keep saying that?' Laura had protested, and much as she loved having arguments about absolutely nothing with her gorgeous dark-eyed boy, she'd known that they were just delaying the inevitable. 'I'm never going to get this packing finished if you keep draping yourself over my luggage in such a delightful manner.'

It had taken another hour to finish packing and then a further ten minutes to persuade Colonel Meowington to rouse himself from his toasty nest of woollies so they could shut the damn thing. But the final doorstep goodbye had been just as bittersweet and hideous as Laura had suspected.

She was so ready to go to London that all it needed was for someone to stick a fork in her and pronounce her done. But she'd started crying and Tom had had to slowly uncurl her fingers from their death grip around his neck.

'Easy, tiger,' he'd whispered, giving her cheek a final stroke, then before she could snatch him back into her arms, he'd hurried down the path and vaulted over the gate. 'We'll talk every night and don't cop off with any poncy male models,' he'd called over his shoulder. And then he'd become a shadow disappearing into the dark.

It was five forty-five, which technically counted as

night and Tom would be back from footie practice. Besides, it had been almost nineteen hours since their doorstep tryst and the withdrawal symptoms were starting to peak. Laura grabbed her phone. 'I hate it here,' she moaned pitifully, before he'd even had a chance to say hello. 'I'm going to die from sheer boredom and you'll never guess who—'

'Laura? Hey, can I call you back? I'm in the middle of a World Civ essay and I don't want to lose my train of thought. Love you!'

He obviously didn't love her if she came second to World Civ essays, Laura thought, and was just texting Tom to inform him of this new development when there was a banging noise on the door, followed by some excited yelping sounds.

Maybe they'd got a delivery of kittens.

There were no kittens in the lounge. But there was a tall, skinny blonde girl hugging Candy and squealing.

'Oh my God! I am so pysched to be here!' she announced in a breathy, little-girl voice, which was going to get very old very fast. 'Who'd a thunk it?'

Candy looked like she wouldn't have thunk it in a million years from the anguished expression on her face. 'Had . . . Great to see you too . . . Get off me, please!'

Long limbs slowly disentangled, like a modern sculpture slowly coming to life, and Laura found herself staring at a standard-issue, pretty blonde girl with the most vapid expression she'd ever seen in her life. Hey, and she'd shared a flat with eleven other wannabe models.

'Hi,' the blonde girl said shyly, and now the vapidness had upgraded to something that seemed more . . . *expectant*.

'I'm Laura.' A handshake seemed like the best way to go, even though the fingers that rested gingerly against hers were so fragile she was worried about crushing them if she applied too much pressure. 'So . . . um, you're a new model too?'

The hand was snatched away with a gasping noise. 'I'm not just a model,' she hissed. 'I'm, like, an actress and a singer and I do a lot of charity work too. I guess really I'm an all-round entertainer.'

'Hadley, sweetie, no one remembers who you are in Britain,' Candy sighed. Laura got the impression that sighing was going to play a large part in all her encounters with Hadley. 'I thought that was the whole point of you coming to London to relaunch your career.'

'Hey, my career does *so* not need relaunching.' Hadley whirled round so Candy could get the full benefit of her outraged face and the impeccably manicured finger she was holding up for emphasis. 'I just had to get away from LA because of, like, the constant press attention. Because, yeah, I had the highest-rated entertainment show three years in a row and, hello, I was the fifth biggest ranking draw at the box office in 1997 . . .'

'I'm going to put the kettle on,' Laura announced because Hadley's pitch was nearing hysterical. Then she looked at her properly, and underneath that fake tan – and could those lips have a little collagen in them? – there was something familiar about her, if only she'd had plump cheeks, pigtails and a lisp. 'Were you in *Hadley's House*? God, I loved that show when I was a kid.'

Candy threw up her arms. 'Don't encourage her!'

'I was. I'm Hadley!' Now it was Laura's turn to be pinned to a bony chest and enveloped in a cloud of Anna Sui's Sweet Dreams. 'It's so adorable that you're a fan.' Before Laura could insist that maybe 'fan' was too strong a word, she was being thrust away and held back by an unexpectedly strong grip on her shoulders. 'But y'know, Lauren—'

'It's Laura . . .'

'I'm a normal girl,' Hadley breathed. 'Just like you. Well, almost like you. And it's really important that where I live is, like, this comfort zone. I can't be in a negative space right now.'

'Well, I'll try not to,' Laura said carefully. 'Make the space negative, that is.'

Hadley hitched up her huge sunglasses, which were slipping down her nose. 'I'm meant to be incognito so please don't tell anyone I'm here. The paparazzi . . .' She tailed off meaningfully.

'But who would I tell?'

26

Candy patted Laura on the shoulder. 'She won't tell anyone, Had. Now why don't we get settled in? Hey, I was hanging out with Kimberly and Kelly before I left and they said . . .'

Laura decided that not following them would be the wisest thing she ever did, especially when she heard Hadley's anguished squawk, 'What do you mean, share a bathroom?'

Chapter Two

Today was the first official day of her modelling career. Laura stretched luxuriously and nearly fell out of the narrow bed, which gave an ominous creak as she sat up and tried to remember where she was. Had the room been this small yesterday? She'd skulked in here all evening, emerging only to make emergency trips to the loo and the kettle and the biscuit tin. She'd spoken to Tom, and reminded him what happened to boyfriends who hung up on their girlfriends in their hour of need, then let him apologize abjectly, before she'd decided to have an early night.

Ten hours of sleep – broken slightly when the people upstairs decided to shift heavy furniture around at three a.m. – was the secret of looking rested and beautiful. That's the impression she wanted to give her new booker anyway.

She climbed out of bed so she could stare at herself in the mirror. It was so cool that it didn't make Laura vain any more. Nah, she was just evaluating the raw material. And the raw material was looking good. There was always something comforting about looking at herself. Her features sat on her face, all working together and grooving along in perfect harmony. Her green eyes were sparkly, apart from the huge piece of sleep clinging to her lashes; her skin had recovered from one of its periodic break-outs. The *Make Me A Model* judges had wanted her to lose a little weight, but when it came to her appearance, Laura knew best. And her booker was just going to have to trust her on that one.

Time to shower and then wrestle her hair into sleek submission. Laura even allowed herself to whistle a jaunty tune as she headed for the bathroom. But it was not to be, because even before she tried the locked door, the shower was audibly powering away and someone was singing a Kelly Clarkson song at the top of their little lungs. By a process of elimination, it had to be Hadley; Irina and Candy didn't seem like they'd be big with the Kelly Clarkson love.

Laura wasted ten minutes sitting outside, before knocking gently on the door. Another ten minutes and she was trying to knock it off its hinges with the power of her fists. 'What are you doing in there?' she screamed.

The shower turned off and she breathed a sigh of relief. A very short-lived sigh of relief, as Hadley opened the door wrapped in a towel and covered in green gloop as far as the eye could see. 'I'm in the middle of exfoliating,' she clarified. 'And then I have to depilate and moisturize.' She closed the door firmly in Laura's furious face.

Washing herself over the kitchen sink was not how this very special day was meant to start. Laura had to alternate chugging down a cup of coffee with frenzied applications of a damp flannel. While still wearing pyjamas. The whole delicate balance of the operation was not helped by Irina sauntering in and calmly reaching past her to fill the kettle.

There was just time to pull on her new black trousers and a white lace camisole and grab her *A to Z*. By some miracle, she was only fifteen minutes late (and red-faced with exertion) when she eventually tracked down Fierce Management to a little alley in Soho.

There were barely seconds to spare to take a deep, centring breath and step into the lift. This wasn't scary. Not really. She could totally handle this. They were lucky to have her, not the other way round. If she hadn't won *Make Me A Model*, then sooner or later, probably sooner, she'd have been scouted by another agency. So why was she shaking as her hand reached for the door that had *Fierce Management* emblazoned on it in a pink, cursive script?

Fierce inhabited a big, white shiny space, which had to be the reason why God invented Cillit Bang. Every now and again a pink sofa broke up the vast minimalism. Far more intimidating though were the people. Apart from one deluded creature swanning about in a taffeta ballgown, they were all dressed down in this artfully thrown together way that was painfully familiar to Laura after twelve weeks of fashion shoots on *Make Me A Model*. Male, female or whatever, they were all wearing an androgynous uniform of skinny jeans, fadeds Ts with retro logos on them and low-key trainers. And every single one of them had a headset clamped on so they could bark into their mouthpieces.

'Ludmilla doesn't do swimwear any more. Not for that kind of money anyway . . .'

'Do you want Clara B or Clara D? Or Kara P?'

'Well, it's much edgier that his last collection. It's kind of urban, kind of fantasy. Kind of *Memoirs Of A Geisha* meets Arctic Monkeys, y'know?'

Awkwardly, Laura shoved her portfolio between her thighs so she could rummage in her bag for the email she'd printed out from someone called—

'I'm Heidi,' said a flat voice behind her.

Laura tried to turn round and her portfolio landed on the wood floor with a dull thwack. She made a frantic attempt to catch it, and succeeded in dropping her bag too so it upended itself at Heidi's feet.

Generally, scrabbling about on the floor after stray tampons and leaky biros was not the best way to make an impression. All Laura had seen of Heidi so far were her Japanese trainers impatiently tapping out a staccato rhythm. It didn't bode well.

Neither did the curdled-milk look on Heidi's face when she finally stood up and held out an ink-stained hand. 'Hey, I'm Laura.'

Heidi's smile was the merest stretching of her facial

muscles. 'I know.' She was one of the impossibly tiny girls that Laura had seen ironing clothes or assisting photographers or manning a press room. Like there was a fashion-girl assembly line in a factory in New York. She had poker-straight brown hair cut in this really complicated, flicky, mullety way, a bright-yellow vest and a pair of jeans that were so trashed-looking that they had to be from some really expensive boutique.

Laura's go-see outfit of black, hip-hugger trousers and lacy cami might have passed for fashionable in Manchester, but in London it was obviously not making that kind of statement. No, if it said anything it was: 'I take style advice from my mother,' especially if you were a too-cool-for-skool trendsetter.

Laura waited for Heidi to show her to a well-appointed room where they could sit and bond and plan out a global strategy and become BFF. Instead she gestured at one of the Calpol-pink sofas.

'The Tube is really weird,' she heard herself saying. 'Like, you think it's going to be pretty straightforward but then the lines go off on all these strange little tributaries and a destination comes up on the board and you don't have a clue—'

'Yeah, really weird,' Heidi echoed, like she didn't give even the smallest damn. 'Portfolio.'

She flicked through the pictures from each of Laura's *Make Me A Model* weekly shoots with a practised ease.

'Well, we can use maybe three of these pictures,' was her summing up.

While she was still reeling from that body blow, Laura realized she was being stared at with an unnerving intensity. 'Well, you have good skin, at least. And your eyes are great but you need to get your hair cut; it's dragging down your features. And you can't go out on appointments wearing those clothes.'

'But Daisy and Magnus – he was the Creative Director on *Make Me A Model* – said that we should wear something plain so we don't distract people from looking at us,' Laura pointed out with just a hint of huffiness. Had Heidi got her confused with some other girl, because she sure as hell wasn't treating her like Fierce's latest star signing? 'That we should be a blank canvas.'

A frown was just about registering on Heidi's face. 'It was a television show, Laura. Half the stuff they told you went out of date sometime around 1987. You want to get booked for fashion jobs, then you need to dress as if you actually like fashion.'

'I do. I mean, normally I wouldn't wear something like this.'

Heidi reached out to pat Laura's arm, then snatched her hand away in case she got infected with fashion backwardness. 'Look, there's no nice way to say this, so I'm just going to come right out with it,' Heidi announced, and while Laura's heart was plummeting towards the floor, she made good on her promise. 'You're at least twenty pounds overweight. I know it worked for you on the show, but in the real world you're not going to cut it.'

'Not twenty pounds,' Laura said feebly, looking down at her thighs, which seemed to have swelled up to elephantine proportions in about five seconds.

'Eighteen at least,' Heidi stated, nodding. 'Sample sizes are usually an eight, sometimes a six, and you know as well as I do, the camera puts on at least ten pounds. You seem to gain a lot of weight in your face, and I need cheekbones. I'm telling you this for your own good.'

It didn't sound like it was for her own good but more like Heidi got a sadistic kick out of it, if the way she kept running her hands over her own size-eight body was anything to go by.

'I'm big boned,' Laura said, trying to win her over with humour – and failing utterly as Heidi stared at her tummy as if it was the most odious thing she'd ever come across. It's not like she was fat; she was curvy. Slightly curvy. Ever so very slightly curvy.

'You're overweight,' she countered, getting up so she could glide across to a little workstation and pick up a sheaf of papers. 'Which doesn't mean you can start skipping meals. You need to drink at least two litres of water a day, try to cut out sugar and fill up on lots of veggies and fruit. Oh, and absolutely no carbs after six. Better yet, make it four. I'll arrange membership at a gym for you.

Concentrate on cardio because that burns fat and do free weights to tone up. Frequent, high-impact reps.'

Heidi was obviously fluent in dolphin. Laura couldn't follow a single word she was saying, but she knew what her agenda really was: bring the new girl down a peg or two so she'd know that Heidi was the boss of her. Which would work if Laura didn't have the kind of exposure that most new models could only dream about.

'So how many bookings have I got?'

'Nothing yet. Well, you have the cover shoot you won and the beauty campaign for Sparkle Cosmetics. I've booked them for the end of next week and I want you to lose at least five pounds before then.'

'Five pounds in ten days . . . ?'

'Eleven days. It'll be fine.'

This was even worse than the nightmare she'd had where she'd turned up for her first job wearing nothing but a pair of fairy wings.

'When Ludmilla first came to us she had three rotting teeth and a wonky hairline. Could be worse, Laura,' Heidi said in the most consoling manner she could muster, which actually not so much. Then she concentrated on scrolling down her BlackBerry to find a gym and a hairdresser that could silk-purse a sow's ear.

When Laura felt this crap, chocolate was the only thing that pulled her through. Not like that was an option any more. Maybe she'd be one of those people who got addicted to the exercise high. 'Right, so I s'pose I'd better hit the gym then,' she muttered, as Heidi gave her a Post-it note with a couple of numbers scrawled on it.

'That's the spirit,' she said with another barely there smile. 'We have an account here, just give them your name and your agency number and I'll have the fees deducted from your earnings.'

At this rate she was going to have to pull double shifts at Maccy D's to pay her rent. 'OK,' she said glumly.

'So, remember you want to go for high-impact cardio, and ask for Guiseppe at the hair place and tell him to ring me before he even picks up the scissors.' Heidi already had her bony knuckles pressed into the small of Laura's back as she guided her out of the door. 'I'll see you back here Friday week five pounds lighter, OK?' she chirped and before Laura could even say goodbye she was plugging in her ear bud and jabbering away in German. Pretentious cow.

Laura looked in the mirror as two stylists lifted up limp strands of her wet hair and peered at it curiously. Guiseppe, who had a goatee and didn't appear to speak or understand basic English, was talking to Heidi and brandishing a vicious-looking pair of scissors.

'I don't want to lose the length,' Laura bleated. 'Maybe to my shoulders?'

'We're going to give you some dark-blonde highlights to

pick up the sheen in your hair,' announced one of the juniors eventually, translating from Guiseppe's rapid-fire Italian. 'And we really want to give you a sixties crop. Edie Sedgwick is so now, and Heidi says you're going to lose weight . . .' She decided that tact was the way to go and didn't finish the sentence.

'That's the plan.' Laura tried to muster an optimistic smile and waited for the girl to insist vociferously that she didn't need to lose so much as a single gram.

'You know, my mum lost over two stone on Atkins. Carbs suck,' the girl stated emphatically. She might just as well have called Laura a fat freak to her face.

No wonder her newly chubby cheeks were stop-light red as Guiseppe sheared away. Huge hanks of hair floated down to the floor, to be immediately swept up as nothing unsightly was allowed to clutter up the salon.

Guiseppe had already swung her chair round so she couldn't look at the horrors being done in the mirror, so she sat there leafing through back issues of *W* and *Vogue* at Amazonian models with limbs like pipecleaners and cheekbones you could cut cheese on.

Laura had to sit there for another aeon with foils on her head, asphyxiating from the hair-dye fumes, which were supposed to be organic, but smelled like something that had been decomposing for several weeks. By the time Guiseppe was supervising as two acolytes wielded hairdryers like blowtorches, Laura was in a state of high anxiety. She couldn't see, but she could feel, and as she reached up to touch her hair there didn't seem to be much left of it.

'Ow!' Laura squealed as Guiseppe slapped her hand away.

'No poking,' he hissed in what sounded suspiciously like a Brummie accent. 'Your hair, eet belong to me right now.'

There was much fussing and tweaking before her chair was ceremonially turned round to face the mirror. Laura's eyes were tightly shut and her citrus tea was threatening to make a comeback.

Slowly she prised her right eyelid to the up position, then the left one. Her hair! Her hair was gone. Totally gone – and in its place was this beautiful sleek cap of brown and gold and hazel and silver and all colours in between, with a thick brushed fringe several miles above her eyebrows. It was a beautiful, edgy cut that sat on top of her head like she'd borrowed it for the day. Underneath, her face in all its hamster-cheeked glory looked like a beach ball. Laura took a deep breath and burst into tears.

Chapter Three

They'd shuffled her out of the door so fast that her feet barely made contact with the floor. Sobbing, chunky-cheeked teenagers didn't really send out the right message. Laura had still been crying as she got on the bus back to Camden, much to the horror of the woman sitting in front of her, who'd moved several seats along.

At least she'd lost the flatmate fear. Laura didn't even pause to wonder if they were in. She slammed the front door so hard that the whole flat shook, burst into the bathroom, and physically hauled Hadley away from the mirror and into the hall so she could lock herself in and collapse in a tear-soaked heap on the lino.

'She's mad!' Hadley screamed, her volume knob all the way up to eleven. 'I was really specific about not sharing with mad people when I signed with the agency.'

It took some effort but Laura managed to haul herself to her knees and crawl over to the bath so she could turn on the taps and wet her hair. It's the law that when you have a bad haircut you have to make it a gazillion times worse by shoving your hair under running water. Sometimes she could be so predictable.

Over the gushing torrent and her own hiccupy sobs Laura could hear someone banging on the door.

'Go away!' she shrieked. 'Leave me alone!'

If you could lose weight from tears shed then Laura figured she was already three pounds lighter and her eyes showed no signs of drying up any time soon. There was another bang on the door.

'Um, hey, er, I've forgotten your name,' called Candy through the door, and her misery was now complete. 'Hey, Had, what's her name?'

'Go away,' she moaned piteously. 'I need to be alone.'

'Laura? It is Laura, isn't it? Why don't you let me in?' Candy tried again, rattling the door handle. 'C'mon, what's the matter?'

There was no way to summon up a reply that encapsulated the full horror of the barnet butchering, so Laura just whimpered slightly and covered her ears.

'You can't stay in there much longer,' Candy continued. 'People need to pee, and Hadley has a face mask on and her skin's getting really tight and itchy.'

'If I break out, I'm gonna sue!'

Laura didn't want to be sued, though she doubted it would have stood up in a court of law. Also her camisole was soaked through and she really needed to change. 'OK, I'm going to come out,' she announced in a trembling voice. 'But everyone has to close their eyes and promise not to look at me.'

'We're stepping away from the door now,' Candy said soothingly, like Laura was a skittish horse who might bolt at any sudden loud noises. 'And closing our eyes.'

Laura had a moment of inspiration and wrapped a towel round her head before she slid the bolt back and opened the door, to be confronted by Candy and Hadley, their eyes wide open.

'Ack!' The only thing for it was to hustle back from whence she came, but Candy had her arm in a vice-like grip and was dragging Laura toward her own bedroom, which was now covered with huge bolts of fabric and a large table with a sewing machine perched on it. 'What the . . . ? *You lied!*'

'Oh, suck it up, honey,' Candy drawled, pulling Laura down on the bed. 'You're being scrutinized, better get used to it. And lose the towel.'

Laura clamped her hands over her head, then rearranged her features into a modified pout. 'When I lose the audience,' she gritted out, as Irina squeezed past and crouched at her feet.

'Whassup, yo?' It sounded really odd in that former-Eastern Bloc accent.

'Nothing's up,' Laura said icily, because her bad hair day to end all bad hair days was not an appropriate topic of conversation.

'Don't need to be a rocket scientist to work out you've

had a disastrous haircut,' Candy clarified. 'Hey, we've all been there.'

'I vant to see,' Irina muttered, and it might have been the longest sentence she ever uttered but Laura was more interested with the way her hand was creeping upwards.

'Touch the towel and you lose full working use of your fingers,' she growled. 'Your call.'

Irina backed away because the menace in Laura's eyes was universal lingo for 'don't mess with me, bitch'.

'Respect.' Irina's grudging look of admiration completely blindsided Laura to Candy snatching the towel off her head and throwing it across the room.

What came out of her mouth was a stream of invective that rivalled anything that Candy herself had ever achieved – but Candy was unmoved. She just yanked down Laura's hands so she couldn't hold them over her head or wrap them around Candy's throat, and assessed her new 'do.

'Well, it could be worse,' was her eventual summing up. 'Not sure it suits your face-shape.'

'It look better on me,' Irina decided, with the smug smile of a girl who thought that everything looked better on her.

'It's awful,' Laura said flatly, all of the fight deserting her. 'I'm awful. My face looks like it has elephantiasis.'

'Well, I don't even know what that is, but it's probably because you've been crying so much,' Candy added in a softer voice. 'It's a good cut and the colours really bring out the green in your eyes – well, when they're not so bloodshot anyway – and . . .'

Candy patted her arm, Irina looked bored and Hadley suddenly got a clue. 'I still don't understand why you're upset,' she announced. Probably because she'd been too engrossed in rifling through Candy's gargantuan collection of clothes. 'So you had a—'

'Shit haircut,' Irina interrupted, standing up and stretching so Laura could see nothing but miles of taut stomach as her vest rode up. 'Is boring,' she added, striding over to the dressing table. 'Yeah, your hair looks crap. Get over it.'

Excuse me? Laura was speechless from the sheer nerve of her. All she'd done in the last twenty-four hours was make smart-arse, monosyllabic digs in some accent that was probably completely faked. Like, it would turn out that she was really from Basingstoke. Candy was also speechless, but that was probably because she'd finally met someone who was ruder than her.

'Are we going to have the champagne yet?' Hadley chirped, completely oblivious to the stomach-churning tension in the room.

Laura was starting to get the nagging throb of a monster headache. 'What's she talking about?'

'I bought some bottles of champagne in a lame attempt at a flat-warming,' Candy explained blithely. 'That's why I had to get you out of the bathroom, because we were meant to be doing some serious bonding.'

'Great,' Laura muttered gracelessly, but the circumstances was beyond extenuating. 'I'm not feeling bond-y. I just want to find a hat so I can wear it until my hair grows back.'

Candy looked highly agitated and Laura wondered nervously if she was about to launch into a major snit, like she did on *The Careless* when things didn't go her way, but she seemed more concerned about Irina, who was rummaging through the assorted potions and lotions on her dresser.

'Can I help you with something?' she enquired coldly, and Irina turned and threw something at her, which she caught one-handed. At any other time Laura would have been impressed.

'Hair serum. It's going to take more than hair serum.' She stood up and pointed at Hadley, who was twirling in front of the mirror. 'Get me your big-ass hairdryer, Had.'

Hadley paused in admiring how her skirt flared up over her toned thighs. 'Huh?'

'Hairdryer. Big black thing with a diffuser stuck on the end of it. Go! Fetch!' Candy turned to Laura. 'You sit on that chair and don't move a muscle. And you, Cavegirl, go and get the champagne in the fridge.'

'I not understand,' Irina grunted with a sour look, but she went. Maybe champagne was still pronounced champagne where she came from.

'What are you going to do?' Laura asked fearfully. 'I

think my hair's been through enough for one day.'

Candy whisked up a huge bristle brush and twirled it between her fingers. 'Look, sweetie, I spent most of her childhood trailing my mother round the New York shows and designers' ateliers. She's, like, best friends with Kate Moss. I know a thing or two about make-overs. Trust me.'

Laura didn't trust her, but she sat still while Candy dried and tonged and coaxed her hair into some semblance of order, and the three of them all stared at her, like she was a performing seal.

'There,' Candy said finally, pinning a couple of sparkly clips above Laura's fringe. 'Now it's a hair do, not a hair don't.'

Laura squinted at herself in the mirror. It didn't look that different from before, except Candy had made it flatter, straighter and, most importantly, longer, so that it was more of an ear-length bob, which hid her complete lack in the cheekbone department.

'Thanks,' Laura said, sounding exactly like the ungrateful wench that she was. So she tried it again. With extra feeling. 'Seriously, Candy, thanks a lot. I really appreciate it.'

'It was no biggie,' she said, waving her hand around. Then checked herself. 'Contrary to popular belief, I am a halfway decent human being. I just don't play one on TV.'

'More champagne, ja?' Irina said, from where she was sprawled out on the floor like an Amazonian starfish.

Chapter Four

After much deep thought, or the ten minutes it took her to eat a bag of Skips, Laura decided the whole weight-loss plan was ridiculous. Like, that whole Nicole Ritchie look was so over.

Besides, she'd rung her mum and then Tom, and neither of them thought she was anything less than perfect. Those had been Tom's exact words, 'You're perfect, Laura. Don't let them try to change you.'

It was also painfully obvious that Heidi had a chip on her shoulder because she was too much of a short-arse to be a model. Those that could did, and those that couldn't became bookers. It was time Heidi realized who actually had the power in their relationship.

At the moment Heidi seemed to think that she was all omnipotent and stuff. She certainly didn't need to say, 'Hi, how are you?' or look pleased to see her newest model. Oh no. That would have weakened her power base. Instead when Laura turned up at Fierce on the morning of her Sparkle Cosmetics shoot, Heidi simply pointed at an object in front of her.

An object which made an army of goosebumps start marching up Laura's arms.

'Jump on,' she said impatiently. 'The car's coming in five minutes.'

'You want me to get on the scales? Here? In front of everyone?' Laura clarified incredulously. 'Like at Weight Watchers?'

'Well, if you've lost weight like I told you then why should it be a problem?'

Laura was starting to dislike Heidi in a very special way. She toed off her sneakers, despite Heidi's contemptuous sniff, then gingerly stepped on the object of evil and watched with a frantically beating heart as the digital display starting spiralling upwards and upwards and then slowed down.

One hundred and forty-six, one hundred and forty-five, one hundred and forty-four, one hundred and forty-three, one hundred and forty-four again, and back to one hundred and forty-three. Laura decided to risk letting out the breath she'd been holding. 'See, I don't need to lose weight,' she crowed triumphantly. 'That's totally within the acceptable weight ratio for my height.'

'It's not in the acceptable weight ratio for a model. You're over ten stone. *Ten stone!*'

There didn't seem to be any point in explaining that she was five feet ten and that those bones weighed a lot. On Planet Fashion, *just over* ten stone was obviously not a healthy weight for a growing girl, especially if you couldn't see every single one of her ribs underneath her skin. 'All the women in my family are curvy,' she insisted. 'My junk in the trunk is genetically predetermined.'

'Cheekbones. Stomach crunches,' Heidi muttered obliquely and pulled out her beeping phone. 'Car's here.'

Despite Heidi being a sucking black hole of negativity, the Sparkle Cosmetics shoot was a breeze. The pretty white summer dress scattered with pink and black polka dots fitted like a dream. The silvery-blue eyeshadow was subtle and went beautifully with the soft pink blush on her lips and cheeks. Oh, and hello, irony! One of the stylists was dispatched to find a fricking wig that matched Laura's original hair. Heidi's lip had curled to monumental proportions for the whole five minutes that the crisis had loomed large and Laura figured that if she could hide a triumphant smirk, then she could rock the shoot just as well.

The only blip was the moment when her co-stars erupted on to the set. Larry, Mo and Curly were a triplet of wriggly Labrador puppies who were totally going to steal her beauty-campaign thunder if she didn't project enough.

There were so many things to keep under control; head up, chin down, stop blinking her eyes, turn her body slightly to the right, keep her hands relaxed so they didn't look like catcher's mitts. That's when she wasn't trying to stop the completely adorable but also completely annoying balls of fur from licking her make-up off. Still, way better than being back at school.

All this was going on before a group of assembled onlookers. After each roll of film, William the photographer, Heidi and the Sparkle Cosmetics suits would gather around a computer monitor to see the pictures, while Laura attempted to stop Larry, or was it Curly, from eating her dress.

For the final roll of film, Laura had to lie flat on the floor while the puppies gambolled excitedly around her and William stood on a ladder and shot from above, while she pouted and made her eyes go so big that it was a wonder that they didn't come clean out of their sockets.

'Great, great, relax your bottom lip slightly,' William ordered. 'And move your left shoulder down, yeah, that's it. Hey, watch that little bugger, he's trying to make a break for freedom. Good, perfect, love it – it's a wrap!'

With a heartfelt sigh Laura let go of the puppies, who scampered over her with excited yelps and headed straight for the food table. Her stomach let out an ungodly rumble because last night's sweet-and-sour chicken from the Golden Wok was just a dim and distant memory. She ambled after the puppies to see if there was anything left. But just as she was scraping out the ends of a bowl of pasta salad, Heidi appeared at her elbow like an evil genie.

'What are you doing?' she hissed, poking at the plate with an accusatory finger. 'Are you going to eat that?'

'I haven't had anything all day,' Laura protested. 'It's salad; it's healthy.'

'But it has carbs!' she said, like the carbs were crack cocaine and Laura was about to go on a week-long bender with Pete Doherty. 'We talked about them.'

'You said no carbs after four and it's actually 3.55 p.m. so I have a five-minute window, and anyway I don't really think that I need to lose any weight,' Laura snapped. But then again, it probably wasn't the wisest thing to say to the woman who was meant to be masterminding her career. Being hungry made her cranky. 'Look, I'm going to have some non-pasta salad too and an apple,' she added in an attempt to mollify Miss Sour Face.

'Whatever,' Heidi said dully. 'It's your waistline, not mine.'

'So are you pleased with the shoot?' Laura asked, mostly to change the subject but also because a little bit of validation would go a long way.

And what do you know? Heidi actually smiled. It almost reached her eyes. 'You were all right,' she admitted. 'A little bit too cutesy for my taste, but very professional. The Sparkle suits were impressed.'

'And that's good, right?'

'It's very good. Now you just need to stay focused for the *Skirt* cover shoot next week. The photographer is a

53

bit . . . difficult.' She narrowed her eyes thoughtfully. 'You'll be all right if you flirt with him. He's such a perv.'

Nothing had ever been said about pervy photographers on *Make Me A Model*. 'Riiight,' Laura said doubtfully. 'Perv. Check.'

'And don't eat any of that until after you've changed. If you get pasta on that dress, you'll have to pay for it.'

And with that inspiring pep-talk she was gone, leaving Laura to work out how the hell she was meant to get home on public transport.

Chapter Five

The studio for the *Skirt* cover shoot was in an old railway arch behind King's Cross station. Laura was buzzed in without any fuss, even without Heidi, who was on appointments most of the day but had promised to drop by later on. Oh joy. Laura was learning that people in the fashion industry didn't have meetings; they had appointments. She wasn't sure exactly what they did on these mythical appointments, but she suspected they just sat around drinking coffee and bitching about the latest trends in hemlines.

That was what most of the people on the shoot were doing. More hipsters with greasy hair wearing distressed jeans and fugly jumpers were slumped on the low brown leather sofas that every photographic studio had, as well as a long, glass coffee table with lots of Japanese fashion magazines stacked on them. They probably got them on discount.

'Hey, I'm Laura. I won *Make Me A Model* and I'm your cover girl for the day.' Her most perky voice came out as more of a strangled squeak.

'Marta,' one angular girl bit out. 'Your creative director for the day.'

There was an outbreak of sniggering at that, like Laura was too dumb to get that she was taking the piss. Inwardly Laura wilted, but this was only six hours out of her entire life. No biggie. Anyway, she was their contractually obligated cover girl and there wasn't a damn thing they could do about it.

'Get into make-up,' someone grunted, pointing a finger at a brightly lit alcove with a counter full of cosmetics, where two girls were hanging clothes on a rail. 'We're still setting up.'

It didn't look like anyone was setting up apart from the stubbly guy who was rolling a joint with expert precision. But Laura wasn't about to argue. She thought about it though.

'God, I hate shooting competition winners,' she heard someone spit out as she scurried off to get ready for her close-up.

At least the stylist and the make-up artist were sweet, even if they did talk in frightened whispers. 'Don't worry,' they kept saying, which just made Laura worry that there was something she should be worried about. '*Skirt* shoots are always like this. It's a very edgy magazine.'

Laura was also fast learning that in fashion-speak 'edgy' actually meant that the clothes would be unwearable, the make-up would be unflattering, and everyone would act like a total arsehole. She hit the jackpot exactly eleven minutes later, standing in the dressing room in her bloody underwear being talked through the clothes, when the guy who'd been rolling the blunt casually strolled in and stood there staring at her.

'Her tits are huge,' he suddenly barked, even though it was none of his business and they were already being diminished by the finest minimizer bra that Marks & Spencer had to offer. 'You're going to have to strap them down. This is a sodding fashion cover not Page Three.'

Laura covered up the offending appendages with her forearms and hoped desperately that her boy-cut panties weren't riding up her butt cheeks as he slowly walked around her. 'She's too fat. Bloody great, I'm going to have to spend hours retouching this,' he added, and then he *slapped her arse*!

Laura froze to the spot while all these warring emotions – shock, outrage, embarrassment – fought it out.

But oh no, he wasn't done. Now he was right in her face, exhaling stale skunk fames, even though she'd always believed that the whole point of spliff was to mellow you out. 'You ever thought of doing nude stuff?' he leered.

'I'm seventeen!'

'Bet I could get you the cover of *Barely Legal*,' he drawled. 'Maybe we should talk about it later.'

Not coming out with the loudest, longest 'Ewwwww!' ever heard was about the hardest thing Laura had attempted in her young, barely legal life. 'You'd have to talk to my booker,' she whimpered. 'Heidi at Fierce.'

'That skinny bitch,' he sneered. 'Wouldn't touch her with yours, sweetheart. Right, better go and get a bigger lens for my camera. Only way I'm going to be able to fit all of you into the shot.'

'He's the *photographer*?' Laura hissed once he'd gone. 'Oh my God, he should be on the Sex Offenders' Register.'

'Gerry's a genius,' the stylist informed her in a hushed whisper. 'Might be a disgusting old letch, but he usually shoots for Russian *Vogue*. You're really lucky.'

Lucky didn't come close to describing it. When Laura finally teetered on set in a pair of nosebleed heels, strapped into an itchy dress, which was pinned at the back because the zip wouldn't do up, Gerry snapped his fingers.

'Jesus Christ,' he breathed, taking in her slicked-back hair and *Stig Of The Dump* make-up. 'Give me something that I can work with.'

Under strict instructions not to smile or pout or arch her eyebrow – any of the stuff she was really good at – Laura just had to stare moodily at the camera like she wanted to wrench it off its tripod and smash it to smithereens. It wasn't too hard, because that's what she really wanted to do as Gerry's assistant clicked away. Apparently, being a famous photographer meant that all Gerry had to do was mouth obscenities at the hapless model.

They'd shot four different outfits and Gerry had pondered aloud on whether Laura was a virgin, what she was like in bed, and exactly who she'd shagged to win *Make Me A Model*.

'Maybe we should just shoot her in her underwear,' Gerry speculated. 'Have we got anything she could actually fit into? Maybe some granny panties? Marta, why don't you give your nan a ring?'

Laura wasn't glaring at the camera any more. Not crying was now her default position, though her bottom lip was quivering frantically like it hadn't got the message.

There were still two more outfits to shoot as she staggered back to the dressing room so she could be extricated from her current ensemble. There was gaffer tape wound round her boobs and she didn't even want to think about what would happen to her nipples when it was peeled off.

Instead, Laura collapsed on to the stool and tried to find her happy place. She was still trying to find it when Heidi wandered in. Today she was wearing different shades of grey – really working that thundercloud metaphor.

Heidi took a minute to gaze at the wonder that was Laura in a flesh-coloured pair of knickers and a bandeau fashioned from black tape, her arms wrapped around her body to hide it from any lurking photographers.

'If we could just get you down to sample size in the next couple of months.'

Her weight was really not the first item on the agenda.

'Heidi,' Laura yelped. 'This is . . . You should have *heard* what he was saying to me!'

She shrugged. 'Told you he was a perv, but he's a genius photographer.'

'He's not even taking the photos!'

Heidi sighed in that way she did when Laura was being way too much of a naive suburban girl to be allowed through the Fashion front door. 'Well, he's supervising Andre, same diff.'

The stylist was already brandishing outfit number five, which was basically a bronze-coloured body suit with some metal patches hanging off it. 'Knickers off,' she instructed Laura cheerfully. It was like that dream when you realize you're at school assembly with no clothes on. But a gazillion times worse.

'I can't . . .' Laura protested, the tears definitely one nanosecond away from falling. 'I'm not.'

'Don't be so silly. Just whip 'em off,' Heidi demanded, studying her fingernails. 'Just wait until you do catwalk, then you'll have to strip off backstage in front of everyone. If we go over time because of this, you'll have to pay the late fees.'

'Can you at least turn your backs before I do a full monty and can someone stand guard, please? *Please?*'

God, even she and Tom had only done the half-monty. Heidi whirled round with a definite flounce as Laura jumped off the stool and skinned off her panties. She yanked her legs through the appropriate holes and pulled the body suit on. It looked dreadful. In fact it had left dreadful a few million miles ago.

'You can turn around now,' she grumped. 'Though you'll wish you hadn't bothered.'

She looked like a prime contestant for liposuction in a pair of tights with ideas above its station. The mesh clung lovingly to every lump and bump, every ripple and bulge.

'Foudre's designs are quite unforgiving,' the stylist said sympathetically. 'Maybe Andre will just do one roll.'

'I look fucking *awful*,' Laura wailed, just in case they didn't understand the full horror.

And how she wished she'd kept her stupid mouth firmly shut because Heidi more or less dragged her back on to set while she went off on this monotone commentary about how modelling wasn't all puppies and glittery lipgloss and she was going to wind up shooting catalogue layouts if she couldn't do high fashion. And that Laura was never, repeat NEVER, to badmouth a designer or a photographer or even the guy who came to drop off the extra rolls of film. Which, yeah, fair point, but she wasn't the one who had to straddle a chair and then hoist her legs into the air while Gerry told her that she'd 'probably spread 'em wider than that last Saturday night'.

The torture dragged on for another hour, and if they had a decent cover shot by the end of it, then colour her amazed. Laura was more concerned with her nipples, which had been rubbed raw from their enforced bondage.

Heidi quickly disappeared on another appointment after making it plain that Laura was her least favourite New Face, and she was left to get back into her clothes. Laura could have kissed every lovely inch of her jeans, as she marvelled at the way they fitted properly and didn't hurt like the stupid clothes that they'd made her wear. It took some time to register Gerry standing at the door, a cigarette clamped between his lips.

'Thank you for shooting me,' Laura said primly, fastening every single hook and eye on her cardigan, even though he'd already seen way more of her than anyone, with the exception of the midwife who'd brought her into the world. How was she meant to get out of there when he was very effectively blocking the one exit? 'It was a real . . . learning experience.'

'Is that a polite way of saying that I'm a wanker?' he grinned. 'I get that a lot. Don't know why.'

Laura shook her head. It was a difficult situation. She couldn't exactly tell him to piss off, as he had half of London convinced that he was some kind of photographic *wunderkind*. But, then again, she didn't want to give him even a smidgeon of encouragement. 'Well, it was challenging, but guess I need to get used to that.'

'You also need to loosen up,' he suggested, uncoiling

himself from the door jamb and walking toward her. 'No use coming to set with a face like wet cement. Not the best way to impress people.'

'Right,' Laura agreed carefully. 'I'll work on that.'

'Like, I could be in a position to recommend you to a lot of clients, if I thought that you were worth it,' Gerry added, standing way too close to Laura. Like, way, way, way too close, so her flesh decided it might be a good time to start crawling off her bones. 'You scratch my back and I'll scratch yours.'

But it wasn't her back he was interested in scratching. Not if the way his meaty paw suddenly clamping around her left buttock was anything to go by. Daisy Bloom had never covered this potential model minefield. Laura glanced up to see if there was even a speck of humanity in his red-rimmed eyes and, when she decided there wasn't, neatly sidestepped out of groping distance and tried to smile sweetly.

'That's very kind of you, um, Gerry,' Laura said between gritted teeth. OK, she didn't sound altogether convincing, but he was disarmed enough to take a step back so she could rest her hand on his shoulder and give him the standard 'mwah mwah' fashion kiss. Then before he could swoop down to turn it into something more tongue-y she skipped away. 'I've got an appointment I really can't be late for.'

'Oh, come back here, darling,' he called cajolingly, but

Laura just gave him a jaunty wave and did her best impersonation of greased lightning.

She knew, like she knew that the sun came up and that grass was green and that Hadley didn't even know how to boil a kettle, that giving some slimy snapper a bit of touch was not how to get ahead in modelling.

Her head was still trying to process every humiliating event that had occurred that day, when she came home to find Irina back from a trip to Tokyo and camped out on the sofa. Laura hadn't even left Zone 1, but Irina got to go to Japan. There was something seriously skewy about that picture.

Laura waited for her to say something about her trip. Or even just *something* – but she stared at the TV without even blinking. It was very unnerving.

'How was Japan?' she asked, plonking herself down with a Snickers. She needed comfort food and no weapon forged was going to come between her and chocolate.

'Japanese,' Irina murmured, leaning closer to the screen so she didn't miss an exciting second of Derek Acorah searching for telltale signs of ectoplasm. 'Food was gross, tea was green.'

Irina was the only thing between Laura and forced exile back to her cupboard. Besides, it seemed as if she'd added some new words to her vocabulary. 'You were gone longer than a week, right? 'Cause I thought you were going to be back on Sunday.'

Irina sighed and folded her arms as it dawned on her that Laura wanted to have an actual conversation. 'Got booked for Japanese *Vogue* and then a fashion show. Like, whatever, y'know?'

'But you've never even done runway before!' Laura couldn't help the aggrieved tone to her voice, even though it was really cool that Irina looked like a Martian but was getting loads and loads of work, and she'd only had two jobs that she'd had to fight twelve other girls for. Really cool.

'You just walk, up, down, up down, like with a firework up your arse, innit?' Irina sniggered at her own joke. 'S'not hard.'

It had taken Laura eight weeks to be able to strut down the runway in measly three-inch heels and not fall over. 'Well, I had my cover shoot today for *Skirt* magazine.'

'Ja?' Irina picked up the remote so she could turn the volume up.

'God, the photographer was this total sexist pig who kept going on about how fat I was, and then he tried to cop a feel after the shoot and was all, "you be nice to me and then I'll be nice to you, oooh I work for Russian *Vogue*",' she ranted. 'And the clothes were vile and I had to have my boobs strapped down, which was beyond embarrassing and—'

'Gerry . . .' Irina grunted. 'You mean Gerry?'

'How do you know Gerry?' Laura asked incredulously.

'I went on go-to in Moscow . . .'

'You mean a go-see . . .'

'Whatever. He funny,' Irina elaborated. 'We smoke spliff together, then he book me for three shoots.'

Laura squinted at her furiously to see if it was some strange practical joke. It was really hard to tell with Irina. 'You're kidding, right?'

'Gerry,' Irina repeated emphatically. 'You shut up now.'

'But did he come on to you? Like, what did you have to do to get booked? Oh my God, Irina, you didn't . . . no, I mean, *you didn't*?'

Irina's face cracked into its one other expression, the smirk. 'What do you think?'

All Laura could do was splutter and make 'ouch' faces. 'No way!'

'Niet,' she clarified. 'No ho. He try and I tell him piss off and then it all cool. Like, respect, innit?'

For about the millionth time that day, Laura's face became a fiery furnace of shame. 'I'm sorry. Of course you're not a ho,' she backtracked. 'That wasn't what I meant.'

Laura paused as the TV let out a bloodcurdling shriek as something unworldly rushed past.

'So did *you*?'

'Hmmm, did I what?' Laura mumbled, her attention now riveted on the telly.

'Did you fuck him?'

'As if!' Laura went from distracted to outraged in three seconds flat, before her shoulders slumped. 'I did seem to have his hand on my bum for a large portion of the day though.'

And as the sense memory replayed, she scrambled up because she needed to go to the bathroom and scrub every inch of body that Gerry had felt, leered at or talked about.

'Next time, kick him in the balls,' Irina advised, stretching her legs out over the spot Laura had just vacated so there was no chance of her sitting back down. 'Always. And make me tea now you up.'

Chapter Six

When Laura had imagined her glamorous career as an internationally renowned model, there had been certain recurring themes. Like the famous fashion designer who'd clap eyes on her across a crowded New York loft party and declared there and then that she was his muse. He'd even name a handbag after her. That idyllic daydream had got her through many a long and boring history class.

Then there was the fantasy about her triumphant strut along the world's catwalks and how some scientist guy (a really good-looking scientist guy) would analyse her forward trajectory and she'd go down in fashion history as the first model who had a 167°-wiggle to her walk and she'd have her hips insured for ten million pounds.

Life would be an endless and giddy buzz of parties and champagne and adulation, with the odd spot of throwing poses in front of a camera so she could pay the mortgage on her several penthouse apartments.

It wasn't anything like that. Not one little bit.

For starters, there hadn't been a single party. Well, not any that she was invited to. Candy seemed to organize most of her days around the nightclub openings, photography exhibits and mobile phone launches that she went to in the evenings. Hadley was a permanent plus one for her boyfriend, George, another former child star and *Hadley's House* veteran, who was now third on the bill of a lame sitcom playing a former child star who'd decamped to Britain to find fame and fortune. Talk about typecasting. And even Irina, when she wasn't surgically attached to the remote control and a family-sized bag of Doritos, was going out with her gang of equally stony-faced Slavs to pretentious fashion parties in dodgy parts of east London that Laura got to hear about the next day from one of the other models she'd bump into at go-sees.

Oh, go-sees, which hadn't featured at all in her life-as-a-model docudramas, starring Laura Parker as herself. Now go-sees, or 'piss-offs' as she'd renamed them, were all that Laura did.

There were positive aspects of the go-see, if she thought long and hard enough about it. Like the London Underground system had given up its mysteries and was now her total bitch. Laura even knew the difference between via Charing Cross and via Bank. And all that pavement pounding had to be burning some fat, even though she had the world's most sluggish metabolism.

And then there were the crappy, soul-sucking, slit-your-wrists-right-now aspects of the go-see. After a sweaty journey halfway across town to some hole-in-the-wall studio that was always up at least three flights of stairs,

Laura would prop herself against the wall with a whole bunch of other girls who all knew each other. 'Let's get together next time we're both in Paris' or 'My booker will only let me work for more than £500 a day' were some of the more down-to-earth conversational gambits.

Finally she'd get called in to see some gum-snapping photographer/designer/editor/fashion pod person who'd leaf through her portfolio at a rate of knots before they grunted, 'Thanks.' Occasionally, just to mix it up, Laura would be asked to change into her high heels and walk across the floor. And that never ended well, or in an actual booking.

What was even worse – and worse was just a relative term at this point – was when they didn't even look at her book but gave her a quick up and down before sneering, 'So you're the girl that won the modelling competition because you mouthed off to Noel Ripley. You were really funny.'

'No, I'm the girl who won the modelling competition because I was prettier than everyone else,' would not have been an acceptable comeback. All Laura could do was stand there like a spare bride at a wedding and not be able to think of anything remotely funny to say.

Not that she was going to tell anyone about the less-than-stellar start to her modelling. Just as well that her mother was more interested in whether she was remembering to wear a vest and eat breakfast; Jen, Chandra and Cath could easily be distracted with little teasers about what Hadley was wearing or who Candy had been speaking to on the phone. Tom, however, could not be duped that easily. Damn him.

'Everything's fine,' Laura would chirp brightly during their nightly phone calls. 'It's all going great.'

There'd be a tense pause before Tom would ask: 'You sound funny. Are you sure you're OK?'

And Laura wouldn't be winning any prizes for Girlfriend Of The Year because during the last week she'd found it much less hassle to text him a breezy: SO BUSY. WILL CALL SOON. XOXOXO.

At least she was putting in serious gym time. Like, the half hour on the treadmill walking really fast cancelled out the odd chocolate muffin or four-cheeses pizza. And she was skipping breakfast too, so that had to help.

As Laura climbed up seven flights of stairs in the FCP Media building because she wasn't allowed to do the lift any more, she tried to visualize her thighs becoming more svelte with each step she took. Then she ran out of oxygen and had to concentrate on not passing out instead.

Although the go-sees had all merged into one seamless blur of minimalist work spaces and black-clad fashion types with frowns on their faces, Laura would admit to just the teensiest smidge of excitement about her appointment with the fashion editor of *Polka Dot* magazine. She'd been a faithful reader for three years and loved the way they ran articles on everything from 'Cut-Out-And-Colour Corsages' to 'Ten Reasons Why You Really Wouldn't Want To Date Seth Cohen, No Really, Trust Us On This'. And they had the best fashion spreads of happy, gap-toothed, freckle-faced girls swinging from trees and rocking out in their bedrooms. She used to rip them out and stick them on her wall at home back in the days . . . well, in the days when she thought that being a model would be fun with a Caps Lock 'F'.

Laura followed the signs and the thumping beat of Goldfrapp until she came to the right office. It was like a really messy bedroom but with desks and computers in it. There were clothes, CDs and lots of pink things strewn over every surface, and the people who worked there were actually – gasp – smiling.

Laura strode purposefully down the office towards a spot at the back where the piles of clothes seemed to have reached a critical mass – she was becoming an expert at finding the fashion department. As she was wrenching her portfolio out of her bag, she felt the back of her neck prickling in a mildly disagreeable way. Maybe this would be the first time that she got blown out before someone had even seen her from the front.

She turned around to see a beautiful girl hovering behind her. She had naturally platinum hair, huge blue eyes and was obviously about to tell Laura to get the hell out because she'd already been booked for the job.

'Oh, hey, you're Laura from *Make Me A Model*,' she exclaimed in a broad Geordie accent. 'You're with Fierce now, right?'

'Er, yeah,' Laura concurred. 'Who are you with?'

This was the standard convo that all models had, closely followed by 'What jobs have you done recently?'

The girl blinked. 'I'm with *Polka Dot* magazine,' she said wryly. 'I'm Alison, deputy fashion editor.'

Foot meet mouth. 'I thought you were a model, sorry.'

Alison held out her hand for her portfolio. 'It's the best compliment I've had all week,' she beamed. 'Could never be a model. I like my chip butties too much. Oooh, I like this one. I remember how Nemi was trying to face you on that shoot by dancing when you were on set. God, she was a bitch.'

Laura waited for the inevitable 'You seemed a lot more peppy on the show', but it never came. 'We were so gutted that *Skirt* got to have a cover shoot with you and we weren't allowed,' Alison said, slipping one of Laura's comp cards out of the back of the book. 'I'd really like to take some Polaroids of you and, God, you have to meet our editor. She's your biggest fan. We had a pizza and beer party . . . hey, follow me, yeah, we had this party for the last episode of *Make Me A Model* and she got everyone to call your number and vote for you.'

Laura followed Alison into the fashion cupboard, not

quite believing what she was hearing and then stopped dead as she saw a plump girl wobbling precariously on one pink five-inch heel and clutching on to another girl for balance. 'Do you think I'd be able to walk in these?' she was asking. 'Or are they more taxi shoes?'

'Kat, you'll never guess who I've got here?' Alison rolled her eyes at Laura as Kat stared reverently down at the pink shoe like it was the most wonderful thing in the history of cobbling.

'I don't know. Adam Brody? That would rock. Oh my God, it's you! You're Laura from *Make Me A Model*,' Kat squealed, kicking off the shoe without any thought for its delicate structure and bouncing towards Laura so she could envelop her in a hug. 'I heart you!'

'This is Kat, our editor,' Alison said somewhat unnecessarily. 'Officially your biggest fan.'

'I so am,' Kat agreed, pushing Laura away so she could grin at her. She was small and lusciously plump, poured into a tight black dress, white curves spilling out at the seams. It shouldn't have worked, but it *so* did. 'Oh God, we love you! Did Alison tell you about the party?'

Laura nodded and tried desperately to think of something cool to say. 'That shoe was nice,' was all she could muster.

Kat looked like she was about to eat her up. Laura wondered if she was just a teeny bit dykeadelic. 'We're doing a winter coat story,' she explained, as Alison slotted a cartridge into the camera. 'On location in Whistler. Can you snowboard?'

'Well, no, but I can fall off a skateboard really well if that helps,' Laura blurted out. 'Especially if there's a camera phone in the vicinity. You should see my best friend's MySpace page.' She really did talk a load of shit sometimes.

But Kat just clapped her hands delightedly. 'That would be cool! We should have all the girls falling off their boards and making snow angels. Lots of energy, Ali, lots of movement.'

'I'll see if Simon's free to shoot,' Alison muttered. 'He's great for those action shots and we might be able to get a beauty story out of it too.' She gestured at Laura. 'Can you go and stand by the door and give me a really happy face? Think of Nemi when she didn't win.'

And it was so unexpected that Laura burst out laughing just as Alison pointed and clicked. She thought she'd get yelled at for shutting her eyes but Alison just snapped a few more, while Kat looked on approvingly.

'Laura'd look great in that emerald-green coat,' she suddenly said. 'The one I want to use for the opener.'

One of the little cupboard minions who'd been crouched on the floor untangling a huge pile of jewellery duly fetched the coat and held it out so Laura could shrug into it.

She could tell right away that it was going to be too small as she worked her arms into the sleeves and felt the complete lack of give as the wool stretched warningly over her shoulders. Laura slowly wriggled her way into it, then gripped the lapels in what she hoped was an insouciant manner and smiled at the assembled throng.

'That's such a good colour on you,' Alison said, pointing the camera again. 'Can you just do up the buttons?'

Cursing her opposable fingers and thumbs, Laura got the first button fastened and pulled at the objecting coat so she could get the second one done. Unfortunately her burgeoning breasts had other ideas.

'It doesn't fit . . .' she started to say, but was drowned out by the loud ripping noise as the entire back seam split down the middle. The noise seemed to go on for ever. And ever. And ever. Such a harsh, ugly sound. And Laura knew that this would be the moment in her life that, fifty years from now, would shock her out of sleep, so she'd wake with a start, soaked in sweat.

Unfortunately, it wasn't fifty years later. It was right now and her *back fat* had destroyed an item of clothing in front of three people, who were trying really hard to pretend it hadn't happened.

Was it possible to die from embarrassment? Apparently not. 'I. Am. So. Sorry.' It was hard to speak through clenched teeth.

Kat held up her hand. 'Don't worry about it,' she said cheerily. 'Sample sizes are always ridiculously tiny.'

There was nothing Laura could do but carefully take off

the hateful coat and school her features into something that she hoped approached mellow calm. Even if inside she was a sobbing, screaming, shaking mess on the floor.

'I *am* losing weight,' she offered helplessly. 'I'm so sorry about this.'

Kat suddenly grabbed her hand, which made getting the hell out of there rather difficult. 'I'll walk you out,' she said, and Laura wished that she wouldn't because her sympathy was way harder to handle than all the blank stares and rejections she'd been collecting like Yugi-Oh trading cards lately.

She hustled Laura out of the cupboard and maybe she knew that Laura was one sniff away from total emotional meltdown because she gave her fingers another tight squeeze and then let go. 'You know why I liked you on the show?' she asked as she opened the office door.

'Because I dissed one of the judges at panel and didn't let anyone walk all over me,' Laura answered by rote. 'Bet I'm a huge disappointment in the actual bountiful flesh, huh?'

'Well, there was that,' Kat conceded with a wry twist of her crimson lips. 'But I'm pretty shallow and I thought you were beautiful too, in this refreshing, believable way so the viewers weren't scared by your looks like some of those other girls who were all hipbones and angles. You're, like, like what our readers could be on their best day ever, if they really lucked out in the face department.'

'You're just saying that to make me feel better,' Laura protested, trying to ignore the first warning prickle at the back of her eyes. She really shouldn't be talking back like this. Heidi would kill her – if she didn't kill her for the whole coat thing first.

'I'm not, and I'd really like to have you in the mag; maybe we could do an interview about what you've been up to since the show ended.' Kat warmed to her theme. 'Like, how glamorous and exciting it all is . . .'

She tailed off partly because Laura was doing a good impersonation of Edvard Munch's *The Scream* and also because she knew that Laura knew that she knew that there was nothing glamorous and exciting about being a model – unless you were Candy or Hadley, or even Irina who was probably back in downtown Tokyo right now asking if she could have ketchup on her tempura.

'Look, thanks for everything,' Laura mumbled, shaking her hand. 'And, oh, I just wanted to say that *Polka Dot* is my favourite magazine and I think you're a great editor and I'm not just saying that to be a suck-ass and God, I'm going to shut up now and actually leave the building.'

Kat gave a bathtap gurgle of laughter and pulled her in for another hug.

Chapter Seven

Laura found herself walking along the Embankment by the Thames, avoiding the hordes of joggers and backpack-wielding tourists as she gazed at the higgledy-piggledy London skyline, framed through the plane trees. She also found herself not answering her phone because Heidi called seven (count 'em!) times over the next hour.

The imposing red brick of the Tate Modern came into view and Laura sighed. She'd only been there once on a school trip when she'd spent the whole day crushing on Tom from a distance, gazing at him out of the corner of her eye rather than the Jackson Pollocks; and on the coach home he'd suddenly sat down next to her, told her she was the most beautiful girl he'd ever seen in real life and asked what she was doing that weekend.

Laura was almost knocked off her feet, not by the great gusts of wind, but a huge wave of Tom-sickness.

'I miss you so much,' she blurted down the phone before he'd even had a chance to say hello. 'I'm just by the Tate Modern and I remember the day you asked me out . . .'

'Hey, hey, Laura,' he said worriedly, because her voice was as shaky as the stray carrier bag blowing in the breeze before her eyes. 'Are you all right?'

'No,' she admitted in a tiny voice. 'I want to come home.'

'Then come home,' he said simply, because that's what Tom did. He narrowed things down to their most basic form. 'Just go to the station, buy a ticket and get on a train.'

'I can't.'

'Have you got a job? That's fantastic! Why didn't you say something?'

'Like, that's ever going to happen,' she scoffed. 'No, I haven't got a job. Because I'm fat! Why did you never tell me that I was fat?'

'You're not fat,' he said immediately, like he didn't even have to think about it, which was slightly gratifying. 'Why are you being like this?'

'You couldn't understand,' she moaned. 'You don't know what it's like here.'

She hadn't even been this whiny in the *Make Me A Model* house. When the other girls were crying down the phone to their boyfriends, she'd entertained Tom with this whole 'Am I bothered though?' riff on what spectacular feats of bitchery had occurred that day.

'Well, no, but life isn't exactly fun times for me,' Tom bit out. 'I have coursework on top of coursework and stacks of university applications to wade through. Plus my dad is still acting like the legal profession is a done deal. And you're not here to talk to, then when you do deign to phone me, you start giving me grief.'

'I'm not giving you grief. Jesus!' She hated it when they had these rows. It didn't happen often, but somehow they'd managed to light the blue touchpaper, and instead of standing well back, she was bellowing into the phone like a Billingsgate fishwife. 'You could at least pretend to be interested in what I'm going through. I'm having to deal with all kinds of serious, grown-up stuff.'

'You get paid to stand in front of a camera and smile, Laura. You're not finding a cure for cancer . . .'

'Oh, excuse me, maybe you could try to sound even more condescending?'

'I'm not doing this,' he suddenly shouted. Like, really shouted so her eardrums twanged in protest. 'You don't speak to me for days and then you phone up and pitch a diva fit for no reason. I do not need this.'

'Well, well, well . . . *fine!*' she hissed in the lamest comeback of all time.

'No, it's not fine. And if you find yourself in a more pleasant mood, you can call me back,' Tom barked and then he had the flaming audacity to hang up.

It took Laura a good forty-five minutes to find a more pleasant mood. Mostly she wandered round the Tate Modern's gift shop, and she must have been depressed because even buying a styling new notebook didn't cheer her up.

It wasn't like Tom to cave under pressure. But when her phone started ringing, Laura knew, without even looking at her caller display, that he'd called to apologize, even though she should have been the one begging for forgiveness because she was a mardy cow.

'I'm sorry,' she squawked. 'I shouldn't have been so pissy with you just because—'

'Laura.' No one but Heidi could ever manage that flat monotone which conveyed so much disappointment. 'I've been calling you for the last two hours.'

'My phone was right at the bottom of my bag.' At least two months in London had taught her to lie fluently. 'I didn't hear it or—'

Heidi cut right through her excuses. 'I spoke to Alison from *Polka Dot.*'

'Oh.'

Heidi gave this short bark of not-laughter. 'Yup, "oh" just about sums it up. You didn't get the booking.'

'Yeah, well about that, see, there—'

'You tore the coat, I know. I heard.'

Laura shuffled out of the gift shop because she was getting filthy looks from the girl on the till and squatted down on the floor outside with the phone tucked against her shoulder. 'It was a really small coat.'

'It was sample size,' Heidi said in an exasperated voice. 'How many more times do we have to have this conversation?'

'But they liked me and the editor was so cool and she—'

'People don't book you just because they like you.

The clothes have to fit.' Heidi dropped the monotone in favour of actually raising her voice. 'You need to come in for a chat.'

Laura had a feeling that Heidi didn't mean a friendly gossip over tea and buns. In fact 'chat' was sounding a lot like a euphemism for taking her round the back of the agency for death by firing squad.

'Umm, well I guess I could come in tomorrow,' she prevaricated, because her phone was beeping and Tom was probably languishing in Call Waiting. 'Someone else is calling me, Heidi.'

'Now,' she intoned ominously. 'You need to come in now. Ted wants to see you.'

Ted was the senior booker. In fact, he was Irina's booker because the Idiot Savant Of Modelling had only lasted two weeks on the New Faces board before they bumped her up to greener pastures. Ted was also Heidi's boss. Things were really not looking good for the little girl from Manchester.

'Are you sure it can't wait until tomorrow?' Laura pleaded, but, even over the phone, Heidi could do bitch-ass like no one else.

Laura felt as if she was walking the green mile; going willingly to her own execution. Or at least to see the headmaster. But she wasn't at school. She was an adult. Or as near as you could be, when you were seven months away from your eighteenth birthday. Heidi, and even the famous Ted, weren't the boss of her. Technically, she was self-employed. And technically, she didn't seem to be heading in the direction of the agency. Maybe it was the red mist settling around her, which made it difficult to see where she was going? Or maybe it was the fact that Laura's legs were acting independently of her brain and climbing on the bus back to Camden and the stupid, poxy flat where she was forced to live with three other stupid, poxy girls who got booked for stupid, poxy jobs and generally thought they were all that when they were actually the stupidest, most poxiest people to ever strut the earth. She was prettier than them. If you lined the four of them up in front of an impartial jury, she was the prettiest. Why didn't that count for anything?

'Who the *hell* left that there?' Laura hissed under her breath as she almost tripped over a rubbish bag when she walked in. Snatching it up, she marched into the living room, and bingo! Full house! The Three Stooges were on the sofa and one of them was going to deal with the rubbish. 'This needs to go *out in the street*!'

And just in case they didn't get the message because they were all looking at her like she'd just taken a dump on the sea-grass rug, she threw the garbage bag at their feet.

Hadley and Candy looked at the rubbish, looked at each other, and then decided that this had nothing to do with either of them. Only Irina roused herself from where she'd been staring at the Fashion Channel and no doubt picking up tips for her inevitable world domination.

'You make tea, ja?'

Laura opened her mouth and then shut it again. Nothing wanted to come out except a high-pitched scream of pure rage. She settled for a mid-volume growl and clenched her fists to stop them from punching Irina in her angular, ugly face.

'No, I'm not making any bloody tea!' she shrieked. 'I don't make tea. I don't wait on people. I'm not here to fetch and carry and put out the rubbish and serve you endless hot drinks. You've been here two months, learn to say please and thank you already!'

It would take a direct hit from a weapon of mass destruction to dent Irina's sizeable ego, because she just gave one of her ubiquitous shrugs and sank back on the sofa. 'Whatever,' she sighed.

'Hard day at the office?' Candy asked, putting down the nail file, which had been getting her full attention. 'You seem a little excitable.'

'I'm not excitable,' Laura snapped. 'I'm *so* far from a state of excitement. I'm just sick of being the only one who ever does anything around here. Like, do any of you even know where we keep the Dyson?'

'Of course I do,' Candy demurred, which didn't exactly mean she'd ever used it. 'It's in the cupboard outside the kitchen.'

'Oh, yeah, that thing,' Hadley chirped. 'I wondered what that was for.'

'You all make me bloody sick! I hate it here. I bloody well, sodding hate it. And you can all rot in your own filth because I'm going home and . . . and . . . and I hope you don't get a single booking!' Somewhere in the middle of her heartfelt rant, the anger had given way to big, stinky depression. Leaving her standing aimlessly in the middle of the lounge while her three flatmates all sent her to hell with the power of their combined glaring.

'Well, we'll get right on that, sweetie,' Candy drawled. 'And you can work on that bitch routine because it's a little sloppy round the edges.'

'I'll be sure to pick up some pointers from watching your show,' Laura bit back, before whirling around and nearly colliding with the coat-stand mid-flounce.

And the worst thing was that she couldn't even comfort eat. The diet started right here. She was heading back to Manchester and going nil by mouth for a week. Then she'd come back to London all slender and bookable, and Ted and Heidi could choke on their surprise when the phone started ringing off the hook with bookings for her.

That was the plan. Right then, Laura had to content herself with barking down the phone at her mum as she issued a series of instructions about being picked up from Manchester Piccadilly the following afternoon and then not calling Tom because their fraught relationship really couldn't stand two hissy fits in the space of one day.

Chapter Eight

Ah, Manchester, Manchester, so much to answer for. Rain was lashing down from colourless skies as Laura wheeled her suitcase along the platform and scanned the crowds at the gate for her father.

He wasn't hard to find, as he was wearing his spoddy, red mac with no discernible sign of irony. The fashion gene must have skipped a generation.

Laura clunked him in the knees with her suitcase by way of greeting and huddled into her jacket. The wool had gone soggy and was giving off Eau de Wet Dog.

'I hope you're parked somewhere close,' she grumbled, proffering her cheek for a kiss and then giving him the other one, before remembering that he was her dad and she could probably ixnay on the air kissing.

His frown suggested much the same thing. 'And hello to you too,' he said mildly, giving her set features a curious glance. 'You all right? Your mother said that you sounded a bit upset on the phone yesterday.'

God, she hadn't been in Manchester more than five minutes and she was already getting the Mancunian Inquisition. 'I'm fine,' she said flatly, striding on ahead, and then coming to a grinding halt as crowds of commuters kept pouring on to the station concourse.

'Bloody rush hour,' her father muttered behind her. 'Going to be murder getting home.'

He didn't say another word about her obviously less-than-sunny disposition, but one of the best things about her dad was that he could always be relied upon to take the path of least resistance.

Unfortunately, the same couldn't be said of her mother, who was waiting for them on the doorstep.

Inside, the house looked warm and inviting. There was the faint sound of meowing coming from behind her mum, as well as a savoury and garlicky fragrance wafting out of the open door and hitting Laura square in the face. She just had to get past her mother, who folded her arms and showed no signs of budging even though Laura was soaked through.

'My goodness, you look as sulky as you sounded on the phone last night,' she exclaimed. 'And peaky. Are you going down with something? Is that why you've come home? I knew there was a smell of damp in that flat.'

Laura opened her mouth to begin a furious rebuttal but was shouldered aside by her father. 'For God's sake, Wendy, it's *pouring*. Can you stop blocking the doorway and let us in?'

She shrugged off her jacket, aware of her mother's pursed lips.

'Have I got time for a shower before dinner?' Laura

asked, pressing her hands to her damp jeans. 'Unless you want me to catch pneumonia.'

'There's no need to take that tone of voice, young lady. And we are going to have A Talk after dinner,' her mother called as she took the stairs two at a time. She was the only woman in the world who could speak in capital letters. It was freaky and scary in equal measure.

Freshly showered and in her sagging Hello Kitty pyjamas and one of her dad's jumpers, Laura sat at her usual spot in the dining room. Normally they ate in the kitchen, but the return of the prodigal daughter called for a formal venue and the second-best china.

Her stomach sent out rapturous gurgles of delight as her mother set down a platter of home-made garlic bread, which she did her level best to ignore. She hadn't had anything to eat all day, except a fat-free plain yoghurt, which she'd found at the back of the fridge. 'I made your favourite, spaghetti Bolognese, with the fresh egg pasta that you like,' her mum said, because she was an evil, food-toting genius. 'Had to send your dad out to Tesco's specially.' Also an evil genius when it came to applying a metric ass-load of maternal guilt.

'And it was raining then too,' her father added, because he had his own sneaky skill-set too. 'Why don't I dish up the spaghetti?'

They'd never buy a sudden wheat intolerance, Laura thought, anxiously watching her father ladle huge mounds of pasta on to her plate. 'Is there salad?' she asked, as her mother sat down.

'Why do you need salad? There's vegetables in the Bolognese sauce,' she said a tad haughtily, because dissing her cooking was like saying that she smelled of wee.

'I just want some green stuff,' Laura said, taking her plate and giving the pasta a baleful look. 'What vegetables are in it?'

'The same vegetables that were in it the last five hundred times I cooked it for you,' her mother sniffed. 'Carrots, mushrooms, tomatoes, fresh parsley, garlic . . . hmmm, I think I might have used a little basil. Would you like me to check for you?'

'There's no need to get huffy.'

'She's not getting huffy,' her father said, because they always tag-teamed. 'Have some garlic bread.'

Laura took a deep breath, all the better to inhale her dinner with. 'Look, I'm not doing carbs after fo— ever. I don't do carbs any more.'

'I beg your pardon?' her mother asked incredulously.

'It's really hard for my body to metabolize them . . . and don't give me one of those looks. I'm not on a stupid crash diet and I'm like so far from being anorexic that it's not even true, I just need to lose some weight,' she finished savagely. There was a moment of silence, during which her mother downed a good half of her glass of Pinot Noir. 'And modelling has different rules and different standards and you wouldn't understand, but I'm big boned and the camera adds at least ten pounds and I'm not eating the pasta or the garlic bread. End of discussion.'

'No, it bloody well isn't,' shouted her mother, banging her glass down on the table. And she must have been mad, because she totally missed the coaster. 'I'm sure that food deprivation must be at least half the reason why you're in such a filthy mood. I don't care what you get up to in London but when you're in this house, you'll eat what's put in front of you and you'll damn well like it!'

'Do what your mother tells you,' her father added helpfully. 'You're all skin and bone.'

Yeah, dream on. And if watching Irina stuff her face with KFC every night was hard, pushing away a plate of her desert island meal was well nigh impossible. But somehow Laura managed it. The stakes were too high. 'I'm not eating it. I'll have the sauce and I'll have, like, some extra tomatoes if there's any left, but I'm not having carbs.'

'You're not leaving this table until you finish what's on your plate,' her mother insisted, forcing down a forkful of food like it was liberally dosed with arsenic. 'And thank you for ruining dinner for the rest of us.'

Laura looked her mother straight in the eye, then made a great show of scraping a mushroom free from a piece of spaghetti and putting in her mouth. 'Are you going to force-feed me?'

'Laura, you're being ridiculous,' her father pointed out,

like she needed any reminding. 'Just eat the pasta and forget about the garlic bread.'

'Don't do that,' her mother snapped, turning her wrath on him, and giving Laura a respite. 'You always give in to her.'

'No, I don't. I just prefer to have a harmonious meal, which doesn't give me indigestion.'

'I'm not eating the pasta.' It was a point of pride. 'But the sauce is really nice.'

The sauce *was* really nice, but not very filling. Laura pressed the heel of her hand against her stomach, which was saying loud and proud that it wanted more food in it right now. It would be so easy to twirl those fat strands of spaghetti around her fork and slide them down her throat. She could see little globules of the sauce clinging to it, and what the hell, she could always go for an extra-long run tomorrow . . . Then she heard a grim little voice in her head, which sounded far too much like Heidi for her liking.

'She can't get into sample size. She's had no bookings. She's too fat to be a model. She's too fat to be good for anything.'

Then she visualized her slimmer, happier self (which was a tip she'd picked up from this bizarro, weight-loss, hypnosis CD she'd bought to listen to on the train). Her slimmer, happier self was sashaying down the runway during Milan Fashion Week in a barely there wisp of white chiffon. And she was all cheekbones and prancing legs, because her slimmer, happier self had also totally nailed a signature walk.

'Do you want to try a cup of my green tea?' she asked her mother in an attempt to make peace. 'I promise it's not as gross as it sounds.'

'No, thank you,' her mother bit out. 'Your father and I will be having tiramisu, despite its horrific calorie content, and you'll be making a start on the washing up.'

'Fine,' Laura announced, pushing her chair back.

'Fine,' her mother echoed, scraping the plentiful remains of her own dinner back into the serving dish. 'And then you can go to your room.'

It was strange being back in her room. Even though it was about ten times the size of her cupboard in London, it felt like she'd outgrown it. Laura lay on her bed, inhaling the welcome whiff of posh fabric conditioner and not the cheapest own-brand washing powder she used in London, and stared at the pictures on her wall. There was one shot that she loved. Three girls racing down a cobbled hill on bikes, their hair streaming in the wind. Faces stretched open in joyous screams. Not that you could hear them, but you kinda could because the picture captured the moment so well that you could almost feel the breeze lifting your own hair and the bike picking up speed as you got nearer and nearer the bottom. Laura wanted to be one of those girls. She wanted to shoot those kinds of pictures. And not eating a bowl of pasta was totally worth it.

But there was still one unpleasant task to get through before the end of one of the suckiest days since records began. She dug out her phone and pressed 1, because Tom was the most important person on her speed dial. Or he used to be.

The phone rang and rang, even though it was Thursday night and he should be doing homework or watching television or a million other activities, which meant he could get to his phone before the voicemail clicked in.

'Hey, this is Tom. Leave a message. No, please leave a message. Don't just hang up because it's really annoying.' Laura smiled faintly because it was cute, even if he had no business to be away from the phone when they were in the middle of a fight.

'It's me,' she mumbled, curling up on the bed. 'It took me ages to find a more pleasant mood. Not sure that I was one hundred per cent successful but I am one hundred per cent sorry. So, anyway, if you're talking to me again, I'm back in Manchester for a week and I'd like to see you. And I thought maybe we could go to a club or something this Saturday . . .' She paused because this was all sounding a little disjointed and desperate. 'Look, just call me back and we'll sort out the fine-tuning then. Love you.'

She placed her phone carefully on the pillow next to her

and stared at it expectantly, waiting for it to ring. Five minutes later, it was still annoyingly silent.

God, it was nine-thirty on a Thursday night and she was languishing in her room with no telly because it was in London. Her parents weren't speaking to her. Her boyfriend was AWOL. And her entire future was hanging by a perilous thread. Life sucked. Someone should make a rubber stamp to that effect. Laura was just rifling through her bookshelves for something mindless to read when there was a tentative tap on the door.

'It's all right,' she called out. 'You can come in. I'm not throwing up or anything.'

'Nobody thought for one moment that you were,' her father said, opening the door. He shuffled restlessly on the threshold, as he didn't like being in her inner sanctum ever since she'd spray-painted the walls silver. It offended his inner DIY geek. 'Would you like to come downstairs . . . ?'

'For what? Like, the second part of the bollocking?' she demanded furiously, snatching up a book, before realizing it was *Great Expectations* and shoving it back on the shelf.

'I thought we'd banned that word,' her father said automatically. 'And actually your mother and I thought we'd watch a DVD and enjoy your charming company. Well, one out of two would be good.'

'Very funny.' The edge had gone out of her voice. Laura stood up and stretched tiredly. 'What DVD? Not *Pride And Prejudice* again?'

Her father shuddered. 'Something with Johnny Depp in it, I believe. Your mother was quite specific about that.'

'Well, I guess there's not much else to do.' Laura was already sidling towards the door and his outstretched arm so he could pull her towards him and kiss the top of her head. 'You're a stupid kid,' he said gruffly. 'God knows how you manage to get dressed in the morning.'

It was an opinion that her mother obviously shared, because she was sitting stiff-backed on the sofa with thin lips. But she made room for Laura next to her and gestured at the plate on the coffee table.

'I made you a little snack,' she said in a permafrost voice. 'It's absolutely carb-free.'

Her mother was so infuriating sometimes. Like, she made it impossible to stay mad at her. And by the time she'd finished her cheese and apple slices and a glass of semi-skimmed milk, Laura had her head on her mother's shoulder and they were holding hands.

Chapter Nine

Tom finally deigned to call at 9.07 p.m. the next night. Not like she was staring at the display on her phone and watching the minutes change.

'Oh, so you suddenly remembered how to use your mobile,' she snapped, forgetting all her good intentions to play the apologetic girlfriend and settling for mardy bitch again.

Tom sighed. 'I left my phone in my locker and then I had footie practice after school, but if I'd known you were going to be so pleased to hear from me, I'd have called you in the middle of English Lit,' he snapped right back.

Laura bit her lip back on the bitter retort that was bubbling up. Would it have killed him to call her at lunch or act like he was pleased that she was in town and a mere five minutes' walk away?

'Well, I'm home for a few days,' she said, deciding it was best not to continue the cold war and just concentrate on the facts. 'Do you want to see me?'

Another sigh, which was so heartfelt, she could have sworn the hairs on the back of her neck rippled in its slipstream. 'Of course I do – but God, Laura, did you have a personality transplant while you were in London?'

'No, I bloody well didn't . . .' Just the facts, go toward the facts, Laura. 'Can we just stop with the insults and make some arrangements? What's happening this weekend?'

'Nothing in particular. I think Johnny P's having an eighteenth birthday bash at the golf club tomorrow night.' Tom sounded a little cagey. If he'd been planning to go with some other girl, like that skank Marina Holloway for instance, then she was going to pull his head off his neck. 'There's no rush to sort anything out. You've only been home for five minutes.'

'I've been home for over twenty-four hours,' Laura pointed out significantly. 'And maybe we could round up the gang and go out for something to eat first.'

'Yeah, I suppose we could do that.'

'Could you give me a little enthusiasm to work with here? Hell, you could even go out on a limb and pretend that you're pleased I'm back instead of acting like it's a huge inconvenience.' For a second, she contemplated hanging up – but only for a second, because it would just make this weird scratchy argument last even longer than three days and counting. 'Look, I'm sorry that I was a humungous bitch when I spoke to you before. You know what I'm like when I get into a mood.'

Tom paused. 'Well, actually I don't, because you never used to get into moods, even when you were doing *Make Me A Model*. And this last month—'

'I've been a rollercoaster of different emotions and none

of them good ones,' Laura finished for him. 'I know I'm all schizo lately but it's been— hang on, there's someone at the door.' She put the phone down and stuck her head out of her bedroom. 'Mum! Door!' Why did they have to have the TV on so loud anyway? 'Muuuuummmmm!'

She started heading down the stairs. 'I don't know how my 'rents managed without me,' she grumbled down the phone. 'Anyway, so look, I'm sorry, I'm really, really sorry. I don't know how many ways to say it.'

'I think I got the message,' Tom said, as she wrestled with the chain on the front door to find him standing there, phone clamped to his ear. 'Had to keep you talking so we could have this romantic moment. It's like something out of a film, right?'

'A really naff, cheesy film,' scoffed Laura, switching her phone off so she could hurl herself into Tom's outstretched arms. 'I thought you were on the verge of breaking up with me, you pig.'

Colonel Meowington, wandering in after a heavy day of fanging around the nabe, was shocked by their display of public affection. Laura felt his tail twitching disapprovingly about her legs as he sidled past her.

But it felt so good to be wrapped up in Tom, like she was finally home at last. He cupped the back of her head and stroked the raggedy ends of her hair between his fingers before swooping in to plant a row of devastating kisses along her neck. He wasn't the only one with the wandering hands or mouth; Laura was currently stroking the hinterlands between Tom's shoulder blades and had her mouth pressed against his collarbone so she could inhale great whiffs of him. She'd missed his toasty boy smell.

'Let's take it upstairs,' she whispered. 'Then we can make up properly.'

'Parents?' enquired Tom, snaking his arms round her waist so they could shuffle across the hall like a boy/girl Siamese twin combo.

'Engrossed in *Desperate Housewives* with the door closed.'

It was a good fifteen minutes before either of them spoke again. Probably because his mouth was locked on hers for most of that time, but eventually they had to regroup to get with the half-montying.

Tom's eyes were fixed on her as she whipped off her top, and actually she'd have been pretty mad if they hadn't been. 'I thought you'd be all modelly and aloof and that I'd be scared to touch you,' he said softly. 'But I like your hair.'

Then he was the only person in the world, apart from Guiseppe and Heidi, who did. 'Thank you, because I do know that my hair looks like it fell on top of my head from a great height,' Laura smiled wryly. 'And you never, ever have to be scared to touch me.'

'You promise?' He sounded so unsure of himself, so unlike Tom in that moment, with the lamplight casting half-shadows across his face so he seemed younger, more vulnerable.

Laura pulled him towards her, into the light, so the little-boy-lost look she could hardly bear to see changed into something more familiar – well, actually something downright lecherous – which she could handle.

'So what you're saying is that you want me to touch you?' he leered, with a wolfish smile. 'Well, how very interesting.'

'Oh, cut out the fake Casanova routine.' She let her fingers walk across the planes of his face. 'God, I missed you so much. That's why I didn't phone much, because it just made the lack of Tom-ness even worse.' And that wasn't a *complete* lie. Just a fraction of one.

Tom ducked his head, trying to hide his pleased smile. 'Y'know, I reckon we've got a good half hour before your mother realizes that I'm in your bedroom and intent on doing unspeakably rude things to her only daughter.'

Laura made a show of looking at her watch. 'Only thirty minutes? Well, you'd better get on with those unspeakably rude things, mister, we're on the clock.'

She hadn't just missed Tom, but missed this too. How they'd cling to each other, legs entwined and mouths soft from kisses and all the sweet nonsense they'd whisper. She'd missed being his girl.

So she'd scurried home rather than being lectured about her lardiness and its coat-wrecking abilities? So what! She wasn't going to spend another second worrying about her weight or Heidi, bookings – any of it. She was going to live in the moment a bit more, starting with tomorrow night when she was going to hang with her gang, drink some, dance some, kiss *a lot*. She could go back to angst mode sometime in the future. Right now, she wasn't going to ruin her Tom-time by getting all introspective. 'That's so emo of you,' Candy would have said with a sneer. Even Hadley would have told her that only Botox got rid of the frown-lines. 'And that's only a temporary fix, sweetie.'

Her face felt strange. Unfamiliar. She was smiling, properly smiling for the first time in weeks.

'Why have you stopped kissing me?' she asked Tom, still grinning from ear to ear. 'Kiss me right now!'

'What are you so happy about?' Tom asked, stroking his fingers through what was left of her hair.

Laura wound her arms round his neck. 'Nothing. Everything. Hey, aren't you meant to be kissing me?'

Chapter Ten

Laura was always the last one to arrive. Even before she got sort of famous, she'd always had an uncanny knack of being fifteen minutes late for everything, so her grand entrance was inevitable. Tom never even came to pick her up any more because he got so tired of waiting for her to narrow down her wardrobe choices. If you had to make people wait, then it was best to be worth waiting for, in her humble opinion.

Tonight it had been easy though. No doubt about it, her outfit was seriously stylin'. She was wearing a broderie anglaise petticoat she'd found on a stall in Portobello Market, over footless black tights with her silver ballet slippers. She'd even improvised a pink satin sash with a ribbon from one of her Sparkle gift baskets. If she hadn't vowed to not think about You Know What until an unspecified later date, then she'd be seriously considering it as a fashion-forwards, go-see outfit.

Laura followed the waiter through the crowded restaurant, which was actually just a burger bar masquerading as a swank eaterie. And just around the corner, tucked into an alcove, were her gang. Jen and Paul were still surgically attached; Chris was crushing on

Chandra, who remained oblivious; and Cath and Dan were already bickering, because it was the foundation on which their relationship was built.

Laura paused, until one by one they all looked up and she could strike a pose. Just a casual one; hand on hip, face tilted ever so slightly to the left. 'Hey guys, did you miss me?'

Seemed that they had, because within a nanosecond she was in the middle of a four girl cuddle-athon.

'What *are* you wearing?' Cath gasped, when she'd finally stopped squeeing about Laura's hair. 'It's a bit Gothic Lolita.'

Laura adjusted her ribbon sash. 'It's kind of what Miu Miu were doing for Spring/Summer.'

'Huh?'

Oh my God, she was speaking fluent fashion! All those 'directionals' and 'on trends' and 'very Marc Jacobs' had finally infiltrated her neuron space. 'I mean, I think this is going to be a big look for summer and it will be comfy to dance in. Summer! Summer in *The OC*, she wears this kind of look.'

Jen nodded slowly, then looked down at her own low-rider jeans and camisole uncertainly. 'I bet everyone in London really dresses up all the time.'

'Not so much. Well, Candy and Hadley do, but Irina – she's from Russia, right – she wears shell suits with, like, woolly tights underneath them. And when I go with her on appointments all the stylists think she's making this daring fashion statement. It's really deluded.'

'I hope that tonight's going to be glamorous enough for you,' Chandra teased.

Laura let the statement percolate a little, just to process whether Chandra was taking the piss. Was she actually beginning to sound like some uppity little model who was too good to kick it with her friends? 'I'm still me, right?' she said eventually. 'You know that, don't you?'

'Well, who the hell else would you be, you daft cow?' Cath snorted, giving her the finger. 'Believe me, if you started with the diva antics, we'd be the first to tell you. Then we'd sell our video footage of you singing *Pretty Fly For A White Guy* at karaoke to the highest bidder.'

'But I never signed a release form,' Laura gasped dramatically, clutching her hand to her forehead. 'My people will sue.'

Cath snorted again. 'What*ever*. Look, I'm starving, sit down so we can order.'

Laura slid into the seat next to Tom and looked around to check that nothing alarming had been going on in her absence. That was when she spotted a boy and a girl who must have been seated at their table by mistake. Both were blonde, blue-eyed and supremely at home with her five best friends.

'Who are the new kids on the block?' she hissed in Tom's ear. 'Why did no one tell me about them? They look like an Aryan breeding experiment.'

'Shall we skip the wine and I'll just order you a saucer

of milk?' Tom whispered back. He leaned forward and cleared his throat. 'Cassie, James, this is Laura, my girlfriend. Laura, this is Cassie and James, we met them at the Camera Obscura gig last month.'

'God, it was so funny,' Jen butted in. 'The rail collapsed in the cloakroom and we all had to hunt for our coats and Cassie had exactly the same jacket as me, that green one from New Look, and then she had to chase me through St Anne's Square to get it back.'

'Oh, hi. Um, great taste in jackets.' Laura never knew what to say when she was introduced to new people. Candy usually cooed 'Cute shoes' in similar situations, but Laura couldn't see either of their feet under the table.

'So you're the famous Laura?' the Cassie girl said, and Laura wasn't imagining the challenge or the self-satisfied way she ran a hand through her shiny, blonde, rich-girl hair, as if to say, you might be a model but I'm much prettier than you. Which, not even. 'We saw you on that show.'

'Nice to meet you,' her boyfriend said, or grunted to be more accurate, and then went back to talking about football with Dan.

'Cassie works at this really cute little boutique and she gets us all discounts,' Chandra said, rustling the menu. 'Are we going to order, because the waiters are getting restless?'

Cassie might be the go-to-girl for cute little boutique discounts but she was also a bitch from way back, Laura could tell. Sometimes she thought that she must have some invisible radar on top of her head, which picked up other people's evil bitch rays. At least she had a boyfriend, because otherwise she'd be worried about Tom. Not about Tom, but about him being in close proximity with a girl like Cassie who was pure predator under all that girly blonde hair and glittery eyeshadow.

'So how long have you two been going out?' Laura asked sweetly. 'You look pretty serious.'

As questions go, it was fairly innocuous. Certainly no reason for everyone to start giggling and clapping like she'd spent the last two months honing her stand-up skills.

'Ewwwww! Cassie and James are brother and sister. They're, like, twins, you freak!' Jen managed to spit out, because she was one small step away from crying with laughter.

They were twins and *she* was the freak? Hey, she hadn't had to share womb space with anyone else! 'Silly me.' Laura pressed against Tom, to let him know he could stop laughing any time soon. Cassie smiled faintly, as if people assuming she was getting jiggy with her brother was her own personal cross to bear.

'It's all right,' she sighed, straightening her knife and fork. 'Happens all the time, doesn't it, Tom?'

Tom just chuckled all the more but didn't seem inclined to explain any further, and Laura's mind was already racing through a variety of possibilities all more lurid than the last, until she was saved by Cath, who was picking up on her telepathic distress signals.

'Can we order before I start chewing on the tablecloth,' she complained with just a tad too much eyebrow to be really convincing, but it worked. The next ten minutes were lost in a flurry over menus and exactly how many side orders of chilli fries were appropriate.

Laura finally exhaled and gestured to Tom to refill her wineglass.

'You OK?' he asked, tracing the back of her hand with the tip of his finger. 'Is this happening enough for you?'

She had to smile at that. 'What do you think I get up to in London? I spend most evenings fighting Irina for control of the remote and Hadley for visitation rights to the bathroom. This is about a thousand steps up, believe me.'

And he moved in close for a little smooch that was sweet enough to make up for the fact that she couldn't have dessert.

It's always the small things that make up a world. Holding hands with Tom, listening to Chandra and Jen giggling about the retro swimming hats they bought with flowers on them, Dan tossing olives into the air so he could catch most of them in his mouth. Laura felt flushed and glowing – though that might have had something to do with a glass of wine on an empty stomach and the forest of nightlights on the table.

She was just spacing out on the quiet bliss of it all when she realized that the waiter was standing next to her with pad poised. 'Can I have the Caesar salad? But I want the starter portion for my main course and no dressing. Oh, and no croutons.'

'God, Laura's gone totally ana,' Chandra announced to the table once the waiter had gone, because she'd had two glasses of wine and she so couldn't hold her drink. One hour from now, she'd be puking on some poor twat. Fact.

'I have not gone ana,' Laura said icily. 'I just watch what I eat now.'

'If we get fries to share, will it be all triggery for you?' Jen wanted to know.

'Don't be stupid,' Laura spluttered. It was out of her mouth before she could rein it back in. 'Do you think I'm fat?'

'No, you look slim,' Cath breathed, but she was a size sixteen so of course she was going to say that. 'And you always look great.'

'Yeah, Laura's slim but she isn't celebrity slim,' noted Chandra, who was definitely not getting any designer cast-offs that might come Laura's way. 'Celebrity slim is like about fifteen pounds lighter than normal slim.'

'Exactly,' Laura nodded emphatically. 'It's not like I'm going to become a lollipop, it's just that a lot of clothes that are sent to shoots are a size eight, or even a size six.'

'Who's a size six?' Tom frowned, eyes slightly glazed

over because this fell into the category of girltalk. 'Is that even possible?'

'Jacinta is, but her mum's from the Phillipines so it doesn't count – and Posh is a like a size zero!'

'But you're eating healthily, right?' Jen asked, snatching up a breadstick in a manner that could only be described as defiant. 'You don't just live on Diet Coke and cigarettes?'

Laura slumped against Tom; only the grounding weight of his hand on her thigh kept her from launching into the mother of all snits. 'Don't be an idiot, Jen.'

Support came from a really unlikely source. 'All models have to be careful about what they eat,' Cassie chimed in. 'I have a friend from New York whose sister is a model and she's *much* slimmer than you.'

Game on, bitch. Game fucking on. Well, not right at that moment because Laura couldn't think of a single cutting comeback, but Cassie had shot straight to the top of her shit list in fifteen minutes flat. That had to be some sort of record. Laura was forced to retreat.

But by the time their food had arrived, situation normal had resumed. She didn't want to come across like the Big I Am of modelling, but they wouldn't stop asking questions. After dishing the dirt on Candy and Hadley (and assuring a goggle-eyed Chandra that only half the dirt actually appeared in the gossip mags), they got on to the topic of her glittering career.

After extolling the glories of her Sparkle shoot (the puppies getting the requisite 'aw' noises), there wasn't much else to say. Laura glossed over the horrors of the *Skirt* cover and racked her brains for something to keep their expressions rapt. Even Cassie was concentrating more on Laura than her Garden Burger.

And she didn't mean to exaggerate, or like flat out lie, but it seemed easier to swap some names around. Maybe that's why Irina's constant stream of jobs seemed to have Laura in the starring role. It wasn't like her friends had a regular subscription to Japanese *Vogue* or *Ja*, Russia's best-selling fashion magazine.

'There's not really a language barrier,' Laura explained, warming to her theme. 'All photographers say "Love it, love it, make your eyes go big, great". I think there must be some fashion vocab book that they pass around.'

'Do you get to keep the clothes?' Jen asked, through a mouth full of fries. 'Is that a designer dress?'

Laura allowed herself a rueful chuckle. If modelling didn't pan out, she should really think about acting. 'It's vintage actually,' she admitted bashfully. 'You're not allowed to keep the clothes. They're just borrowed from the fashion houses, but sometimes you can buy them at discount. Still cost a fortune though.'

'Yeah, but you'll be able to afford them soon with the amount of work you're getting.' Tom had never sounded that proud of her before. Not even when she'd pretended that she understood the off-side rule. 'Sounds like you'll probably stay up there once the year's up.'

'We'll see,' Laura hedged. Man, would she have some explaining to do if they sacked her for ripping any more clothes.

'So you have been to Russia or Japan?' Cassie asked. 'I've always wanted to go to Tokyo.'

To the casual onlooker it seemed like an innocent-enough remark, but Laura knew better. 'You don't actually have to go abroad to shoot for foreign magazines,' she said patiently, like Cassie was a total philistine who couldn't be expected to understand the inner-workings of the industry. 'London is one of the centres of the fashion world. Loads of people come here to shoot actually.'

'Oh, it's just that—'

Shut up. Just shut up! 'It's a bit of secret but I'm probably going to New York in a month or so,' Laura improvised. It was like she'd swallowed the opposite of a truth serum. 'There are lots of clients out there who want to meet me. Anyway, I'm getting sick of the sound of my own voice and you must be too. Tell me again how much you missed me!'

If only she had a fraction of this confidence (or should that be bare-faced cheek?) when she went out on go-sees. Laura's hand was shaking slightly as she picked up her glass and drained the contents.

'Are you sure you're OK?' Tom whispered in her ear,

gesturing at her hand, which was still trembling. 'You've seemed on edge all night.'

'I'm still getting used to being the centre of attention.'

'You love it! You always did,' he teased, pinching the end of her nose even though she'd told him a million times that it worked her last nerve. 'Aw, my little supermodel.'

'I'm practically the same height as you,' she reminded him, digging her purse out of her bag as the waiter placed the bill on the table. If Cassie said anything about it being Laura's treat because she was super-successful then she'd be wearing the remains of her Chocolate Brownie Surprise.

Thankfully there was a God and he wasn't too annoyed about Laura flouting the ninth commandment, because Cassie got into one of the other cabs for the trek up to the golf club for Johnny P's birthday extravaganza. Laura had never really liked him anyway ever since he compared her to a giraffe when they went on a school trip to the zoo. OK, he'd been eleven at the time but she was *still* five inches taller than him.

There was a collective sigh as they followed the thundering bass into the function room. Laura would have been happy to die on the spot if it meant that she never had to have an eighteenth birthday party as crap as this one.

Paper streamers and a few anaemic balloons hung at strategic points along the room. There was a table laden with platters of limp sandwiches and jugs of orange squash.

True, there was a bar, but it was manned by a hefty man in a pink V-neck, who she knew for a fact played golf with her dad, so she couldn't even dull the senses with alcohol.

Even worse were the other party-goers, mainly hordes of hyperactive children, hopped up on too much sugar, careering off tables and trying to trip up people flailing around the dance floor. Bratty ankle-biters were one thing, but actual *old* people were quite another.

'Well, the joint's rocking,' Tom said heavily, looking behind him, but the others had disappeared, probably sloped off to have a sneaky fag at the third hole. 'Think it's too late to chase after the cabs?'

'It's horrible, I can barely look,' whimpered Laura. 'That woman's wearing a skirt so short I can see her pants. Just kill me now.'

'Let's find Johnny, shove the box of chocs at him and get out of here,' Tom decided. He could be very goal-orientated in a crisis situation. 'Five minutes. Ten minutes, tops.'

Laura reached out to clutch his hand, entwining their fingers so they weren't rent asunder by any wayward rug-rats. Tom was looking neither right or left, but dragging her across the dance floor on a one-man mission towards the bar, where he waved the battered box of chocolates that they'd bought at a garage en route hopefully in the air. 'Where's Johnny?' he asked the cluster of men drinking pints of bitter, who were all super-short and super-rat-faced, so there was a definite family resemblance.

One of them gestured in the direction of an open door to the left. 'Him and his friends are out back,' he grunted.

Laura winced as she prised one of her ballet flats off the sticky floor. Out back was a little ante room at the end of a corridor where someone had rigged up decks and a massive pair of woofers, all the better to be deafened by the sound of drill 'n' bass. The skankiest girls from her old school were all hoochie dancing like they were in a Pussycat Dolls video. She was really racking up points on the gusset tally for tonight.

'There he is,' she hissed at Tom, pointing at the furthest corner of the room, where the elusive Johnny P was downing a pint in one, to the accompaniment of encouraging bellows from his Neanderthal friends. 'Why did we think this party would be any good? He's a little git from way back.'

Tom shrugged, hand at her elbow to guide her away from a girl who was bogling hard enough to dislocate her hips. 'He's all right sometimes. He just shows off when his friends are around.'

'Whatevs.' Laura hung back as Tom strode to Johnny, who clasped him in a bear hug, slapping his back heartily so no one would think he was gay. As if any self-respecting gay guy would look twice at him.

'Tom, my man!' he cried, peering over his shoulder at Laura, who gave him a slightly less evil eye than she'd been planning. Hey, she even managed to raise one hand and limply wave it. 'Laura! Get your skinny arse over here!'

Well, at least he'd used a slightly inoffensive adjective. Laura shuffled over but kept her distance, because if he spilled beer on her white dress, then she'd have to kill him, birthday or not.

'Happy birthday, Johnny,' she parroted dutifully, pulling the card out of her bag. 'Had to write this in the cab so it might not be that legible.'

Johnny held the card aloft as if it was a holy relic at the very least. 'You got me a card?' he gasped. 'Didn't have to do that.'

Laura exchanged a look with Tom that said very clearly, 'Just how many pints has he had to drink?'

'I hope you're having a nice time,' she continued politely. Damn having good manners instilled at a young age. 'So, you can vote now, yay!'

Actually not yay, but ewwww! Because it was her turn to be wrapped in a sweaty hug. 'Can't believe you turned up, Laura.' Johnny sounded like he was very near to crying. That wasn't the usual reaction she got from him.

Tom was absolutely no help as he rifled in a plastic bin full of ice for what had better be two bottles of beer.

'Well, I'm back in town and I couldn't miss your birthday,' she said, gently disentangling herself. 'We've known each other since junior school.'

Johnny rubbed his beaky nose and looked shifty. 'You

brought any of your model mates with you?'

And the mystery of Johnny being her new best friend was now solved. 'Sadly, no. They had to stay in London, I begged them to come,' she added, taking the beer and ignoring Tom's warning look. 'Just me, I'm afraid.'

Johnny's attention was wavering now that the subject of her model mates was a non-starter. They didn't really have much else to talk about unless she brought up the whole giraffe thing or the time that he wet himself during the nativity play rehearsals and tried to hide the puddle by pushing Baby Jesus' crib over it.

'Nice one,' Johnny mumbled in lieu of anything else to say.

'Yeah, you too,' Laura said sweetly. 'Have a really great birthday.'

Out of the corner of her eye, she spotted Cath and Jen on the other side of the room and skidded over. 'Urgh, I just had to give Johnny P a birthday hug,' she groaned. 'I need to be fumigated when I get home.'

'Our little man's drinking enough for someone twice his size,' Cath noted and the three of them grinned. 'How long has it been since we've had a really good bitching session?'

Way too long. 'Hold that thought,' Laura said. 'I need to pee.'

'You mean even top models still go to the loo? Another dream shattered,' Jen called after her.

Laura thought about a cheeky two-fingered salute, but

beer and wine were sloshing about in her almost-empty stomach and finding a loo was her number one priority.

She joined the tail-end of a long queue snaking out of the Ladies and down the corridor.

Ten agonizing minutes later she was next. Jiggling frantically and clenching everything she had in the way of pelvic floor muscles was the only way to stop herself from . . . well, it was too awful to contemplate.

She heard a flush and the rattle of the lock, and took an eager step forward, when Chandra and Cassie pushed past her and crowded round the opening door.

'Hey, back up. There's a queue,' Laura pointed out, though they'd have had to have been legally blind to have missed out on the long line of tutting women. 'I'm next.'

Both girls turned around like a two-headed, glarey monster. 'I'm busting, Laur,' Chandra said belligerently. 'We'll just be a sec.'

Maybe she could have let it go if she hadn't been in far greater need than them. 'Look, I've been waiting for ages and so has everyone else . . .'

A little girl stood trembling in the now-open doorway. 'I was as quick as I could be,' she protested.

'. . .so you're just going to have to join the back of the line,' Laura continued. Being desperate for a wee gave her balls of steel.

'A great friend you are,' spat Chandra, squaring up so Laura could see exactly how broad her shoulders were in a boob tube that was under a lot of strain. 'Don't start disrespecting me, Laura.'

Oh God. Chandra when she was pissed up was a force of evil. 'I'm not disrespecting you,' Laura said far more calmly than she felt. 'You just have to wait your turn.'

And it would have been really cool if any one of the, oooh, ten other women waiting had jumped in with a bit of well-timed sisterly solidarity, but they'd all gone quiet.

Laura took a step forward towards the not-very-clean toilet, which had assumed almost mythic proportions, and found her way barred as Cassie placed her arm against the door frame. 'I can see through you,' she smirked. 'You think that because you won a low-rent modelling contest on the telly, it makes you better than the rest of us.'

'No, I don't,' Laura shot back, evil-eyeing Chandra so she'd know that the moment they were alone, she was going to open up a huge can of whupass on her two-faced head.

Chandra was beyond bothered. 'Yeah, you do. You always did. You're the only one who thinks you're something special. Even Tom—'

'Even Tom what?' There was no way humanly possible that the situation could have got any worse, but it just had. Cassie and Chandra shared a look. A knowing, spiteful look and if all her bodily fluids weren't currently in her bladder, Laura was pretty sure she'd have broken out in a cold sweat. Laura took another step forward, immensely grateful that she was five foot ten inches and could loom menacingly over Cassie and Chandra. 'Tom what?' she repeated in a low growl.

Cassie wasn't phased in the least. 'It's just like Chandra said, he didn't seem to think you were anything special when he was all over me.' Before Laura could process that bolt from the blue and wait for the ringing in her ears to stop, Cassie continued. 'And you were the ugliest cow on that show and I'm going to the loo and so is Chandra and I hope you piss yourself!'

A meaty hand landed hard on Laura's shoulder, sending her skidding back against the sink as the door slammed behind them. 'I'm not going to cry,' she told herself, rubbing her hip and trying not to look at the other girls who'd all found their voices and were whispering variations on 'Did you hear what they just said?'

And the worst thing of all, was that she *still* needed a wee and was just going to have to stand there and sweat it out (almost literally) and probably have another confrontation with the two nastiest skank-bag, bitch whores in Greater Manchester. She wouldn't put it past them to pee all over the seat.

The loo flushed again and they traipsed out, making sure to hold the door open for her. 'There you are, Your Majesty,' Cassie giggled, making sure to bump Laura as she scurried into the cubicle. 'See, you still need to piss just like everyone else. Now, I wonder where Tom's got to?'

It wasn't so bad. Not really. Chandra was someone she could do without and Cassie was lying. Cassie *had* to be lying, because Tom would never do that to her, and Jen and Cath would have said something. It would be a great story to tell Candy when she got back to London, Laura decided as she carefully covered the seat with neatly folded loo roll. They had to have a whole slew of scabby diseases between them. After all that, it took a good few seconds for her to relax enough to actually attend to the matter in hand.

Luckily, they weren't waiting for her outside to start round two, or should that be round three? Laura ignored the curious glances she was still getting, washed her hands, gave a cursory look at her blotchy, lip-trembly reflection, then pushed past the rest of the line, which seemed to have doubled in length, so she could storm out and get someone to tell her what the hell had been going on in the last two months.

She'd been through worse than this – most of it beamed into the nation's living rooms – so why were tears running down her cheeks faster than a windy day at Niagara Falls? She was practically going into convulsions from the shoving and the swearing and the look of utter hatred on Cassie's pug-ugly face as she'd torn into her. And Chandra? She was in for some nasty surprises. OK, Laura might live in London right now but she was still popular enough to call in some favours and ensure that the last year of Chandra's school career would be never-ending misery.

Laura shoved her way across the dance floor to where Jen and Cath were propped up against a speaker stack. She took a moment to rub her fingers under her eyes to curb the mascara streaks. There was no point in getting hysterical. It was obvious that Cassie had to scam on other girls' boyfriends because she had severe personality flaws. And thin lips. Quite frankly, compared to Irina or Candy, when it came to playing people, Cassie was strictly amateur league. Cath and Jen would know what had really happened and it could all be nipped in the bud calmly . . .

'What the hell has been going on?' she screamed. Well, it had sounded calm in her head. 'Why are you hanging around with that thin-lipped bitch?'

Cath's arms were around her in a second. 'Oh, you mean—'

'How many thin-lipped bitches do we know?' Jen shouted over the music. 'We've been keeping an eye on her, don't worry,' she added darkly, looking over her shoulder as if she expected Cassie to materialize in a puff of glittery smoke. 'The situation was spelled out loud and clear. I even used flash cards.'

That didn't sound good. It sounded like a world of no good. Also, it was really hard to hug Cath back when she was so tense that she thought her arms might snap in two. 'Oh yeah? What situation would that be?' Laura gritted her teeth. She had the answer narrowed down to only one possibility.

'Tom,' they said in perfect unison.

'What about him? What did he do?'

'He was the innocent victim. Cassie thought that having a girlfriend in London meant that Tom was free to be at her beck and call. You know what he's like, Laura? He can't say no to anyone.'

'I'm going to fricking *kill* him!'

Cath's consoling pat just made Laura feel worse. She couldn't bear to be touched when she was five seconds away from a homicidal rage. It was just as well there were no pickaxes in the immediate vicinity.

'The boy's oblivious,' Jen said rationally. 'He has five thoughts in his head: you, football, passing his driving test, Oxbridge and football again. He's not used to sneaky boyfriend-stealers.'

'Yeah, he's way too dumb to pick up on the stuff she was doing.'

'Stuff? Stuff?!' Laura's voice was so high that something in the back of her throat felt like it had just ruptured. 'Define stuff!'

'Y'know, *stuff*.' If Jen didn't stop being big with the cryptic, then things were going to get really ugly. 'Cassie was doing stuff. Like evil-girl, boyfriend-stealing stuff. Looking at his mouth when he spoke to her . . .'

'And touching his arm all the time,' Cath added helpfully.

'Oh, and once she even patted him on the bum as he

125

walked past her, but it was really crowded and I don't think he noticed.' Jen gave her a crooked smile as if it was OK for Tom to have his butt stroked as long as he didn't realize it. Wrong. If anyone was going to get in petting distance of that posterior, it was going to be Laura.

She took a deep breath to centre herself, which was as much use as peeing on a forest fire. 'I knew something was up with him,' she spat. 'I bloody well knew it!'

Except actually she hadn't, because she'd been too busy plumbing new depths of self-obsession and thinking only about the wobble factor of various parts of her body. 'How could he not know that she was copping a feel of his arse? It's not like it's Teflon-coated or something. And she said he was all over her, which implies kissing! Was there kissing? Did you see kissing?' Laura stamped her foot because the occasion really merited it. 'I could tell she was a ho-bag the moment I clapped eyes on her.'

'But you're a top model,' Jen protested, slinging a sweaty arm round Laura's shoulder. 'Like, she's any competition. So can we please talk about something else or start dancing again?'

'Kissing! Was there any?' Why was she repeating herself? And why were Jen and Cath looking at each other like that? She was so sick of people exchanging looks when she asked them stuff. 'Oh my God, there so was!'

Cath was mechanically patting her arm again. 'Look, Laura, don't make a fuss about this,' she said, with an edge of exasperation. 'There might have been a teensy bit of kissage, but I took it upon myself to have a friendly little chat with her. The words "back off, bitch" featured quite heavily, so let it go.'

No way was Laura going to let it go. 'Why didn't you tell me?' she demanded, and people were starting to stare even though this was a private conversation which was none of their damn business. She seized a wrist apiece and dragged them into the corridor, even though Jen dug her heels in all the way.

'You're totally overreacting,' she complained, rubbing her wrist reproachfully. 'We had the sitch under control. There was no point in upsetting you.'

'But that wasn't your decision to make,' Laura pointed out angrily. Oh, she was mainlining on moral indignation. 'You should have called me.'

'Yeah, we should have,' Cath agreed and a little bit of validation was very welcome at this point, even if her delivery lacked credibility. 'But then you'd actually have had to return the call and you're not very good at doing that.'

Laura stared at Cath as if she had ectoplasm spurting out of her nostrils. 'I return calls,' she insisted. 'Most of the time. I've been really busy!'

Really busy not being really busy.

'Well, whatever.' Jen shrugged. 'You weren't here, and Cath and I didn't see the point in dragging you into it.'

Laura thought about stamping her foot again and settled for clenching her fists extra hard. 'But it was about me!'

'When is it *not* about you?' Cath suddenly shouted, taking a couple of angry steps forward so she was in Laura's face. 'It's always about you. God, you haven't asked me a single question all evening about what I've been up to. So, excuse us for not wanting you to completely overreact about something that was under control.'

They'd all had too much to drink. Cath and Jen's faces were red and belligerent and, from the flush heating up her own cheeks, Laura guessed she was a perfect match. Except, really she was the odd one out, which was an entirely new look and not one that brought out the green in her eyes.

It wasn't always about her. It was just *stuff* happened to Laura. Not just the same old school, homework, one big night out a week that Cath and Jen had to look forward to. She might be having troubles kick-starting her career, but she was still a model. And she was still the pretty one and they just couldn't stand it.

'I bet it's been great not having me here to get all the attention,' Laura hissed. Tonight was turning up all sorts of nasty surprises, and learning that her two best friends in the entire world had been managing just fine without her was the easiest one to deal with. 'That's why you didn't tell me, because you couldn't wait to see me fall off my pedestal.'

'Oh, believe me, you were never on a pedestal,' Jen snapped. 'We *were* looking out for you – but I don't know why we bothered because you've become even more self-obsessed than you used to be, and that's saying something!'

'Not self-obsessed,' Cath hastily interjected as Laura's mouth gaped open. 'You're a little bit spoilt, Laura – and really you should be having this out with Tom, not us.'

Laura was sick of people making a shopping list of her supposed flaws. She'd had two months of it from Heidi and now her best friends thought they could slag her off to her face. God knows what they'd been saying about her behind her back. 'No wonder Cassie's your new best friend if I'm such a pain to be around,' she sniffed. Her voice was meant to resonate with icy disdain but it just came out as a petulant whine. 'I'll see you later, or whatever.'

'Don't be so ridiculous,' Cath called after her, but Laura didn't bother to turn around as she pushed open the fire door and collapsed on the step outside.

She hugged her knees and hoped that she looked deep in thought, rather than one sniff away from a full-on crying jag. There were a group of kids further down the yard passing a joint around and all staring at her. In London, no one knew who she was but here, back home, she was the local girl made good. The one that got away. She was living the dream and all those other stupid clichéd phrases that made no sense when her life was unravelling as surely as that coat she'd torn the day before yesterday.

She dabbed at her eyes, which were starting to leak, with the hem of her dress, watching dispassionately as streaks of black mascara desecrated the pristine white lace. It was all messed and she didn't know how to put it right.

'Laura! There you are!'

She looked up, eyes glassy with tears yet to be shed, to see Tom. Bet Cassie was looking a much more attractive proposition right now.

'Hey, what's the matter?' he asked softly, climbing over her so he could crouch down and take her frozen hands in his. 'Are you crying?'

Laura turned her head away from that befuddled gaze of his, which was beginning to become a permanent feature every time he looked at her. 'They said . . .' she choked out, and couldn't finish the sentence because it had never happened. If she said it, it would become real.

'Who said what?'

Furiously, she wiped her eyes with the back of her hand and willed herself to hiccup out the words. 'I had an argument with Jen and Cath,' she said in a rusty voice.

He definitely looked wary. His eyes were darting in all directions, rather than focusing on Laura. 'Oh yeah, what did you argue about?'

'Stuff,' she said obliquely. 'Cassie . . .' Laura tailed off and waited to see if he'd take the bait.

He didn't just take it; he flailed helplessly like he really was trapped at the end of a fishing line. Tom dropped her hands so he could scratch his neck and stare at her bug-eyed. 'They told you? But they said they wouldn't!'

This conversation was going nowhere that she wanted it to go. 'So what's going on?'

'Who told you what was going on?' he repeated back at her, and it was like some dumb drama-group exercise to see who could get the most amount of anguish in their voice.

'Well, what *is* going on?' Ha! She was the winner! Funny, but Laura didn't feel like crying any more. She faced him down with suddenly dry eyes and a fast-beating heart. 'What's going on, Tom?'

And she knew what he was going to say before he'd even opened his mouth. Could tell from the way he hesitated as he tried to come up with something that wouldn't sound quite so bad. Guess he couldn't manage it. 'Cassie and me,' he said. 'We hooked up.'

There were long moments when she just stared at Tom's stricken face; stricken because he'd done things that he never should have. To *her*. Cheated. Betrayed. Destroyed. Horrible, ugly words that barely described the way he'd just ripped out her heart.

He was waiting for her to say something, but all she could do was flash him a bright smile that made her cheeks ache. 'You know, you could have just denied everything and I would have believed you.'

'But nothing happened. Not really,' Tom croaked and when he tried to take Laura's hand she was glad, because it was an excuse to slap his fingers away. To hurt him. 'Will you let me explain, please?'

Laura stood up, which seemed like an amazing feat. 'There's nothing to explain. Who do you think told me in the first place but Cassie? Congratulations, Tom, she's a real catch if you like skeevy, spiteful bitches, which you obviously do.'

As speeches go, it was a pretty good one. Tom seemed to think so because his face started to crumble and, as he took a step towards her into the light above the door, Laura could see tears coating his lashes. 'You've got it all wrong,' he started to say, but was interrupted by the little coterie of dope-smokers strolling over.

'Hey, Tom, Laura,' one of them said. 'You guys having a fight?'

'We're not fighting,' Laura said sweetly, watching Tom's shoulders sag with relief. 'We're breaking up.'

Everything speeded up to a constant flicker and flash of images: Tom's hand on her arm, before she wrenched away from him. Cath and Jen's perplexed expressions as Laura grabbed her bag and stormed out. Even Chandra daring to come up to her as she dived for the main doors, then falling back as she saw Laura's face.

Time only righted itself as she started trudging down the hill that led back into town, fumbling in her bag for her phone.

Thank God her dad answered and not her mum. He just listened to her garbled plea for a lift, told her to wait at the garage round the corner, and within ten minutes he was pulling up. Must have lead-footed it all the way. It was toasty warm in the car, but she still couldn't stop shivering even with the heater turned up.

'You'd better do something about your face,' her father said. 'Otherwise your mother will want to know what happened.'

Laura snapped on the light and looked helplessly at her red face. She licked at a tissue so she could get rid of the black tear tracks marching down her cheeks, before dabbing on some tinted moisturizer.

'Do you want to talk about it?' he asked, which was sweet. But she could sense his panic about having to offer advice on a Saturday-night situation that would probably fall way outside of his remit.

Laura shook her head and dived for her phone, which had burst merrily into life. Tom's name was flashing and she switched it off. 'When we get home, if anyone calls, I don't want to speak to them,' she mumbled. 'Say that I've gone to bed.'

Then she closed her eyes so that he'd get the message that she didn't want to talk any more. If only her mother was as unconfrontational. Despite the hurried repair job, she took one look at Laura's face and launched into a series of questions, each one designed to make her heart flip over.

'Did you have a row with Tom? Or one of the girls? The phone hasn't stopped ringing. Have you been crying? You look like you've been crying. Why won't you tell me what's wrong? You were in such good spirits when you set out, I just don't know what could have happened in such a short time. I'll make us a cup of tea and we can have a chat,' she banged on, without coming up for air.

Sometimes Laura wondered if her mother had ever worked for a clandestine branch of the special forces, because there had to be some explanation for her mad interrogation skill. 'I don't want tea,' she insisted, her voice croaky from all the tears. 'I just want to go to bed.'

'What about some hot chocolate then, with marshmallows, and I made some fruit cake today . . .' She was relentless. All Laura could do was wave her hand vaguely, which might have meant yes, no or shut the hell up, and back out of the kitchen slowly.

It wasn't just avoidance tactics (though that was about thirty-seven per cent of it), she was struggling under a huge wave of tiredness as she skinned out of her clothes and fell into bed. She didn't want to think about any of it; Tom and Cassie, or why Tom should suddenly be linked by an ampersand to a girl's name that didn't belong to her. Or why she'd decided to come home in the first place. It was far easier to burrow down under her duvet and force herself into the welcoming arms of sleep.

Chapter Eleven

Fourteen hours of sleep nearly became fifteen, but for an insistent tap on the door, followed by her mother with a breakfast tray.

Even the wonderful denial land of slumber couldn't compete with the smell of bacon and freshly brewed coffee. Laura sat up and frowned.

'I only get breakfast in bed on my birthday,' she yawned. And just as she was all ready to snap out a reprimand about bacon sandwiches not being on any diet that she knew about, she realized that a) they were smothered in brown sauce and b) she wanted to be a model more than anything in the world. Wanted it far more than she ever had.

Maybe it was the first time that a bacon sandwich had ever led to such a startling epiphany, but it was true. She didn't have anything else left. No Tom because he was sucking face with that twenty-per-cent-discount-wielding skank. Her friends weren't her friends any more. She'd missed too much school to be able to catch up without repeating a year. Being pretty was the only thing she had going for her. She had to make the modelling thing work because her life really did depend on it.

Laura could feel her face crumple in on itself as her eyes started spurting out more tears.

'Oh love,' her mum cooed, sitting down on the bed. 'Why won't you tell me what the matter is?'

'Tom and I broke up.' She was never going to get used to saying that. 'He's been copping off with this horrible bitch—'

'Language, Laura!'

'OK, she's a supercilious *cow* and he . . . he . . . how could he?'

'Eat your breakfast.' Her mother was employing the sneakiest tactic she had in her arsenal: the comforting hair-stroke. 'You'll feel better with some food inside you. Honestly, Laura, you've got a lovely figure, how could anyone think you need to lose weight?'

Laura found a resolve she didn't know she had as she pushed away the breakfast tray. 'Do you know how many fat units are in a single rasher of bacon?' Not that she knew herself, but there had to be a lot. 'Mum, I'm going back to London today. I've got all these jobs coming up and I need to get ready for them.'

Lies that you told your parents to get them off your back really didn't count. But it still took three hours of pleading and threats and promises before she was back on the London train. All she could hope was that their mother/daughter bond was strong enough to survive this temporary blip, because she hadn't even got a kiss goodbye, just a terse: 'Do your coat up. It looks like it's going to rain.'

But her mother's disapproval she could handle. Heidi's disapproval was something else entirely. Laura had her mobile number, which was strictly for emergencies. Heidi had been really specific about that. But getting her career back on track was an emergency. Like, duh!

A Virgin train toilet wasn't the most auspicious venue to relaunch herself back on the fashion scene (and why did some people think they were too good to flush a loo?), but Laura didn't have that many options.

'Hi, Heidi, it's me, Laura,' she said as perkily as she could. 'Sorry about calling you on a Sunday.'

'You've got some explaining to do. I'm not impressed with your little disappearing act.'

Oh, *crap*. After two days without her, Heidi was still the same sunny soul.

'I was going to call you on my mobile but, um, it's broken. There was a thing with my mum and I had to go home really suddenly . . .'

'Are you coming back to London? You'd better be.' Heidi sounded very definite about that. Which had to be a good thing, right? 'We need to have a talk.'

'I thought we could just have a little chat on the phone,' Laura demanded plaintively. 'Like, clear the air, because I really am committed to being a model and I just wanted you to know th—'

'I'm not going into this now, Laura. Ted and I want to see you tomorrow morning. Make it eight-thirty, and believe me, I'm not happy about having to get up at the arse-crack of dawn either. And if you know what's good for you, then you'll be there.'

'You're not going to sack me, are you?' The question leaked out of her mouth as an anguished moan. 'Oh God, if you are, please don't.'

'It can all wait until tomorrow,' Heidi stated firmly. 'I do have a social life and, right now, I'd like to get back to it.'

Obviously whatever it was that had to be said would be more effective if they could see her falling into tiny, sobbing pieces right in front of them.

'OK, I'll see you tomorrow morning.' Laura's perkiness was a mere husk of its former self.

It was starting to feel less like a glorious return to London to reclaim her crown and move of a forced march to have what was left of her dreams smashed into smithereens.

Chapter Twelve

After a sleepless night in a bed that hadn't miraculously grown a few inches in her absence, Laura was up at six. Anything was better than watching the shadows on the wall lengthen and get angry about Tom. And then get even angrier with herself for missing him.

It didn't look like anyone had been within glancing distance of a supermarket since she'd been gone, so she sat on the sofa, nibbling at a Zone bar she'd found at the back of one of the cupboards. But she was just delaying the inevitable. It was time. Time to haul her phone out of her bag and switch it on for the first time since Saturday night.

It burst into action, bleeping, flashing and vibrating like an electronic emissary from the underworld. There were twenty-three voice messages, forty-seven texts and eighty-four missed calls. This must have been exactly how Pandora felt when she opened the box.

Tom's voice messages started off with frantic enquiries as to where Laura had gone, and impassioned entreaties about how he could explain. But by the evening he was vibrating with a quiet, dull anger because it was all Laura's fault. She'd gone to London, she hadn't returned his calls or when she had, she'd been a moody bitch. She'd practically thrown him into Cassie's welcoming arms. By Sunday afternoon, he was in a more conciliatory mood because 'We've both acted like a pair of twats and would you just call me, Laura, because this silent treatment isn't achieving anything'. And on Sunday night, he was done. 'You could at least have had the guts to talk to me, Laura but facing up to reality has never been your thing, has it?'

Interspersed with Tom's ever changeable moods were calls from Jen and Cath trying to explain their reasons for getting economical with the truth. 'We didn't think you'd ever find out. So what was the point of telling you all the gory details and making you upset? And you're really not *that* self-obsessed.' Cath rattled on for so long that the message cut out, but she was back in an instant, intent on saving her own skin.

Oh, and there was a call from Candy asking for instructions on how to use the blender. If she hadn't been silently weeping so as not to wake the others, Laura might have raised a feeble titter.

She was just starting on the text messages, which were all pretty much the same, apart from the complete absence of any vowels, when she heard one of the doors creak open. Laura shoved the phone between the couch cushions and tried to appear nonchalant as Hadley appeared in the doorway.

It was gratifying to note that little Miss California Toothpaste had severe bedhead and pillow creases pressed

140

into her cheeks. In fact, she looked like a girl who was just starting to crest the wave of a serious hangover, especially when she moaned pitifully, 'I need water!'

In fact, she needed water so desperately that she didn't even go to the fridge for the filtered variety but grabbed a mug and filled it straight from the tap. Laura concentrated on nibbling at her Zone bar and holding her tears at bay but, what joy, Hadders was in sharing mode.

'I'm so dehydrated,' she announced, flinging herself down on the armchair. 'Candy's Margaritas are lethal.'

Laura had heard the sounds of tequila-induced carousing until about two a.m., so she nodded without much sympathy and concentrated on a tiny white patch on Hadley's ankle where the fake tan hadn't quite taken.

'Why are you up so early? Have you got a shoot? Lucky you.' Even a hangover couldn't shut Hadley up. 'I can't even get arrested. Like, literally. Even when I get papped being drunk and disorderly.'

'Hadley, why the hell would you want to get arrested?' On the other hand, Hadley's deep and frequent vapidness was always distracting.

'Y'know, column inches. My publicist is trying to market me as the new wild child, 'cept he calls it something French. Infant . . .'

'*Enfant terrible*,' Laura supplied with the ghost of a grin, which felt strange on her face. 'You should probably go back to bed and sleep it off.'

Hadley grimaced. Without her hour-long application of make-up and hair products, she looked like a bleached-out photograph; a shadow of her usually sparkly self. 'I might throw up in a minute,' she confessed, curling her legs up under her. 'So, anyway, like, were you just crying?'

Laura's response was automatic. 'Of course not!'

'I cry all the time.' Too much tequila had really loosened Hadley's tongue. 'But in the bathroom, so you guys won't hear.'

'What do you cry about?' Laura asked curiously, because she hadn't even realized that Hadley had enough depth to actually, well, have genuine emotions.

Hadley waved her hand around. 'The usual, I guess. Like, I miss LA and Mr Chow-Chow – he's my Chihuahua; my mom's looking after him but she's a very cold person. And I think about how famous I used to be. I was a household name and now people think I ODed at a *Playboy* party. George showed me the post on defamer.com.'

There really wasn't a lot that Laura could say to that. The household name stuff anyway. 'I miss Colonel Meowington,' she admitted. 'My cat. And, well, my friends sometimes.'

Not right now, admittedly, but generally she missed them.

'Yeah, I love that little picture board thing in your room,' Hadley remarked. 'All those birthday parties and stuff. Y'know, I never had a proper birthday party when I was little, with cake and presents that people had actually chosen. It was just, like, this photo op and my mom would have a gift registry at Saks for, like, diamond necklaces. I always wanted to go to Chuck E Cheese, and she'd get really mad about it. Boy, she'd just blow up.'

Laura could remember each individual birthday party she'd ever had, and the time her mum spent on everything from baking a triple-chocolate cake to selecting presents for the goodie bags. 'The diamond necklaces sound cool, though.'

'Not like I ever got to keep them,' Hadley yawned. 'Anyways, I think it's cool to have pictures of your friends. Maybe I should see if there's a photo of Mr Chow-Chow on the Internet.'

It was time to go, seriously. Five more minutes and she'd be running late, but now Laura wasn't just feeling miserable about her own sorry existence but miserable for Hadley too, who sounded like she had cuddle deficiency syndrome or something. 'I split up with my boyfriend,' she heard herself say. 'He cheated on me and my friends knew about it and they didn't tell me, that's why I was crying.'

Hadley leaned forward excitedly. 'Oh my God, that's rank,' she breathed, her face squinching up into exactly the same expression she'd worn on the poster for her movie franchise, *Little Girl Lost 1, 2, 3* and *4*, which had gone straight to DVD. 'If I had a boyfriend and he did that to me, I'd like leak a story to E!News that he had substance abuse issues.' She thought about it for a second. 'But I do have a boyfriend.' Just in case Laura was in any doubt. 'George is my boyfriend and I know for a fact he'd never screw around with another girl behind my back.'

And if Laura was unsure if George might possibly play for the other team, now she was one hundred per cent convinced. 'I don't think E!News would be interested in whether Tom had a substance abuse problem,' she mused. 'Might be able to work on his footie coach though. But also my eyes are all swollen, I have this huge zit on my chin and I'm due at Fierce for a major, major bollocking.'

But Hadley had given her undivided attention for all often minutes and was fading fast. 'Yeah, that sucks,' she yawned again. 'Going back to bed.'

It's not like Laura had really expected any deep understanding from Hadley. 'I'd better get gone,' Laura said, standing up. 'You should probably drink some more water and then you won't feel so bad next time you wake up.'

Hadley was already beetling out of the room. 'Whatever.'

Laura checked her bag and opened the front door. She'd never felt less like having her life destroyed. Well, what was left of it.

'Hey, Laura, wait up!' Hadley was hurrying down the stairs after her, even though her tank top and sleep shorts were better suited to Malibu than Camden. Laura turned around in time to have an armful of Hadley.

'I forgot to wish you good luck,' she gasped. 'I'm so "It's all about me" sometimes.'

Laura could do nothing but yelp as Hadley's hands were like little miniature blocks of ice. 'You're freezing,' she pointed out. 'Go back inside.'

'Oh, see, that's why I came after you.' Hadley pulled two cans of Diet Coke out from behind her. 'They're super cold,' she added helpfully.

'Right, OK.' Laura was starting to wonder if Hadley hadn't done a whole bunch of mind-altering drugs the night before, as well as margaritas. 'Um, thanks, I'll drink them when I get back.'

Hadley giggled. 'Don't be silly. They're not to drink. You put them on your eyes and they'll reduce the puffiness. My make-up artist on *Hadley's House* used to swear by it.'

'That's so sweet, Hadders.' And it *was* really sweet, even if she would have to strap-hang on the Tube with two cans of fizzy pop pressed against her eyes. 'Thanks. Well, I'll see you later.'

Hadley gave a tired little wave as she traipsed back up the stairs.

Heidi was waiting by the big sliding doors, with a scowling face.

'I'm here,' Laura announced unnecessarily, but with fifty per cent added pep.

Heidi thrust something into her hand. 'Go and put this on and then come into the conference room.'

'This' was a black bikini. Obviously they meant business

and making her step on the scales just wouldn't be humiliating enough.

At least heels made her legs look longer and slimmer. Laura sucked in her stomach until she almost couldn't breathe and attempted to stroll into the conference room with a strut in her step.

'Ah, Laura, we meet at last,' said the famous Ted, and what do you know? He had a posh Mancunian accent that would have made her homesick if she wasn't concentrating on clenching her tummy muscles. He also had a black polo-neck, nerdy glasses and a supercilious attitude. *Quelle surprise.* 'Go and have a look in the mirror and tell me what you see.'

The back wall of the conference room was one gigantic mirror, lit up by the sun glinting in from the big picture windows. Laura had no choice but to walk slowly towards it and take stock.

Preening in front of the mirror was pretty much a vocation with her, but never in a bikini and never under such unflattering lighting. Laura gave the tiniest shimmy imaginable and watched in horror as her belly rippled. And worse, she definitely had muffin top spilling over the boy-cut bikini bottoms. She turned round, craned her neck, and winced at the faintest traces of cellulite dimpling the backs of her thighs. She'd actually put on weight.

How was that possible? It was possible because although

she'd not eaten any carbs for three days and walked briskly on a treadmill when the mood took her (which wasn't often), she'd hadn't made the slightest effort to cut back on her junk food intake.

'Back to me, Laura,' Ted ordered, with a beckoning finger. When Laura finally got to her destination, that same finger gently prodded her in the belly.

'Hi,' Laura mumbled because it seemed rude not to say anything, even when someone was giving you a fat assessment check.

'You all right, love?' Ted peered around her hipbone and made an 'ah' noise.

If Ted jabbed his finger into her for much longer then she was going to yank it off. Instead, Laura contented herself with gazing at the mole on Kate Moss's shoulder on the black-and-white portrait that hung behind Ted.

'There's no point measuring anything. It's pretty obvious. She's naturally curvy but most of this is puppy-fat!' Ted diagnosed triumphantly. 'Should be easy enough to lose.'

'But I've been working out,' Laura reminded them plaintively. 'Most days anyway.'

Heidi stared disconsolately at Laura's pelvic cradle as if it were personally responsible for all the wrongs in the world, including global warming and *Laguna Beach*. 'Yeah, I spoke to Gustave, your trainer, and he said that he's lucky if he can get you on the treadmill, never mind actually breaking a sweat. We talked about this. I was really clear.'

Laura gasped at the unfairness. Hadn't Gustave taken the personal-trainer equivalent of the Hippocratic oath? Did client confidentiality mean nothing to him?

'I've been trying,' she insisted and, in that second, she really believed it. 'I have. I've cut out meals, and short of sticking my fingers down my throat, what else do you want me to do?'

The 'I'm not just a senior booker but a fun guy too' expression slid off Ted's face in a nanosecond. 'That might go on at other agencies, but it does not happen at Fierce,' he bit out. 'Is that clear, Laura?'

The flush of shame even mottled her tummy. 'Yes,' she whispered, painfully aware that every time she opened her mouth she either lied or made the situation even more horrific than it already was. 'I'm sorry.'

Ted gave her a warm smile, which she really didn't deserve. 'So sweetie, how much chocolate do you eat?'

It was on the tip of her tongue to deny all knowledge of chocolate or crisps or sausages fried in batter, but Ted was already pursing his lips in a way which said very clearly, 'Come on, kid. You can't bullshit a bullshitter'.

'Like, maybe two or three bars a day,' Laura admitted grudgingly.

'If you stuck to three healthy meals and a couple of snacks and worked out, the weight would drop off,' Heidi insisted, but it was easy enough for her to say. She was one of those tiny, elfin women who probably had to buy children's sizes so they'd fit properly. 'If you want this, if you really, really want this, then you're going to have to make sacrifices. Chunky KitKats or modelling – make a choice, Laura. You can't have them both.'

Never eat chocolate again? Laura already felt light-headed from the imminent deprivation. 'I can do that,' she heard herself say with a grim determination, which surprised the hell out of her. 'I will lose weight sensibly. And I'll get all hot and sweaty at the gym, I promise.'

'You'd be great for swimwear and under . . .' Ted mused, and Laura's face squinched up as if she'd just been forced to down an entire pot of curdled yoghurt.

She was no Gisele or Heidi Klum. She'd end up in her undies, boobs thrust out, in some tacky lad's mag. If she was going to be a model, and that was the mootest of points right now, then she wanted to wear beautiful clothes in pictures that she was proud to have in her book.

'I just . . . I want to do high fashion,' she pleaded, ignoring Heidi's unimpressed stare and concentrating on the encouraging nods and head-tilts she was getting from Ted. 'I know I can do it if you give me another chance.'

And it wasn't just the terror she felt about having to slink back to Manchester with the words 'abject failure' tattooed across her forehead so Cassie and Chandra, and probably even Jen and Cath, could line up to laugh at her.

Not even close. It was because now that it could all get taken away from her, she had that feeling again; the one she used to have when she'd spend all her Saturdays trailing around the Trafford Centre hoping to get spotted. That she wanted to be a model; the next Kate Moss, a muse, an inspiration. Laura wanted to be in the kind of shoots that she used to rip out of magazines and pin on her walls. If she could actually get booked, then she'd work that camera like no model ever had.

'Is this really what you want, Laura?' Ted asked gently. 'Because you don't seem as motivated as a lot of the other girls. Irina, for instance, she's hungry for it.'

Irina was hungry for anything, especially if it was in the fridge with Laura's name stuck on it. 'Don't talk to me about being hungry,' Laura said mournfully and Ted sniggered slightly before scratching his chin with the end of his pen.

'Now if you could just show a little more bit of that sass at go-sees, I'm sure this dry spell would become a veritable monsoon. See, it's all to do with how you pose; how you hold yourself,' Ted said, gesturing at Kate Moss pouting on the wall. 'Kate was too small but she redefined attitude. Irina has a really prominent jaw but she knows how to disguise it when she's in front of the camera. Every single model has flaws, but the successful ones know how to hide them.'

Maybe, just maybe, she could practise in front of

the mirror and see which poses made her look slimmer, and if she was shot at a three-quarters profile instead of . . .

'So that's the weight thing covered . . .'

Ted's voice broke Laura out of her reverie where she was dressed in a severely cut, black Louis Vuitton dress that made the most of her curves but not too much of them because she was standing at an angle.

She tilted her chin up so she could look all on-message while they devised her new strategy and told her to up the stomach crunches or whatever.

'But really, sweetie, even if you'd lost a stone I'd still tell you that you've got a month to get your act together.'

Ted didn't believe in pulling any punches. He took advantage of Laura's shell-shock to continue. 'I'm not expecting you to get a *Vogue* cover or a million-pound campaign, but I want you to tone up, get motivated and lose the attitude.'

That was also so unfair. She didn't have an attitude. She was practically attitude-free. 'I *am* motivated,' Laura squeaked indignantly. Had they not heard her impassioned pleas? 'And I don't have an attitude.'

Heidi peeled herself away from the wall she'd been leaning against so she could fold her arms and stare Laura down. 'For someone with very little modelling experience, you've got attitude in spades.'

'I won a nationwide modelling competition,' Laura

reminded her. 'I did twelve weeks of shoots. I think that counts as experience.'

'And that would be the attitude that we want you to lose,' Ted said dryly. 'Laura, I'm going to tell you some cold, hard truths and you're going to hate my guts for it, but then you can either get over it or you can go back home and tell everyone how mean those nasty London modelling people were.'

He paused as if he was waiting for Laura's permission to tear her a new one. And for one second she was tempted to flounce out, because this was going to be one of those conversations that plumbed the depths of her soul. But if they wanted her to pledge her allegiance to the world of modelling, she would. Even if she had to do it while standing in an over-air-conditioned conference room, clad only in a bikini with goosebumps on her goosebumps.

'Shoot me,' she said, and hoped he wouldn't take her literally.

'You're a pretty girl,' Ted started. 'Boys want you. Girls want to be you. Pretty means that you've always been the best-looking fish in a really small pond. But you're swimming in the big sea now and pretty doesn't get bookings. Pretty didn't win you *Make Me A Model*. There were three girls on our own shortlist and you weren't one of them. If we'd had our way, Nemi would have won.'

And before she'd even had time to recover from that

body blow, Ted continued with his jaunty character assassination. God, and it wasn't even nine o'clock. 'You won because it was a public vote and the public know jack all about what makes a model. They liked you because you were a funny girl who stood up to the judges, and they understood your looks and didn't find them too exotic or too challenging. Do you get it, Laura? You won because you had a personality.'

Heidi got off the bench. 'And if you brought an ounce of that personality to your go-sees, you'd get booked. Instead, you just stand there and tell them you won that bloody show like they're meant to be impressed. At shoots, you have no idea how to pose, the photographer has to direct you through every shot, and when I give you constructive criticism, I just get sulks and "whatever"s.'

Never had Laura wanted to spit out a sulky 'what*ever*' so badly. 'If I'm that crap, I don't know why you're even bothering to give me a month's trial.' It had been her intention to sound defiant and sassy but it was whiny. Definitely, seriously whiny. And no wonder, she'd just had her entire belief system smashed beyond repair. She was pretty. It was, like, her *raison d'être*.

'Because we think that if we push you hard enough then we might make a model out of you,' Ted replied, but Laura barely heard him over the ringing in her ears. 'And word is that curves are going to make a comeback.'

'Is there anything you want to say?' Heidi asked gently, which was a whole new look for her.

Laura shook her head dumbly. She was too frozen to even cry. Yay for her. 'I've got to go now,' she mumbled, half expecting her legs to collapse under her as she stood up.

Heidi looked as if she was going to protest, but a terse head-shake from Ted stopped her. 'I'll call you in a couple of days,' she promised.

Laura just about managed to nod, which was impressive given that she'd just lost control of all her motor skills. And as much as it was possible in a bikini that was riding up her arse and a pair of too-high heels, she scurried out of the room with about ninety-nine per cent less saunter than when she'd entered.

Deep-frozen Laura didn't last very long. About five minutes tops, before she started coasting a tsunami of rage. Not pretty? Not motivated? Lost her personality? She'd won *Make Me A Model* and they acted as if it was a bad thing.

None of it was true and they obviously just wanted an excuse to sack her and then keep her winnings so she'd be in breach of contract. Yeah, she could see right through them.

But as she stomped down faceless London streets, pushing brusquely past anyone who got in her way, she wanted to do what she always did when the world was ganging up on her; call Tom. And she couldn't because he was a cheating wanker who'd got over her in the space of thirty-six hours. By voice message!

And she was done with being a whiny-ass little crybaby and silently grieving over him. That was the conclusion Laura had reached after a day spent walking around London in a fugue state. She'd fetched up in Notting Hill, which would explain the blisters as she flung herself on her bed and kicked off her shoes.

But her feet could wait, yanking her phone out of her bag couldn't.

'You've got a fucking nerve!' she screamed as soon as he answered, her banshee-like howl ricocheting off the walls. 'You were the one who copped off with that stuck-up, blonde skank, so don't make out that it was my fault.'

'I didn't. I just—'

'Just shut up and bloody listen! I had to wade through about a gazillion voice messages from you that were full of bullshit and spin, so you can just hear what I have to say. Not only did you cheat on me, but then you double-cheated on me by going behind my back to my friends and getting them to lie about it. And I'm stuck up here all on my own and things are awful. They are *hideous* and now I've got no one I can talk to about it.'

She paused to draw in some much-needed oxygen into her lungs, though Tom seemed to think that it was his cue to talk. Wrong, buster.

'Look, that's not what—'

'I haven't finished!' Laura screeched, wishing that they were doing this in person because it was deeply unsatisfying to scream down the fibre optics when she wanted to stamp her feet and wring her hands and yeah, do some grievous bodily harm on that stupid, pouty face of his. 'You're a liar and a bastard and I hate you and I never want to speak to you again. Ever! Ever!'

She hung up the phone, almost spraining her index finger as she pressed down hard on the little red button. There was a lot to be said for the medicinal effects of slamming a phone down. And now she didn't feel better for getting it off her chest. On the contrary, she was seriously considering going to the gym just so she could get nasty with a punch-bag.

Laura shoved her shaking hands into her jeans pockets and wondered how she was going to get through the rest of the day. In fact, she didn't even know how she was going to get through the next ten seconds when she felt as if she had a rusty, chewed-up metal box where her heart used to be.

There was a sharp tap at the door before it was unceremoniously pushed open so Candy could stand there with a knowing look on her face.

'I know exactly what you need,' she said, coming into the room, with Hadley and Irina on her heels. 'Are you free for a while or are you going to phone up that boy and scream at him a bit more?'

Laura pressed her hands to her burning cheeks, 'What the hell do you want?' The angry girl who currently lived inside her was obviously ready for her encore presentation. 'And FYI, he totally deserved it because he's a no-good, two-timing piece of . . . and again, what do you three want?'

There was no earthly reason why her three flatmates had suddenly appeared, all spiffed up and looking way too pleased with themselves. Well, except Irina, and she never cracked a facial expression if she could help it.

'Well, so like my therapist says that I have issues with over-sharing,' Hadley began, toeing the edge of Laura's throw rug.

'Which means that she can't keep a secret to save her life,' Candy supplied. 'She told us all about your fucktard of a boyfriend and so we decided to do something about him.'

'Like what? Put a contract on him?' Laura mused. 'Or even just take out his kneecaps; that would work for me.'

Irina smiled. Possibly. 'I know Russian mafia.'

Candy shook her head. 'Nuh-huh. I have the cure for what ails you – and it's the limo that's parked on the double-yellow line outside with several bottles of Cristal chilling in the ice buckets. We're getting you back on the horse,' Candy suggested.

'I was never on a horse!'

'I'm, like, working a metaphor. What do you do when

157

you fall off a horse? You get straight back on. Same with boys. You find some cute little popsy, climb on board, take him for a ride and, well, treacherous ex-boyfriends don't factor too highly any more. I speak from bitter experience.'

Chapter Thirteen

If Laura had known that saying the words 'actually, I'm a model' was the secret password to a world of foxy boys, then she'd have dumped Tom before she ever came to London. Really, she would.

Because, as they limo-hopped from club to club, there was a never-ending stream of the foxiest members of boy-kind all ready with appreciative smiles and offers to buy her drinks and take her out to dinner. Laura could feel her market value going through the roof. It was like a domino effect: more and more guys moving in on her, until she found herself perched on a banquette with an adoring audience of men in designer jeans and trainers laughing at her jokes and offering to get her backstage passes to any band that she might want to see.

There was always a glass in her hand, always full to the brim, because as soon as she drained the contents, it was filled up again with as little regard for £200 bottles of champagne than if they'd been tap water. It was a million miles away from birthday parties held at golf clubs.

Didn't matter how hard she tamped them down, the memories of that night wouldn't disappear.

'Don't do that,' the boy sitting next to her whispered.

'Do what?'

'Don't look so unhappy. Here, have some more champagne.'

The fizzy bubbles, light and effervescent, tickled the back of her throat and chased the blues away. But it wasn't just the alcohol that was taking her halfway to hammered. It was the attention. Yes, she was ripe for a bit of attention from the foxy boys, but what Laura really dug was the girls. Not in a gay way, but how they were looking at her, in the jeans and sneakers that she'd first put on that morning, like she was a threat, like she was competition, like she was more beautiful than them.

Maybe she was. She felt like it as she twirled around the postage-stamp-sized dance floor of yet another club, watching the girls watch the men watch her. Not bad for someone who just wasn't pretty enough.

Eventually they hunkered down in the grimiest place Laura had ever seen. The walls were nothing more than roughly hewn concrete, and the décor was a couple of orange crates for the DJ's decks and sagging sofas that attacked you with a vicious spring action if you dared to sit down. Irina was jabbering away to a foreign-looking boy in something that sounded like Spanish, her face unusually animated. Hadley had hooked up with George, but they were both gazing adoringly at Candy's stepbrother, Reed, who'd arrived with a stunning Brazilian girl but was tapping away at his BlackBerry while Candy looked over his shoulder.

Eventually the music stopped and the lights came on, shocking Laura back into a harsh reality where nothing looked as glowy or as soft as it had done. She stumbled against the boy who'd given her more champagne, who held out his arms so she could snuggle against him.

'Tell them to turn the lights off,' she slurred. 'It's too bright.'

'It's three in the morning. It's time to go home before we turn into pumpkins.'

'Do you think I'm pretty?' Laura asked him, because now that she thought about it, though her brain wasn't really working at its optimum performance level, he'd been welded to her side all evening: the more men who thronged around her, the tighter he clung.

He gave her a crooked smile and she reached out so she could press her finger into the cleft of his chin. 'You're beautiful,' he said firmly. 'You have really symmetrical features.'

He was kinda beautiful too. With long-lashed, sleepy blue eyes and straw-blonde hair that was longer than hers. Laura could feel the tight muscles in his arms and chest as he held her, and he had a mouth. Mouths were good. Mouths were for kissing.

And if it was easy to lose herself in champagne, it was even easier to lose herself in the feel of someone else. He didn't feel like Tom, or smell like him, and he certainly didn't taste like him when he tilted her head back and explored the inside of her mouth with a practised ease that should have had her alarm bells ringing. Guess all that champagne had turned them off.

It was scary kissing someone new. But rollercoaster-scary, rather than serial-killer-scary. This boy knew what he was doing and then did it, while Laura was still struggling to catch up.

As he slid his arms round her waist, stroking the smooth skin where her top had ridden up, Laura wondered if this is what it had been like for Tom. If he'd got off on the difference, on how Cassie wasn't her.

She didn't want to think about that. So she kissed him again, eyes closed to get that swoony feeling when he bit her bottom lip and slid his tongue into her mouth.

'I don't want to go home yet,' Laura mumbled against his lips. 'I like kissing you too much.'

Out of the corner of her eye, she could see Candy waving frantically at her.

'I could come back to yours,' he offered casually, which was at odds with the heavy-lidded way he was staring at her. 'Then I could kiss you some more.'

'I like the sound of that. Kissing, and also toast. I'm starving.' Eating might be a problem. Her mouth felt as if it was an entirely separate part of her body. It was only good for kissing right now. 'Wouldn't it be great if we could just wish hard enough and be there?' Laura tried to click the heels of her tatty plimsolls together and nearly fell over. It probably only worked in *The Wizard Of Oz*.

'Russian girls hold their drink,' Irina declared snottily, from somewhere behind her. 'We get back in car now.'

At least she wasn't as drunk as Hadley, who was lying on the floor. 'I love limos!' she announced dreamily, as Laura fell over her. 'I love that they have tinted windows so that all the people who can't look in know that you're famous. You're too famous to be looked at. It's so cool!'

Laura settled back on the boy's lap. She really should ask him his name, but Candy was hissing in her ear, 'You're really wasted. Do you want me to get rid of him for you?' She nodded her head in the direction of Laura's random, who was contentedly nibbling away at her neck. 'I don't think you're fit for anything but throwing up and I have an A grade in holding back people's hair when they puke.'

Turned out that Candy couldn't hold back her hair because she crashed out in the hall as soon as they got in. And Laura didn't need to puke, so it worked out.

Reed looked like he would have volunteered, but he was busy forcing Hadley to drink a huge bottle of water while she lolled on the sofa, and Irina and someone she'd grudgingly introduced as Javier had made their excuses and disappeared into her room.

Laura's own overnight guest was already peeling off his

shirt, so the moonlight coming in from the window turned the taut lines of his chest pearly-white. She was drunk. Drunk as a trunk full of drunk skunks. It made it easier to say it. 'I'm not having sex with you,' she blurted out, shutting the door of her room and leaning back against it. Standing unaided was just not going to happen. 'It's too messy. Everything will just be . . . y'know, *messy.*'

Because it wouldn't be about making sweet and tender love, or any of the other gentle adjectives she'd used when she'd thought about losing her virginity. It would be about getting naked and having sex. Messy, graceless sex with a boy who didn't even have a name.

'I have condoms,' he offered, hands now hovering over his belt buckle. 'It doesn't have to get messy.'

When he put it like that, it made Laura's mouth curl up in an 'ewwwww!' that she couldn't quite articulate, so she just settled for an echo: 'I am not having sex.'

Maybe he didn't hear over the sound of his belt swishing out of the loops of his jeans. But then he shrugged. 'OK, we can do other things.'

So they did other things that would have felt really good, if they hadn't felt really wrong at the same time.

Afterwards he sprawled out in a long tangle of limbs, pushing Laura right up into the wall, while he snored away and she stared at a tiny, torn patch of wallpaper and contemplated what a great, big ho she'd turned into. Maybe ho was too harsh. She was like the poster girl for rebounding. But Laura couldn't be content with a little kiss and cuddle, when she could go so close to home base that she'd almost scored a winning touchdown. And she was thinking in sporting metaphors, which was a sure sign that things were totally and utterly FUBAR.

She must have fallen asleep at some point because she was woken by the furtive shuffling of the boy as he got dressed. Blinking warily, as even the weak sunlight leaking through the chink in the curtains was sending all kinds of agony to her cerebral cortex, Laura turned over and carefully raised her head from the two inches of pillow she'd managed to liberate.

'You going, then?' Her voice sounded strange, like she didn't get to use it very often.

He looked up from tugging on his socks. 'Yeah, I've got stuff to do.'

Laura squinted at her alarm clock. It was seven. No one had anything to do at seven freaking a.m., unless it involved delivering papers. This must be the awkward Morning After that she'd read about.

'I've got stuff to do too,' she said, like spending the day in bed and trying really hard not to die because it felt as if someone had replaced her brain with a box of thumb tacks. Laura hauled the duvet around her because she was naked. It took a moment for the sheer lunacy of the moment to hit and then she had to close her eyes and pretend that she hadn't . . . last night . . . with the . . . and the . . . 'Oh, shit!' she groaned.

'It was fun,' he said, as if that pithy summing up would make everything all right. 'You were cool.'

Laura wished that he'd stop talking, get dressed and leave, so the agony wouldn't keep stretching onandonand-onandonandon. 'Thanks. I guess I'll see you around.'

She recognized that shifty look. Tom had worn an identical one last time she'd seen him. 'It was fun,' he repeated, like if he said it enough times then it would be true. 'And you're really beautiful, and I couldn't even believe that you were interested in me, but the thing is I'm kinda seeing someone.'

Laura didn't know what was worse. The fact that she now only attracted boy-sluts who couldn't be faithful to one girl at a time, or that she knew for ever more she'd be 'the one time I copped off with a model' in this guy's personal shag history.

'Whatever,' she said mechanically. 'I don't really care. Can you be quiet when you leave? I've got a terrible headache.'

Chapter Fourteen

'Honestly, Candy, we just fooled around a bit.' Laura closed her eyes as another wave of not-quite-throwing-up hit her, then wished she hadn't because it made her head spin. Fooling around implied that they'd rolled about on her bed, fighting back the giggles. 'It's just, it was intimate, it should have been a big deal and it wasn't. I'm never actually having sex anyway. Not until I'm thirty and I've been married to the guy for at least ten years. And good God, it's bloody *hot* in here.'

'I told you, spa days are great for broken heart, and saunas are the best cure for a hangover.' Candy lifted up a leg and watched a bead of sweat trickle down her shapely calf. 'Look, you had too much to drink, you were hurting, shit happens.'

Candy really needed to work on her pep-talks. They lacked warmth. 'So who was that Spanish guy that Irina hooked up with?' Laura asked because she was sick of talking about herself, which had to be an all-time first.

'Some photographer's assistant she met in Tokyo. I think he's Argentine and he must have the patience of a whole cathedral full of saints. He called her a bitch this morning when she was kicking off about something.' Candy smiled gleefully as if the memory was still giving her untold amounts of pleasure. 'They're totally having sex and she's not freaking about it.'

'Does Irina freak out about anything, because that would assume she actually has an emotion other than . . . ?'

'. . . Sneering condescension? I had to bang on the wall at four this morning because her headboard was thumping and she was moaning in Russian. It was majorly disturbing.'

Laura managed to sit up. Gossip was proving a really effective hangover cure. 'And what's the story with Hadley and George?'

'You mean Mr *Brokeback Mountain* and his beard?' Candy paused and waited for Laura to get the reference. 'Only a fully paid up, card-carrying gay boy could love Hadley. She's the campest girl I've ever met.'

'So why do they pretend that they're going out with each other? I mean, even I could tell that Tab A wasn't going into Slot B.' Laura grimaced as she got a frightening visual of Hadley and George doing the nasty and having to stop because their collective blonde hair was getting mussed up.

'Hadley has this bullshit idea that people actually care about her and that a fake relationship will be good publicity,' Candy said savagely. 'She's such a little media whore.'

'Harsh. Hadders is OK. She can be quite sweet, sometimes. Anyway, are you seeing anyone?'

And just like that, Candy's face closed down. Asking her a personal question was like sticking your head in a lion's mouth and hoping it wouldn't chomp down too hard. 'No,' she bit out.

Laura crossed her legs and tucked her towel in a little tighter so she didn't flash her lady parts. 'You can tell me stuff, Candy,' she said gently. 'If you wanted to unload sometimes. I wouldn't tell anyone. And you know for sure that I don't have a hidden tape recorder stashed anywhere.'

Candy sniggered, and then her features softened; a rueful twist of the mouth, like she had secrets that were weighing heavy.

'I met this guy just after the show had first started airing. He was in a band, though they were kinda sucky.' Candy wrinkled her perfect smudge of a nose. 'But he was a fox and, shit, I thought I loved him. But he dumped me because I didn't want him to get mixed up with the show, and then he tried to sell the story of his "Torrid Nights Of Passion With Candy Careless" to one of the gossip rags. And now I don't date. I don't even flirt with guys any more. I'm like a nun, but much better dressed,' She flashed a defiant smile at Laura. 'That which does not destroy me makes me strong, yo.'

'What happened to the story he was trying to sell?' Laura breathed, because compared to Candy's tale from the dating frontline, she had no right to claim the Miss Angst 2007 crown.

'He changed his mind after my lawyer unleashed a metric load of pain on his sorry ass,' Candy said with grim satisfaction. 'Scratch me and I'll get one of my people to claw your eyes out.'

Note to self, thought Laura, *never, ever do anything to piss Candy off*. 'OK, I'll bear that in mind,' she said, in a voice that only trembled very slightly.

'We should get out of you here.' Candy stood up and teetered as she got the mother of all head-rushes. 'You must have sweated out all the toxins by now.'

After the sauna, they were ushered into a room that must have been a Bedouin tent in a former life. Then every inch of skin Laura possessed was flayed from her body with a sea salt scrub and a loofah. Conversation wasn't happening when all she could vocalize was the odd anguished squeak as she moved on to the deep, intense tissue-massage portion of the jam-packed beautification schedule.

Candy had saved the fun stuff for the last two hours. Laura's flesh was shiny, glowing and redolent with jasmine. Her eyebrows were exquisitely shaped into pleasing arches. Her hair was sadly still lacking but was as glossy as a dressage pony's mane, and her toenails were painted what Candy called 'whore red' and her fingernails a fetching shade of what she called 'ballet-slipper pink'.

'My treat,' Candy insisted as the receptionist totalled up the final bill. 'Put your hard-earned pounds away.'

Laura caught a glimpse of a sum that had at least four

figures before the decimal point, and conceded without a struggle. 'Have you got plans for tonight 'cause I can just about stump up for a takeaway and a DVD?'

Candy tapped in her pin number. 'No jedis or hobbits and you've got yourself a deal.'

It wasn't until they got in the cab that Laura switched on her phone. Even the sight of the little phone icon flashing made her break out in a cold sweat, but it was only Hadley. 'Laura,' she whispered urgently after the beep. 'It's four p.m., or is that, like 1600 hours in British? Anyway, you have to come back to the apartment right now. We're on a total code red.' There was a long pause. 'That means a total emergency. OK? Bye!'

That was weird, even for Hadley. 'I swear to God that girl's on crack,' Laura muttered, deciding to call and find out what the big panic was. She'd probably blocked the sink again.

'Ja?'

'Irina? Is Hadley there? It's Laura. She left me this really strange message.'

There was a moment's silence punctuated by the sound of a door slamming, before Irina spoke in the same fierce whisper that Hadley had used. 'Ja, you come home now. Code red.'

Laura rolled her eyes at Candy, who was straining to hear and making no attempt to hide it. 'Irina, do you even know what a code red is?'

'Yeah, and it's sitting on the sofa. Get your ass back right now.'

'But . . . but . . .'

'You're a stupid girl,' Irina hissed. 'You come home and clean up your own shit.'

Laura chewed off most of the ballet-slipper pink polish as they sat in traffic on the Euston Road.

'I'm sure it's nothing,' Candy breezed. 'Those two are drama queens from way back. It's probably your hook-up back to confess his undying love or to tell you that he's got an STI and you need to see a doctor.'

'You're really not helping, Candy!'

Candy pouted. 'Excuse me for trying to lighten the tension with a little topical humour.'

'I think I'm going to be sick again.' Laura hoisted up the window and took great gulps of heavily polluted air. 'Jesus! I bet it's Heidi come round to sack me after all. I hate her!'

And that was her starter for ten and she was off on the Heidi bitchfest – officially sponsored by the taxi driver, who absolutely refused to beep his horn or break the speed limit so they'd get home faster.

Laura was still bending Candy's ear as they trooped up the stairs. 'Other bookers hug their models when they come into the agency and ask how they're doing, but all I get is a sour smile and a shove in the direction of the scales.'

'Yeah, she's a real bitch.' Candy drawled in a monotone. 'Goddamn weight fascist.'

'I know.' Laura jabbed her key in the lock. 'I'm not going down without a fight, I'm going to tell her exactly what I . . . think . . . of . . . her . . .'

Candy shoved her in the back. 'Move it! Don't just stand there.'

But standing there was all that Laura was capable of, because it wasn't Heidi sitting on the sofa with her trademark scowl but Tom, hiding behind a bedraggled bunch of mixed blooms, his face pinched and miserable, until he saw her and lit up like the Blackpool Illuminations.

'Hey, Laura, surprise, eh?'

Chapter Fifteen

Laura stood there, still in her coat, and folded her arms. Now he was here, in her lounge, wearing that lopsided smile that broke what was left of her heart, she realized with a sudden clarity that she didn't hate Tom. Not even close.

'You shouldn't have come,' she gasped, turning to make a quick getaway and finding her path blocked by Irina, who was standing there staring at her coldly.

'You stay,' she insisted fiercely, though it was no business of hers. 'You stay and talk and stop acting like a big baby. We're going out. Hadley!'

Hadley stuck her head round her door. 'I can't find my scarf.'

'You won't die without your scarf,' Candy snorted, beetling towards the door. 'We're just going to the Greek place next door. C'mon, stat!'

Laura watched helplessly as they filed past her, Candy stopping to pat her cheek. 'Don't hurt the boy too much. He looks like he bruises easily.'

'Yeah, but he heals really fast,' Laura muttered, but she was already talking to a closed door.

She went into the kitchen and put the kettle on. It was

like a reflex action when life pulled the rug out from under your feet: have a cup of tea. Because this time yesterday she'd still been the injured party, fuelled up on righteous indignation. Now she was just a stupid tart who'd done worse things with Mr No Name than Tom had ever done with Cassie. Unless Tom and Cassie had . . . Oh, she *so* wasn't going there.

Tom shuffled into the kitchen as she was pouring milk into two mugs. 'I made you some tea,' she said tonelessly. 'Irina and Hadley aren't big with the social niceties.'

'They were OK.' He leaned against the counter and blew on his tea. 'It took about ten minutes of explanations and hand gestures before they'd let me in though.'

Laura sneaked a glance at him from under her lashes as he sipped his tea. She'd been picturing him with devil horns and a pitchfork so it was weird to see him looking, well, Tom-like in a stripy jumper and jeans as he stared at her quizzically.

'It's Tuesday so, like, don't you have school tomorrow?'

Tom shrugged. 'I s'pose. But I don't think they'll expel for me for skipping one day.'

'Are you hungry? I doubt that there's any food that's actually mould-free but I could—'

'Laura, it was five seconds of kissing when I was really drunk,' Tom suddenly said, clumsily putting his mug down on the worktop so that tea slopped over the edges. 'It didn't mean anything.'

She knew that was a lie. Kisses always meant something, even if the something was because you were hurt and lonely. 'It doesn't matter,' she said, fishing a dishrag out of the sink and mopping up the muddle of spilled tea.

'Yes, it does.' Tom took the cloth out of Laura's hands and turned her round so she had to look at him. 'It matters because I hate myself for hurting you.'

She didn't even realize that she was crying until his mouth followed the damp path of her tears. 'Don't look at me like that,' she pleaded, because his face was scrunching up as well and she was the biggest bitch in Bitchdom. 'Tom, please . . . I'm OK.'

Tom pulled at his jumper then nodded his head in the direction of the door. 'Can we go in there and try . . . no, we're not going to try, we *are* going to sort this out.'

Laura tucked her legs under her and sipped at her lukewarm mug of tea as Tom unburdened. He seemed to think it was necessary to go into over-share mode about Cassie. Which would have been a sound plan twenty-four hours ago when she didn't have anything to over-share about. Full disclosure sucked.

It was exactly as Jen and Cath had said. He hadn't realized that Cassie was coming on to him, or was even that interested, until one night at some party she'd suddenly plonked herself down on his lap and attached her mouth to his.

That was incident number one for her consideration, and it all sounded like a simple case of mixed signals + nasty skank = unwelcome kissage. But then there was incident two, which had involved more of the same but with added booze.

'I'd already told her I had a girlfriend,' Tom insisted, elbows on his knees as he hunched forwards and stared at the spot on the rug where Hadley had had an accident with her nail polish. 'But then I was drunk and I hadn't spoken to you in a week and she tried it on again and, yeah, for, like five seconds, I kissed her back. It was five seconds of kissing, Laura. Five freaking seconds, and if I'd told you, you'd have yelled at me for a bit and then it would have all been forgotten. But Jen and Cath saw and it got blown up into this big thing with all these phone calls and cover-up plans, and I was just a dumb boy who couldn't possibly understand the intricacies of the female psyche and I wasn't to tell you. And that's it. And I'm sorry but I'm not prepared to chuck away two years for five seconds of drunken snogging, y'know?'

She did know. It all sounded really reasonable when he put it like that. She'd have torn several bloody strips off him, he'd have shouted back, then they'd have made up with some pre-watershed loving. It would have been so simple.

'You should have listened to your instincts,' Laura said. 'Just called me and explained and then I wouldn't have been angry 'cause you know how I get when I'm angry. Like, me and rational thinking aren't on speaking terms.'

'Would you have left permanent marks?' Tom asked, arching his eyebrow because he thought they were almost done. That this was the part of the conversation where they swapped some snarky banter before vowing undying love.

'Maybe a black eye,' she prevaricated, and then she just had to come out with it. Like ripping off a plaster in super-quick time. 'Or maybe I wouldn't have . . . last night . . . I was so *mad* at you and I felt so ugly and OK, I was drunk too . . .'

Tom went from floppy to rigid in a nanosecond. 'What did you do?'

Laura shut her eyes and opened her mouth. 'I slept with this guy. I didn't have sex with him but it was more than just five seconds of drunken snogging. Tom, I'm so sorry . . .'

She reached out to touch him because yeah, she could make it all go away with just a few random pats along his arm, but he flinched away from her as if she was wielding a blowtorch. 'Don't bloody touch me! What did you do?'

'I told you,' Laura said helplessly, because going into the gory details wasn't going to help. 'We didn't go all the way.' Because the fact that they only went five-sixths of the way made everything OK. Yeah, right.

'What did you do?' Tom repeated, voice mechanical in that way that it went when he was so angry he couldn't trust himself to speak. 'I want to know what you did with him.'

Laura's face heated up as every other part of body went icy-cold, which was an interesting combination. 'No, you don't,' she said miserably.

But he did, and he wasn't satisfied until he'd made her repeat every single second of it, each piece of clothing removed, each place she'd touched and been touched, all the stupid words that you say when you're butt-naked and mindlessly writhing against someone who isn't your boyfriend.

It felt like she was cheating on Tom all over again, but this time he was standing in a shadowy corner of the room watching her and that boy re-enact scenes from *The Lover's Guide*.

'How is that not having sex?' he demanded when she finally got to the end of the inquisition, stammering and stumbling over words that he'd made her repeat until they stopped making sense. He'd be a natural successor if Judge Judy ever decided to retire.

'Because he didn't, y'know, put his penis in my vagina,' she spat out angrily, trying to work herself into a frenzy of moral outrage before she realized that she didn't have that right any more.

'You're a stupid bitch!'

It hurt much worse than Tom slapping her around the face. He practically crawled off the sofa as if he was going to catch some contagious, pus-heavy disease from being so close to her, then stood there glowering. Laura hadn't even known that he could glower, but he was surprisingly good at it.

'We are *so* over,' he announced in tones that were so final that if their relationship was a TV show, they could replace the end credits. 'You're disgusting, Laura.'

All she could do was nod dumbly in agreement as they heard a key turn in the lock and the other three girls stumbled in.

'Aw, have you two kissed and made up?' Hadley cooed. She must be drunk. Again.

Tom shoved his hands in his pockets and stared at the floor. 'I'm going. How do I get back to Euston from here?'

That roused Laura from her stupor. 'Can't you stay a bit longer so we can talk this out?' she asked quietly, even though her flatmates already had ringside seats to watch the closing scenes of her getting gloriously dumped. 'Please, Tom . . .'

'I don't even want to look at you right now, so having a cosy chat about what a two-faced cow you are isn't really on my list of things to do.'

There was a shocked little gasp from the doorway. Now turning Tom into a bitter, venom-spewing misanthrope could be added to her list of crimes.

'I'm not a two-faced cow, I was acting under the information I had at the time.' Laura sprang to her feet.

'How was I to know that you'd got jumped by Cassie and hey, you still kissed her back? Even if it was only for five seconds, you still kissed her.'

'Yeah, well at least I didn't have to get naked to do that!'

'I bet you would have if Jen and Cath hadn't been around. I mean, I've only got your word for it that you suddenly had an attack of conscience.'

'Don't you dare turn this on me, Laura! You're always happier being the victim and going off to sulk instead of dealing with stuff. You're such a lightweight!'

'Fine, I'm a lightweight and a bitch and a cow and I've probably been shagging half of London,' she screamed, because it was better than being in a state of collapse on the sofa, helpless as a day-old puppy, while Tom bludgeoned her over the head with his tongue, which was a really bad case of mixed metaphors but thinking clearly wasn't her priority right now, 'Go on, then, get the hell out. I don't care!'

And just to show how much she didn't care, Laura started this flounce out of the room, which would have totally rocked if Candy hadn't pushed her back. 'It's gone eleven,' she pointed out. 'He can't schlep all over London—'

'It's a five-minute bus ride to the station,' Laura interjected coldly. 'Even *he* can manage that.'

'I'm standing right here, Laura.'

'Yeah, don't remind me,' she snapped, and she was ready

to hurl a few more choice epithets about, but Irina was stomping to the sofa because she hadn't watched any TV for a couple of hours and the withdrawal symptoms were getting to her.

'Always drama with you,' she informed Laura with a wagging finger, which made Laura want to hurl herself on the floor and indulge in a full-on hissy fit. 'Just chill the fuck out, ja?'

'Yeah, this is really harshing me out,' Hadley added, clutching a hand to her forehead. 'I'm going to have an aromatherapy bath.'

'She's so drunk she'll probably drown in the tub,' Laura muttered savagely, as Hadley staggered down the hall. No one was safe from her all-powerful bitch ray.

'You've probably missed the last train or whatever,' Candy said to Tom, with a wave of her hands. 'Man, this country is so primitive. Stuff closes way early. Anyway, you can sleep in Laura's room and she can either sleep with me or crash on the sofa if she wants to carry on being such an evil douchebag.'

'I don't want to stay here,' Tom said stiffly, drowning out the sound of Laura's furious intake of breath. And then he stopped being angry for the second it took to realize that he was speaking to someone so famous that she was immediately recognizable just from her first name. A look of dopey stupefaction hit him before he had time to do anything about it.

'Oh, she's way out of your league, sad boy,' Laura snarled, and if she managed to elbow him right in the ribs on her second attempt at flouncing out of the room, then, hey, bonus.

Of course there was nowhere to go that wasn't Candy's room, which rather dented her dramatic exit, especially as Candy waltzed in after her with the air of a girl who also wished that Laura had somewhere else to go.

'When you fuck up, you really go that extra mile,' was her opening shot. 'I thought you were meant to be the injured party.'

'I am,' Laura reminded her, picking up one of Candy's many cushions and hugging it. 'But it turns out there were certain facts that I wasn't privy to.'

Candy sat down and began tugging off her boots. 'Sorry, honey, but you've now been cast as the villain of this piece. It's just how it is. You've broken his heart and he gets to be all quivery and victim-y.' Candy paused for breath. 'God, you're *stupid*.'

It was obviously National Dump On Laura Day.

'Why did you tell him?' Candy continued. 'What he didn't know wouldn't have turned him into a big ball of misery.'

It was hard to come up with a good answer. 'Because he asked,' Laura said listlessly. 'But, like, it was more the way he asked.'

'Well, you should have just lied. It's not like you're

religious or something. Boys can never handle the truth. They're all pussies.'

It was almost tempting to go back and face the wrath of Tom rather than listen to Candy explain in painstaking detail just how she should have played the scene so it would still have been all Tom's fault and then they could have made up and Laura would seem like a forgiving, sweet paragon of girlfriend-dom. 'I bet you'd have got presents,' Candy added helpfully. 'Maybe even jewellery.'

They lay there in silence and after a few minutes and a couple of whuffling sounds, Candy was asleep and Laura was left with the voice of her conscience. Wow, the voice of her conscience really didn't know when to shut up.

It was as if she could feel Tom's pain permeating through the walls and, telling herself it was because she needed to get her pyjamas, Laura found herself tip-toeing out of the door and across the hall.

She was damned if she was going to knock, because she wasn't feeling *that* conciliatory and besides, he'd just tell her to piss off anyway.

Laura nudged open the door and all those words she was going to say about how they'd both behaved like idiots fluttered away and she was melting at the sight of Tom slumped on the floor, holding a photo that he'd pulled off her pinboard, and crying. Boys shouldn't cry. It defied all the manly laws of nature.

'Oh, Tom,' she sighed.

He looked up and immediately began to scrub furiously at his eyes. 'What do you want?' he asked gruffly.

'Pyjamas.' But she was already crouching down because it was her turn to stroke his hair. Not that he wanted her to, because he tipped his head back and gave her one of those vengeful glares he was getting really good at. 'I knew you were in here feeling like ten shades of crap and I know that I'm the one who's to blame for that, but I just couldn't—'

'Why did you never return my calls?' he asked baldly, cutting straight through her garbled attempt at something apologetic. ''Cause for those five seconds I was tempted to cop off with Cassie, I already felt like I didn't have a girlfriend any more.'

Respecting his no-touching rule, Laura sat down on the floor next to him. 'I was going through stuff that was hard to talk about,' she tried to explain. 'If I'd spoken to you, I knew it would all come pouring out and I couldn't deal with it.'

Tom grunted. It was a grunt that didn't exactly beg her to continue, but it was a grunt of mild interest.

There were still untruths that she had to truth. 'It's been really *hard*. I'm on my own without my mum and dad or you. And I thought it would be easy, that people would be falling over themselves to book me. Like, hello, I beat twelve thousand other girls to win *Make Me A Model*.'

Tom roused himself long enough for another grunt.

'What about all those shoots for foreign magazines and poncing off to New York in a few weeks? Sounds pretty bloody successful to me.'

It did to her to when she'd made it all up to impress the cheap seats. 'I lied,' she whispered, because saying that was always going to be difficult. 'I'm too fat and supposedly I have a bad attitude and my booker hates me and do you know what they told me yesterday?'

Tom shook his head, which was marginally better than the grunting. 'Go on, surprise me.'

'That I've got a month to get my shit together or they're going to sack me.'

She wasn't going to cry. Laura was adamant about that. This wasn't one of those times when she'd turn on the tears to get Tom to feel sorry for her. But she could feel that warning prickle which meant her tear ducts were ready to unleash.

'I just can't do this,' she summed up, in case Tom wasn't on the same page. 'And when I came home I didn't want everyone to feel sorry for me.'

It was unbelievable, but she looked down and Tom's hand was resting on her knee, rubbing soothing circles, his thumb tracing the loose piece of cartilage, a legacy from falling off her bike the first time her father had taken the training wheels off. But his voice was anything but gentle. 'You're so spoilt, Laura,' he said dryly. 'You've never had to work for anything in your life.'

That wasn't fair, or even halfway to being true. 'I've had to work for lots of things! I won that dumb modelling competition, didn't I?'

Tom carried on with the rubbing but added some snorting into the mix. 'You just had to do what you're good at, which is being pretty and perky. It wasn't that difficult 'cause the other girls all had severe personality disorders.'

'But I had to pose underwater and get winched on a harness which cut right into my girl parts and . . .' Yes, compared to soldiers on the frontline of the war on terror and ER doctors and basically anyone in the world who wasn't a model, it didn't seem that hard. Time to try another tack. 'And I had to work hard at school. I had a B+ average . . .'

'You coasted,' Tom interrupted. 'The rest of us slogged our guts out to get As, but you were happy to put less effort in and pout sorrowfully at the teachers if it helped. You're pretty, Laura. You don't live in the same world as the rest of us.'

'I don't see what being pretty has got to do with it.' Sure, it was cool to get wolf-whistles on days when she was feeling rank, but it wasn't a passport to the land of easy rides. 'I've been smiling on go-sees until my cheek muscles ache from the strain. OK, I haven't led the downtrodden in social revolution, but it's still work.'

'Still, about being pretty,' Tom remarked implacably. 'You're the only person I know who can actually say, "I didn't have a chance to go to the cashpoint but it doesn't matter, I'll just find someone to buy me drinks", like that's an acceptable way to live your life. Well, the free drinks have run out.'

'So, I'm two-faced, I'm spoilt, I'm a cow and a bitch and I'm lazy.' She stopped with the unflattering adjectives because she was going to have to use the fingers of her other hand. 'I wonder why you stuck around as long as you did.'

Tom grinned with a predatory flash of teeth because he had the punch line already gift-wrapped. 'Well, you're pretty.'

'I don't feel very pretty right now,' she informed with an angry harrumph, which was deeply unsatisfying. 'Maybe I can shove a paper bag over my head if my face is that objectionable.'

Tom stretched out his legs so they were brushing against hers. 'You know what really pisses me off?'

It could be any one of a number of the crimes on her rap sheet, so Laura shrugged. 'Enlighten me.'

Tom leaned in close so he could cup her chin in an echo of how they used to be. 'That even when I'm so angry with you, the sight of you still makes my heart skip a beat. This would be much simpler if you looked like the back end of a bus. I could just get up and walk away from you.'

'Yay, for being pretty,' Laura said bitterly. 'You're not in it because of my winning personality or that we both like

Belle And Sebastian or because we love each other, I'm just really good arm-candy.'

'Scored me plenty of macho points with the rest of the team,' Tom drawled, and his anger had been easier to read. Not this poke and prod as he got in touch with his bitchy side.

'Glad I was able to help. I'm going back to Candy's room now that we've got all that sorted out.'

Her exit would have been more graceful if she hadn't tripped over one of her trainers, which were lying in the middle of the room. Laura teetered, uncertain if she was about to plummet to the floor in an inelegant heap. She started her descent with a squeak until Tom gripped her elbows and hauled her back to vertical.

It was only four steps to the door so why was she relaxing back against his chest? Because he was kissing the back of her neck; tender little presses of his lips against a spot of skin that had become so sensitive that even her toes wriggled in response.

'I noticed you because you were beautiful,' he purred in her ear. 'Way out of my league, but then do you remember the day we came up to London on that trip to the Tate Modern? I watched you stand and gaze at this chaotic, grey Jackson Pollock for nine minutes and everything I thought I knew about you changed.'

Laura remembered the moment. It was the only brief respite during the whole day that she hadn't been mooning over Tom but staring in amazement as the fugly splodges of paint transformed themselves the longer she looked at the picture, like cloud-watching or staring into a fire.

'See, I can be deep,' she mumbled as they mutually and silently agreed that she should turn round.

The first kiss was inevitable. It had taken them many angry words to get to where they were now; just a boy and a girl standing in a dimly lit room, pressed so tightly against each other that not even a feather could come between them.

The spiky, tense, end-of-the-world days since they'd last kissed didn't exist any more. Reality was her hands twisting in Tom's hair, his arms clinging tight round her waist, and nothing else mattered.

When they sank to the floor, it was as if Laura had suddenly mastered a complicated dance that she'd never known the steps to. Clothes just got in the way of being close to each other, and although they'd never done *this* before, it felt utterly right. Her body curved into Tom's, fitting neatly, as she reached for the pretty prize of his lips again. Even the brief pause as she asked, 'Have you got something?' didn't feel awkward.

He fumbled for his jeans so he could pull something out of his wallet. 'My dad gave them to me six months ago just in case,' he admitted bashfully.

'Is this weird?' She sounded like she was talking to herself. 'This is weird.'

'Too weird?'

Laura ran a hand through her hair, then traced her tongue across kiss-bruised lips, stopping when she saw Tom's expression darken again.

Later she nestled into the crook of his arm and wondered if this had been a special, unique experience with someone she loved or just a textbook case of break-up sex.

'It's complicated, Laura,' Tom said, as if he had a CCTV set up in her brain. 'This doesn't automatically make everything OK between us. Not even close.'

She didn't deserve any more than that. In fact, she was lucky with what she did have, even though the rug was scratchy against her skin. But neither of them made a move to get into bed. The truce was tricky; a delicate, gossamer thin edifice, and sheets that might smell of another boy's rather cloying aftershave would render it null and void.

Laura stretched out her hand and groped under the bed for the patchwork quilt that she never used because it was stuffed full of feathers which tickled her nose. She had to learn to be a bit more self-sacrificing and this was a good place to start.

Chapter Sixteen

Things were strained the next morning (they were being abnormally polite to each other, for one thing), but that was only to be expected.

They'd had sex. Proper sex. And it changed everything. Sex meant full-on, big-time commitment and they needed to work out a way for that to happen, even with three hundred miles of motorway between them.

Maybe that's why Tom was sat on the sofa wearing his most pensive expression. But then it could have been because he was getting the glorious Technicolour, now with added surround sound, show that Laura had to put up with every day. Candy was packing to go to New York, which consisted of screaming about how much she hated packing and then collapsing into Laura's arms with pitiful requests for hot beverages. Hadley was working her way through the tabs and totting up how many times she got a mention in her pink Sidekick and exclaiming excitedly every time she hit paydirt. And Irina, God love her, was strolling about in a bra and thong and eating stinky sausage. Just a bog-standard day *chez* the Fierce flat.

Laura had decided that this morning was going to be the start of her life do-over. Tom and she were halfway back to love-shaped, so she could cross that off her list. The next thing to work out was how to cook oatmeal, because every diet article she'd ever read extolled its lumpy, tasteless virtues.

'You can have some of my blueberries to put on top, otherwise it tastes kind of gross,' Hadley murmured as Laura lifted the bowl out of the microwave. 'They're a superfood. You on a diet?'

The old Laura would have denied it vociferously, but new, improved Laura pinched a love handle disconsolately and nodded, after making sure that Irina wasn't in earshot. 'I either lose weight or I lose my contract with Fierce.'

Hadley smiled sympathetically. 'Hey, I haven't eaten anything that contains white sugar since I was eight. I even look at a doughnut and I put on, like, two pounds. How much do you need to lose?' She ran her eyes over Laura's pyjama-clad body. 'About fifteen pounds, right?'

'Well, I guess . . .'

''Cause you should start running. Anything that increases your heart rate makes you burn fat quicker. And also I swear by raw almonds and sushi but, like, not at the same time. You want any tips, just yell. Man, can you believe what Paris Hilton is wearing in this picture?'

Hadley's focus had already shifted back to the *Sun* and Laura took the opportunity to grab a handful of the proffered blueberries and sprinkle them on her oatmeal.

Tom was staring at Hadley with barely concealed

wonder. But he wasn't exhibiting any clear signs of morning-after freak-out, or making noises about trains. Laura gazed at him as she took an unenthusiastic mouthful and tried not to gag.

'Urgh, that stuff is disgusting,' Candy said, coming into the kitchen and rummaging in the laundry basket perched on top of the washing machine. 'You know if you want to lose weight, just cut the crap. Stop eating so much take-out and switch to skimmed milk and shit.'

'How come everyone but me is such an expert on dieting?' Laura complained. 'Ted and Heidi said I can never eat chocolate again.'

'Sucks to be you,' Candy grinned, holding aloft a pink, polka-dot bra. 'But don't go too mad, 'cause nipped-in waists and a defined silhouette are going to be all over the runways for Autumn/Winter. That's what my mom's friend, Isaac, says.'

Laura swallowed down another spoonful of oatmeal. It was OK-ish if she didn't inhale. 'I don't speak fluent fashion.'

Candy rolled her eyes. 'Curves are going to come back,' she informed Laura smugly. 'Face it, Laur, you're never going to be super-skinny but you've got an hour-glass figure underneath all that jelly. You could clean up if you lose enough weight in time for the new season.'

'You think?' Laura asked doubtfully. It was odd to get advice, rather than give it. Cath and Jen had hung on her every word when it came to what was in and what wasn't. They'd never dared to return the favour.

'I've got some look-books in my room, I'll show you,' Candy offered, her arms full of clean clothes.

'Laura, can we go out or something?'

Tom's plaintive whine from the doorway disrupted the heated argument she and Candy had been having for the last ten minutes about skinny versus bootleg jeans.

'Sorry, I forgot you were here,' she blurted out, which was the most tactless thing she could say. Tom's scowl seemed to agree with her. Candy made an 'ouch' face as Laura shifted a pile of fashion magazines off her lap. 'I mean . . . you're my Manchester life and y'know . . .' Her size-eight feet were stomping all over the eggshells she was meant to be walking on. 'Yeah, let's go out. I'll show you round the market.'

It should have felt right and normal to walk along Camden High Street with Tom, her hand clasped tightly in his. But he didn't want to look at the stalls selling bootleg concert DVDs or oh-so-ironic slogan T-shirts. He just dragged her along as if they were taking part in a speed-walking competition, but the tourists kept buffeting into them, so in the end, Laura had to let go of his hand for her own safety.

'We could go to Regent's Park and visit the zoo?'

she suggested half-heartedly, because he'd already nixed her other plans to show him the MTV studios and the Stables markets and the vintage clothing stalls in the Electric Ballroom. 'They have a monkey house.'

Tom shook his head. 'Let's find a café. I'm starving. You don't have any proper food in your flat,' he added accusingly. Maybe his bad mood would evaporate if he had a full English breakfast. God, she'd even pay for it if it made him smile.

They ended up in a greasy spoon on the Chalk Farm Road.

'Full breakfast, right?' she asked Tom, and then waved her hand urgently at the waitress and shouted out an order across the crowded room. 'And cancel one of the teas. I'll have a skinny decaff latté,' she added. This dieting thing was pretty easy once you got the hang of it.

She turned back to Tom with a pleased smile, only to see him staring at her curiously. Laura surreptitiously touched her face to make sure she didn't have a bogey hanging out of her nose. Not even Tyra Banks could make *that* look fierce.

'What?' she asked defensively. 'Why are you looking at me like that?'

'You're different in London,' he said. 'All shiny and glossy.'

'Tom, I have second-day hair and this hoodie is going to jump into the washing machine all by itself . . .'

'I don't mean your hair, I mean you. You're all glowy.'

Maybe the sex had given her a new womanly glow. That, or her new bronzer.

'It's like I'm seeing this whole new side of you,' he clarified. 'You have these close friends that I've never met and you talk about stuff I don't understand. It's a bit of a culture shock, y'know.'

'But I'm still me,' Laura insisted, smiling at the waitress as she placed their mugs on the table. 'And to tell you the truth, half the time I don't know what Candy and Hadley are talking about. They're so sophisticated and I'm just from Manchester.'

'There's nothing wrong in coming from Manchester,' Tom snapped automatically, every Manchesterly inch of him bristling at the mere thought. 'Those girls quack on about clothes and their bodies all the time, like, like they don't even belong to them. They're just this collection of parts to be auctioned off to the highest bidder.'

'You get used to it.' Laura wrinkled her nose. 'Kind of. Like, when you're doing a shoot, everyone is fussing around you but at the same time they're talking about you like you're not even in the room.'

But when she tried to explain to Tom in finer detail that five people discussing how best to disguise her slight overbite didn't piss her off that much, he wore his blankest expression. He even picked at a hangnail, before stifling a yawn. She'd known Tom too long to find either of those moves endearing.

'All right, I'm obviously boring you rigid,' she said at last. They should be A-OK now that they'd had sex. Wasn't that how it was meant to work? 'This mood, is it about last night? Do you think we should talk . . .'

Tom's head shot up from his silent contemplation of a puddle of ketchup at the side of his plate. 'Do you love me, Laura?'

At least that was a no-brainer. 'Of course I do. Is this because of all that stuff I screamed down the phone at you?'

Tom pushed his empty cup away so he could reach for her hand and stroke his finger across the back of her knuckles in a feathery caress. 'But how much do you love me?'

It wasn't like Tom to be the needy one, but Laura could relate. Could she ever. 'It can't be quantified,' she said firmly. 'But a lot. Really a lot.'

Really a lot didn't seem to cut it, as his fingers tightened painfully against hers. 'Do you love me more than you love modelling?'

'*Tom* . . .'

'Do you love me enough that you'd give it up if I asked you to?'

At first, Laura thought it was a test. A cruel bluff. Like that story from Sunday School about King Solomon

199

threatening to slice and dice a little nipper so he could prove who its rightful baby mother was.

But there was something defiant in Tom's eyes, like he was forcing himself to stick his hand in a vat of flesh-eating maggots. And just in case she was in any doubt, he said quietly: 'If you really love me, you'll give it up.'

She'd always thought that Tom was a little bit more in love with her than she was with him. Or the old Laura had. New, improved Laura knew it wasn't so. That he didn't love her more, or wisely, or well.

'Y'know that's like me asking you not to go to Oxford, or, like, never to play football again,' she protested. 'If you loved me, you wouldn't ask me to give up something that's so important to me.'

'It's completely different,' Tom snapped with a stubborn flash to his eyes. 'When I play football or prepare for my Oxford interview, I manage not to turn into an emotional wrecking ball.'

And now they were having *that* conversation. 'So is this about me sleeping with that other guy?'

Tom didn't say anything but his face squinched up long enough for her second cup of coffee to arrive and for Laura to take the first cautious sip.

'You have to start trusting me again,' she said calmly. But she didn't feel calm as she shook her hand free of his grip. 'I know I'm to blame, Tom, but if you can't forgive me then how can we be together?'

He shrugged. 'Beats me.'

'But we had *sex*,' she hissed the word across the table at him. 'I know that the timing was slightly off, but it made things right between us. Didn't it?'

And this was Tom's cue to rush in with reassurances about how he was sleep-deprived and taking it out on her just because she was there.

'It doesn't make all the crap you've pulled magically disappear,' Tom said bluntly, conveniently forgetting all the endearments he'd husked in her ear while they were doing it. 'You just went from him to me in the space of twenty-four hours, so no, I don't know how I'm meant to trust you. Not sure I even can,'

The cold hard facts of her sluttiness weren't a reasonable argument. Because yeah, that was one way of looking at it, but then there was an entirely different view from Laura's side of the fence. 'You kissed *her* back,' she pointed out. 'You admitted it. And you didn't even care enough to make sure that she stayed away from me so I never found out.' She reached out to stroke his arm, to *touch* him, because the pleading note of her voice, the bloody desperation that had to be oozing from her every pore, wasn't working. Tom flinched away from her hand before she could even make contact and then Laura knew. 'You're not going to find a way for us to work this out? You're just going to issue a really dumbass ultimatum that you *knew* I wasn't going to agree to so I become the bad guy.' Laura could feel the indignation welling in her chest like a particularly nasty case of acid reflux.

'You *are* the bad guy,' Tom reminded her, and he needed to start singing another tune. 'You slept with some guy, you don't even know his name, and you're never around and you're chasing after a stupid dream, Laura. Getting in training for the poncy frocks of the new season? That's not real.'

'It's real to me,' Laura said hotly, and she was ready to rally her troops for one last over-the-top charge because they, she and Tom, were worth going into battle for. If she'd learned anything over the last two months, it was that it wasn't enough to just want something; you had to fight for it. 'This is my world now and I'm trying to change. This stuff with you is making me realize that I need to take a long, hard look at myself because there are things I have to fix.'

'But that's just it,' Tom sighed, looking out of the window as if he'd give anything to be outside in the rain, rather than with her where it was toasty and dry. 'You have changed. You used to be cool, Laura, and now you're shallow. All you care about is how you look and what other people think of how you look.'

And two months ago, he'd have been right. But now she was big with the personal development, as well as big with the excess poundage. 'Y'know, even if I went with the big dramatic gesture and promised to never stand in front of a camera ever again, we'd still end up in Splitsville,' Laura realized out loud. And it was odd, but even though he was sitting across from her, his knee brushing against hers under the cramped confines of the table, Tom seemed more distant that when there were at least five counties separating them.

'We'd still end up in Splitsville because you slept with someone else and you take no responsibility for anything that happens to you because it's too much like hard work.'

Sooner or later, this would stop – this horrible dredging up of bitter words that she really didn't want to hear. 'I do take responsibility for stuff. I do!'

Tom was unmoved. 'Yeah, I'll believe it when I see you on the cover of *Vogue*. You'll be back home in a month, Laura, tops. You just haven't got the guts to stick it out.'

'Stop it! Just stop it,' she begged, hands clamped over her ears. 'How can you be like this after last night? You were my first . . . my first everything.' Laura wanted to say something deep and profound that would serve as a tribute to the crumbling remains of their relationship, but she couldn't think of anything. 'God, this is so crappy,' would have to do.

'It really is,' Tom agreed, snagging his jacket from the back of the chair. 'So, I guess this is it then?'

Laura nodded. She was determined that she wasn't going to cry – couldn't couldn't bear the thought that he'd go back to Manchester and tell people, *Cassie*, that he'd left her sobbing over the debris of his all-day breakfast special.

'Well, I don't think we'll see each other around,' Tom continued and way to point out the painful and bloody obvious. 'You should get in touch with Jen and Cath. They're really upset.'

And with that non-sequitur of a last goodbye, he walked off into the sunset. Or rather ran out into the road straight into the path of a Number 24 bus, which, sadly, swerved to avoid him.

Chapter Seventeen

Stasis. It was a good word to describe the complete non-event that was the next week.

The go-sees had dried up like a riverbed in the middle of a drought, forcing Laura to either go to the gym or stay in the flat obsessing about Tom and her trial period, which actually felt more like she'd been given a month to live. Then obsessing about Tom again, for a nice change of pace.

She hated that it was a clean break. No possible hope of a cure, so they had to amputate. She couldn't ring him. Or email him. Or send him a mix CD of carefully chosen songs designed to break down the stone walls around his heart. All she could do was brood about her total lack of relationship success. Or her total lack of modelling success. The odds were spectacularly sucky either way.

But if Laura was sure of one thing, it was no way, no how, no shit was she going back to Manchester with the word 'failure' practically tattooed on her forehead. Tom might have royally dumped her but he didn't get to pass judgement on her career choices too. She was going to be a model even if it meant subsisting on a diet of lettuce leaves and somehow obtaining this mysterious 'it' quality that she didn't possess and didn't know where to find it.

Though moping about in her pyjamas all day probably wasn't helping. But on the plus side, her appetite had disappeared along with Tom. If Laura didn't want to comfort eat, then she must be in a really bad way.

At least the flat was hers alone. Candy had extended her stay in New York, Irina had pissed off to Munich and Hadley was shooting a TV sitcom with George, which was good going for a girl whose only talent was falling down drunk every night.

So, stasis. Until one Wednesday morning, Laura was woken up by some arsehole ringing the bell at seven-thirty. They wouldn't stop either. She clomped down the stairs all ready to scream at the postman or whoever, only to find Pei-Yi, Candy's yoga teacher, leaning on the bell.

'She's still in New York,' Laura growled, only bothering to open one eye. 'Somebody should have called you.'

Pei-Yi was too mellow to even frown. Must have been all that downward dogging that chilled him out. So he just shrugged in this fluid way, like water trickling off stones. 'She's paid me until the end of the month,' he mused. 'Do you want a yoga lesson?'

Laura didn't. She wanted to go back to bed and sleep until *This Morning* started, but Pei-Yi was already gently leading her up the stairs. There was a definite *Karate Kid* vibe to the proceedings, which was the only explanation as to why five minutes later, she was in neutral spine and trying to feel the chakras which Pei-Yi insisted she had.

Laura had mistakenly thought that yoga was for housewives. Her mum did it, for Christ's sake, but after two hours she was covered in a fine film of sweat and muscles that she didn't know she had were trembling from overexertion.

'I'll be back tomorrow,' Pei-Yi said firmly, rolling up his yoga mat. 'You should probably detox for the next three days. I felt a lot of negative energy blocking your chakras. Lots of water or chai tea and only raw fruit and vegetables. No citrus. And I recommend some vigorous exercise to clear your head.'

'OK,' Laura agreed brightly. The minute he was gone, she was heading straight for the comforting embrace of her duvet.

Pei-Yi gave her a serene smile. 'I'll know if you lie to me. I can tell from the whites of your eyes.'

Which was all kinds of scary, but not as scary as the discovery she made later when she was in Irina's room on a search-and-destroy mission for her lost Miss Sixty top. Irina's room was a no-go zone. There was a very real possibility that Irina would murder anyone who dared to breach its hallowed portals. And no wonder; mixed in with the ratty grey tracksuits heaped on the floor were more designer threads than the fashion floor of Selfridges. Laura wriggled in and out of a few dresses, all size eights, and didn't need the newsflash that the zips wouldn't do up.

But before she could throw a pity party, her attention was seized by Irina's idiosyncratic taste in décor. The walls were plastered in pictures torn out of magazines. Stuck on top of each one was a Polaroid photo of Irina mimicking the same pose.

'That sneaky cow,' she breathed. Irina wasn't a modelling idiot savant like she thought. She was working her lanky arse off. And ha! That was why she was constantly glued to the Fashion Channel.

Snatching up a Lanvin dress on her way out, Laura felt as if she was teetering on the edge of a major breakthrough. She wasn't sure what it was, but she could ponder it further as she jogged to Sainsbury's to buy her bodyweight in fruit and veg.

Later that evening, she also discovered why Hadley spent so much time in the bathroom – and it wasn't just to take long, tear-soaky, aromatherapy baths. There was really good lighting and a full-length mirror so you could practise posing for hours.

In between making strawberry, celery, apple and ginger smoothies (which weren't quite so gross after the first mouthful) and watching the Fashion Channel, Laura was in the bathroom making all sorts of startling discoveries. Like, if she tilted her head down at a 30° angle, it made her neck wrinkle up in an extremely unattractive manner. And if she turned slightly to the left, she looked thinner than when she turned slightly to the right. And she should never, ever pose with her hands on her hips because she looked like a prize heifer. Laura enrolled in her very own modelling boot-camp. Hell, she even rolled back the rug in the front room so she could practise walking in heels.

But what did it matter anyway? Apart from one call to make sure that she hadn't flung herself off the Westway in a fit of suicidal depression, Heidi had been maintaining radio silence.

'I think she's not talking to me,' she told Cath on the phone. There'd been a furious spate of 'But you said'/'No, but *you* said' emails before they'd both agreed to stop acting like a pair of twats and put the past behind them. Also at some point in the future, Laura had promised to introduce Cath to Orlando Bloom, but she was going to cross that delusional bridge when she came to it. 'Or I'm not talking to her. I can't decide which.'

'You should call her. She probably thinks you're sticking pins into a voodoo doll. You're not, are you?'

'Thought about it, but no,' Laura sighed.

'So, it sounds like you're working hard,' Cath ventured, because caution was the watchword. If they veered off-topic into say, talking about girls who lied to their friends about their glittering modelling careers, it usually ended up in a slanging match. 'Like, you've made a decision to see the modelling thing through.'

'Well, it's more like I'm stuck in the flat with nothing to do but eat myself into a sugar coma, so I thought I'd use the time constructively. But God, Cath, even if I went on a go-see and showed off all my new moves, there's no guarantee I'd get the job. I could be doing it all wrong.'

'But I thought you knew everything about modelling,' Cath said, and Laura could tell she was one breath away from a snicker.

'Well, maybe I didn't know as much as I thought I did,' she conceded after a moment. 'And maybe I wasn't as pretty as I thought I was, but now I know how to fake it, I think.'

Humility was like a new winter coat that she was trying on for size. Laura wasn't sure that it was her colour, but on the day that she could get the zip done up on her skinniest skinny jeans without having to use a coathanger, she rang Heidi.

'About time,' was Heidi's greeting. 'I've got a job for you.'

Six words were all it took for Laura to find her positive attitude.

'You have? That's great!'

'You don't mind working for free, do you?'

And eight words were all it took to lose it again. 'You mean I won't get paid? But I'm in my skinniest skinny jeans.'

'One of my boyfriend's mates is a photographer's assistant and he needs a model for a test shoot. You'll get some pictures for your book and you'll get some shoot experience.' *Which you sorely need*, went unsaid. 'It's up to you.'

Giving Heidi the satisfaction of telling Ted that Laura was still a sulky, talentless loser was not an option. 'OK, I'll do it,' she heard herself say.

The test shoot was like nothing Laura had ever experienced. She met Jared, the trainee photographer, Chloe, the trainee stylist, and Ben, someone's mate who was there to lug equipment, at Chalk Farm Tube station so they could walk to Primrose Hill where Jared wanted to 'take action shots – maybe you running about or something'.

Laura got changed in a public loo, had to do her own hair and make-up, then stood in front of Jared (and a small crowd of lairy kids who'd come over to watch).

'So what do you want me to do?' she asked, swinging her arms aimlessly.

Jared looked perplexed. 'Um, I don't know. Modelly stuff, I guess.'

When she pulled out Pose Number Three, which she'd spent all of yesterday perfecting, the lairy kids started taking the piss. Loudly.

'You're shit and you know you are!' they chanted. Well, at least it was marginally better than 'Who ate all the pies?'

'Could you not be quite so modelly?' Jared suggested

helpfully. 'Like more candid. I saw these Elaine Constantine photos and I wanted that kind of vibe.'

Elaine Constantine. She knew that name. Laura scrolled her way through the photo Rolodex in her head. Elaine Constantine had taken the picture of the fearless girls on bikes that she'd stuck on her bedroom wall.

'OK, I know exactly what you want,' Laura grinned, and then she ran screaming towards the lairy kids, with her fists waving in the air. 'GET OUT OF IT!' she screeched as they scattered like skittles while Jared clicked away.

'Yeah, like that!' he yelped. 'Just like that.'

The shoot was like the most intense workout session she'd ever had. Laura cartwheeled, did handstands, hung upside down from a tree and, as a finale, sweet-talked a gay couple into lending her a pair of Dalmatians so she could be dragged around the park when they set off on full gallop after a yappy dog.

'You were fantastic,' Jared enthused as they sat in a beer garden afterwards, drinking ice-cold Diet Cokes. Pei-Yi had banned caffeine, but the circumstances were extenuating. 'You up for doing another test shoot next weekend?'

Test shoots meant no money. No chance to impress the hell out of a passing fashion editor. But she'd had more fun that afternoon than in for ever. Also, Jared explained why some things hadn't worked, using words of less than three syllables, so she was learning stuff too.

'Sure,' Laura panted. 'I'll give you my number.'

'My friend's looking for a model for a test shoot tomorrow,' Chloe piped up. 'She'll pay you fifty quid and give you some prints.'

'And my girlfriend's a designer,' added Ben. 'She needs a model she can work with to get the fit right on her clothes. You're nearly a size eight, yeah?'

What was the opposite of stasis? Flux? Overexertion? She'd have had to ask Tom because he was better with the book stuff, but for all Laura knew he'd run off to join the Foreign Legion.

When she'd come to London, she'd been resting on her *Make Me A Model* laurels. Then she'd become the Girl Who Couldn't Get Booked and now she was the Go-To Girl For Test Shoots. Since that afternoon in Primrose Hill, her number seemed to have been passed to every aspiring photographer, stylist, designer and hairdresser in London. Not that Laura was complaining. OK, well, maybe she had at the beginning, but now she was too busy to have time to moan. Her shape-up-or-piss-off month's deadline had come and gone, and there hadn't even been time to worry about it.

And she might not be getting paid, but she'd picked up some great shots for her book (and some truly terrible ones from photography students who'd be lucky to scrape a third), some free clothes and, best of all, she did a job for a hair salon who had restored her tresses to almost their former glory with some extensions.

No one seemed that bothered that she *still* couldn't get into a size eight. But even though Pei-Yi had forbidden her from getting on the scales (Laura was sure he'd telepathically know if she had), because she was building muscle which weighed more than fat, something weird was going on with her body. Like, good weird. It was *taut*, and there was firmness where before there'd been floppiness.

It was about time. Apart from one blip where she'd stayed in on a Saturday night with a tub of Ben & Jerry's Chocolate Therapy, she'd become a temple to healthy living. What with the oatmeal (she'd hit on a winning combo of strawberries and flaked almonds), nine pieces of fruit and veg a day and grilled chicken fillets, she didn't even feel like she was on a diet any more. Eating properly had become a habit. So had abandoning the gym and running round Regent's Park with Go! Team on her iPod. But she still wasn't close to getting into the Lanvin dress, which was unfair with added bits of unfairness.

At least a few paid jobs started trickling in, courtesy of her new network of struggling fashion types. A couple of one-page shoots for a teen magazine and a beauty shot for an underground Japanese magazine weren't comparable to Irina getting the cover of Australian *Vogue*, but it was a start.

It was also a good way to check out the competition.

The kind of shoots she was getting booked for were solely the domain of other 'fresh off the train' new models. The Eastern European girls were strike-a-pose automatons. There was a bit of nostril-flaring and hair-tossing in the dressing room if things didn't go their way, but on set they were thoroughbred racehorses compared to Laura, who felt like a pack mule.

But *all* the other girls were thin. Sleek and rangy with legs that went all the way up to their armpits; even the coltish sixteen-year-old on her first job, with her mum in tow, who stood in front of the camera visibly shaking. They were shooting a knitwear story and she and Laura were meant to be acting like best buds instead of two girls who hadn't even been properly introduced.

'Just forget the camera is even there,' she hissed out of the corner of her mouth.

'But it *is* there,' the other girl pointed out. 'And this wool is really itchy.'

Laura could sense the photographer's impatience as he muttered under his breath. She twirled the tassels on her scarf thoughtfully, before whipping it off.

'Here, catch,' she shouted, throwing the scarf at the other girl, then snatching it back as she tried to reach it. No one could be nervous when they were playing tug-of-war with a scarf. It just wasn't possible.

The photographer snapped away until they fell over in a heap on the studio floor. 'You should thank Laura for saving your skin,' he grunted, but the newbie was already rushing to her mother and the box of Krispy Kremes she was holding.

Laura stretched and wriggled. The wool *was* wicked itchy. 'You're with Fierce, right?' the photographer asked, handing her a bottle of water. 'One of Heidi's girls?'

This would have been the time for Laura to brag about her *Make Me A Model* win; instead she just nodded. 'Yeah, and I'm available for shoots, shows and bar mitzvahs,' she drawled.

'I'll remember that. You have very symmetrical features,' he added, before turning away to complain to his assistant about the scuff marks they'd left on the colourama.

Laura couldn't wait to rid herself of the jumper, which was rapidly becoming the bane of her entire existence. The newbie was shovelling doughnuts into her mouth so fast, they barely touched the sides and, just for a second, Laura hated her; her skinny frame and her super-speedy metabolism. Another second and she was over it. Oatmeal for breakfast every freaking day wasn't so bad.

Ten minutes later she was good to go. Just a quick pee-stop before she met a couple of her new photographer mates for a drink.

As she sat on the loo, Laura contemplated her navel. It was definitely surrounded by less flesh. Another girl shut the door of the cubicle next to hers and Laura was shaken out of her daydream. She zipped up her skinniest skinny jeans and then paused at the unmistakable sounds of someone vomiting.

Would it be totally embarrassing if she asked whoever it was if they were OK? Before she had a chance, someone else was coming in and banging on the door.

'Are you nearly finished in there?' a woman called out. 'Make sure you get everything up.'

'Nearly done, Mum, hang on.' The voice of the newbie model drifted over the wall as Laura froze. What the *fu* . . . ?

'It's a pity that you choked in front of the camera,' the woman continued. 'Because you were much prettier and thinner than that other model. We'll work on that when we get home.'

There was no reply, just more puking sounds.

Laura slid down the wall so she was sitting on the floor and pressed the heels of her hands over her eyes. She could barely breathe. If she could have, she'd have reached under the gap and hauled that stupid girl in with her and phoned up Child Protection Services.

So, when Mommie Dearest and her daughter finally left, Laura did something that she never thought she'd do.

'Laura, you have to stop crying 'cause I can't understand a single word you're saying,' Heidi sighed, before handing her a tissue. 'I'm going to get you some water.'

Laura blew her nose and huddled further into the

Calpol-pink sofa. It was way past going-home time; she'd only caught Heidi because she'd been waiting to take a conference call from LA. And she wasn't even sure that it was a good idea to be here and snotting all over Heidi's Eley Kishimoto top, but she'd to do something.

'Here you go.' Heidi handed her a bottle of water and regarded her intently as she sat down. 'OK, now what's upsetting you?'

She managed to hiccup and splutter her way through the story of the mum-enabled puking session with only minimum tear leakage. 'I didn't know what to do so, like, I thought you could help,' she finished doubtfully.

Heidi leaned forward so she could give her a completely spontaneous hug, which freaked Laura out almost as much as the scene in the loos. 'It should be easy to find out what agency she's with and then I'll have a quiet word with her booker, if that will do any good.'

'Her booker should send her to get some help,' Laura sniffed. The tissue was nothing more than pulp at this stage. 'And her mother should be locked up. I guess that's why Ted got so angry when I made that bulimia joke.'

'This is not a nice industry,' Heidi told her, hitching herself up on to the seat and crossing her legs under her. She seemed about three hundred per cent less scary tonight. 'I left my last agency when they sent two size-eight models to the doctor to get a prescription for laxatives a week before a big shoot.'

'That's awful,' Laura gasped. The ice packs on her aching muscles and daily vegetable smoothies weren't even in the same league. 'So, you'll speak to her booker and hope that she's cool about it?'

'Yeah. I might even get Ted to do it. He's more terrifying than I am.'

Laura took a moment to ponder that. Surely Heidi was the most terrifying creature to ever strap on a headset?

'So, to completely change the subject, you should probably come in next week,' said Heidi, as Laura downed half the water in one long gulp. 'We can go through your new pictures and update your portfolio.'

All of a sudden, there were a million things that Laura wanted to bombard her with. Are you still thinking about sacking me? Am I still on Fierce's books? Will you start sending me on go-sees again? Why haven't you asked me to come in for the last seven weeks? She had enough questions to last until Sunday but she settled for a serene, 'OK. I've got rehearsals for a student fashion show but I'm free from Wednesday.' Pei-Yi must have yoga-ed all the surliness out of her. Now that Candy was back, Laura was still gatecrashing the morning sessions; she'd even offered to pay but Candy had just shaken her head. 'At least it gets him off my back, like, fifty per cent of the time,' she'd confessed. ''Cause, man, your Sun Salute sucks.'

Laura stretched out her legs and realized that Heidi was asking her something.

'Sorry, I zoned out for a second.'

'I asked what student show you were doing?'

'Oh, it's at Central Saint Martin's. It's this married couple in their final year that Candy knows from somewhere. They're doing a joint show.' Laura fished around in her bag for the scrabby piece of paper with the details scrawled on it.

'So is that the Jack & Jane show?'

'Um yeah. How did you know that?' Laura asked curiously. 'It's OK that I do the show, isn't it? It's just I've got no catwalk experience and I've been working on my walk. I can do five-inch heels now.'

'My God, is this the same Laura?' Heidi choked out something, which might have been a laugh. 'And of course you can do the show. There's a real buzz about them. They're being touted as the new Antoni + Alison. I'm kinda impressed. In fact, I've been hearing all sorts of good things about you.'

Heidi's praise (or *kinda* praise) was so unexpected that Laura didn't have a clue how to deal with it. 'Like what?'

'It can all wait until next week,' Heidi decided with a maddeningly opaque smile. 'Don't know about you, but I'd quite like to get home before *Lost* starts. You want to get the Tube with me?'

Laura pointed at her plimsolls. 'If it's less than three miles, I walk. I have the blisters to prove it.'

'I swear to God, Laura, you've been taken over by the

pod people.' Heidi stood up and shot Laura another keen look, which gave nothing away. 'You should probably put some ice on your face when you get home, otherwise you're going to be really puffy tomorrow.'

Pretending to be beautiful was a lot more work than just being pretty, that was for sure.

Chapter Eighteen

The atmosphere backstage at the student fashion show was verging on hysterical.

Laura surveyed the madness as she perched on a rickety stool in her knickers and a bandeau top strapping down her boobs, which were still intent on being a lot more than a handful. She continued to painstakingly apply liquid eyeliner as Jane screamed at the top of her lungs, 'Ten bloody minutes, people. I want all models ready to get in their outfits in the next sixty seconds or I start bitch-slapping.'

Her husband, Jack, was chain-smoking away in the corner and no use to anyone.

If Laura concentrated on drawing a sweeping green line across her upper lids, she could ignore the swarm of butterflies doing an energetic four-four-two formation in her tummy. Just a quick slick of gloss on her lips and she slid off the stool and hurried over to Jane.

'OK, outfit me.'

Jane snapped her fingers at one of her mates who'd been roped in to help and between the two of them they helped Laura into a tight red dress. She raised a hand to smooth down the bodice and had it slapped by Jane. Hard.

'Don't touch the fabric,' she snarled, adjusting the material before flouncing out the frill at the bottom of the skirt. 'And remember, be lively and saucy. Go! You're on.'

She wedged her hand under Laura's arm so she could drag her to the billowy curtains then shoved her through, before Laura had time to process that she was on the catwalk. She was on a *freaking* catwalk, God help her.

It loomed long and white, stretching to an infinity and clustered on both sides by a scrum of people and flashing cameras. As she put her first leg forward, she felt it – this huge surge of energy as if someone had stabbed an adrenalin shot right into her heart, *Pulp Fiction* style.

The red satin of Laura's dress swooshed about her thighs as she picked up speed, every inch of her tingling as she tried to remember what she'd learned by watching Daria Werbowy on the Fashion Channel. Don't go too fast. Keep your head up. Do something with your arms. She was already at the end of the catwalk and, before she knew it, she was holding a pose and turning for the walk back. And it wasn't planned, because the move never looked right when she tried it in the bathroom mirror, but Laura threw in an insouciant wiggle of her hips as she slowly rotated.

There was no time to wonder if she'd pulled it off; the next model was already at the top of the runway. She strutted back the way she came, dimly aware that over the soundtrack of Franz Ferdinand's *Do You Want To?*, there was definite applause, maybe even a wolf-whistle. People sure got excited about a few frocks.

The curtain was already lifting as she dived behind it and looked around helplessly for someone to remove her from her dress.

'Laura! What the hell was that booty move?' Jane bellowed, rushing across the room.

'I'm sorry. It seemed like a—'

'I loved it!' Jane screamed. 'Hold your arms up so I can get you out of this. It was perfect. I'm changing your next outfit. I want you to wear the mini-crini wedding dress, so you're going on last. You're the only one with the figure to fill it. And I want you to do something, like, even more outrageous when you do your turn, OK?'

'OK. Um, could you be more specific?'

But Jane couldn't because she'd spotted a hapless model with a stuck zipper and was gone.

If Laura was nervous before, now she was terrified to the power of eleven. The last outfit on the runway, always a wedding dress, was a big deal. No matter if it was a student show or Louis fricking Vuitton, and now there was all this pressure to do *something* spectacular when Laura was astounded that she'd managed to stay upright.

She tried to feel for her Manipura chakra but as she was being laced into a corset, it was all she could do to breathe and stare at her breasts, which were hoisted almost as high as her chin.

'Thirty seconds,' someone shouted as she stepped into the stiff black bombazine of the skirt. Where she came from wedding dresses weren't black or this boobalicious.

Laura lined up behind the other girls and racked her brains for another flirty move. By the time the girl before her was stepping through the curtain, she'd still got nuthin'.

A bouquet of wilted red roses were thrust at her and then she was strutting out on to the runway. She added a bit more sass to her hip-swinging and managed a wink at the cameras on her turn but it wasn't enough. *She* wasn't enough. She'd been kidding herself that she was model material just because she'd lost a bit of puppy-fat, taken some photos that didn't completely suck and admitted that she knew jackshit . . .

Oh, shut up, Laura. Stop whining and do something outrageous right the hell now. Her inner voice sounded a lot like Candy these days – and what would Candy do? What wouldn't Candy do?

As the curtains got nearer, Laura paused, then before she could chicken out she hurled the wilted bouquet into the audience so she had both hands free to lift her skirt, stick out her arse and show the world her day-of-the-week knickers.

There was a moment's silence. Then an unearthly roar went up from the crowd. Laura didn't know whether it was a good roar or a bad one and, quite frankly, she wasn't sticking around to find out. Every instinct she had was shrieking at her to hightail it, but she forced herself to slowly saunter off the runway as if letting a huge group of strangers see the word 'Wednesday' emblazoned across her bottom was a regular occurrence.

She pushed the curtains out of the way and walked straight into Jane's arms. 'I. Love. You,' Jane squeaked. 'For real. I'm divorcing Jack so we can get hitched. Listen to that applause.'

'I'm not sure our union would be legally binding,' Laura said doubtfully. 'Was that cool out there? I wasn't sure, then I just thought I should go with it.'

'If we don't get in the papers tomorrow morning, there is not an ounce of justice in the world,' Jack announced from behind Laura. He had his twentieth cigarette clenched between his teeth as he took Laura's hand and Jane grabbed the other. 'All ready for our victory lap?'

The next morning Laura's sleep was interrupted by her phone ringing, beeping and vibrating at minute intervals, until she was finally forced to get out of bed and switch it off.

It had been a long night and most of it was a blur. She could remember a three-way hug and scream-athon with Hadley and Candy at the after-show party, which had taken place in a working men's club in Shoreditch. Possibly with drag queen karaoke – although that could have been a particularly vivid dream. And she had definite flashbacks to a ferocious dance-off with Chloe, her stylist friend, who she'd completely trounced with her busting moves to *Hollaback Girl*. Also, she was never getting the night bus home with Hadley ever again because it ended with vomit, tears and 'I don't do public transport' shrieked at top volume.

Yeah, she definitely deserved some extra snuggle time with Carrots, her cuddly rabbit.

Bang. Thud. Crash.

'You are not going to believe this!' Candy screamed, hurling the door back on its hinges as a prelude to bouncing up and down on Laura's bed. 'Look at this!'

'Bite me,' Laura suggested sleepily, but Candy was yanking off the duvet and thrusting something in front of her face.

It took a while for her eyes to focus on the newspaper. Even longer for the picture of a pert bum to come into view and the headline: *Bottoms up!*

'You've made the front cover of the *Sun* and there's a long article in the *Daily Mail* about how curves are back,' Candy exclaimed. 'Oh and the *Guardian* have done a piece about days-of-the-week knickers.'

Laura emerged from the quilt and rubbed her eyes blearily. Then she sat up with a gasp. 'God, my mum is gonna kill me!'

She was still on the phone mouthing platitudes – 'but at

least it wasn't a thong so look on the bright side' – when Ted and Heidi turned up. At least, Laura thought it was Ted and Heidi, but it was hard to tell because they were both smiling ear to ear.

'Honestly, Laura, what were you thinking?' her mother bleated. 'Flaunting your underwear. People will think you weren't brought up properly.'

'I know, I know,' Laura muttered, giving Ted and Heidi a feeble wave and wishing that she wasn't wearing a *Die Hipster Scum* T-shirt and her yoga pants. 'It will all be forgotten by tomorrow.'

'It's all very well for you to say that but I don't know how I'll show my face at book group, and your father was *mortified*. He couldn't even look at his cornflakes and—'

'Mum, I have to go,' Laura interrupted frantically. Ted and Heidi were staring at the stacks of magazines and empty Diet Coke cans with obvious distaste. 'I'm really sorry and you can continue telling me off later. I promise.'

'But, I haven't —' She was a bad daughter, hanging up on her mother's anguished shriek like that but matters were pressing. Especially as her Pavlovian response to seeing Ted and Heidi in the ever-loving flesh was for her palms to start sweating.

'Hey,' she began nervously, tugging at the hem of her shirt and taking a hurried step back at Ted suddenly cupped her chin. 'Long time, no see.'

'You've got cheekbones,' he announced, taking Laura by

the shoulder and pulling her toward the window so she was bathed in sunlight.

'I thought she was thinner when she came in, but her face was swollen from crying and she had her coat on,' Heidi noted, sitting down and holding a stray sock gingerly between her finger and thumb. 'This place is a tip.'

'Hmmm, she's definitely thinner, probably because she lost that huge chip on her shoulder. This is all good.' Ted gestured at the papers fanned out on the coffee table where Laura had left them. 'And this, sweetie, is paydirt.'

Laura gaped at Ted and decided that Heidi was the lesser of the two evils. 'Huh?'

'Go and get your latest photos and we can all sit down and have a chat.' Heidi brandished her BlackBerry like a battleaxe. 'Oh, yeah, I managed to repress the memory of the hair extensions.'

Laura paused mid-flee and fingered the ends of her artificial hair. 'They were free,' she said defensively, then scratched her head. 'But they itch.'

Ted and Heidi exchanged a look, which could only be labelled as significant. 'Bathroom?' Heidi asked.

'It's through there, second door on the left,' Laura mumbled vaguely, her mind already on the pile of prints scattered about her bedroom floor. 'Hey? What the . . . ?'

She was being bundled bathroomwards in an unrelenting grip so that she could be propped up in front of the mirror, book-ended by bookers.

'What do you see?' Heidi asked Laura's reflection.

Laura barely glanced at her mirror image. 'I've got a jam-stain on my T-shirt, I need to wash my hair and, er, my eyebrows need plucking.'

There was an extravagant groan from Ted. 'You've gone from narcissist to ostrich in two months. *Look!*'

He gathered her hair in a loose ponytail so Laura had no choice but to stare at her sleep-rumpled face without looking away. Sure, she'd spent more time standing in front of a mirror than was strictly necessary, but mostly she'd been busy concocting new poses and throwing shapes.

She peered at mirror-Laura's familiar features. Then she blinked, and it was like one of those stupid magic eye pictures because slowly, rising up from her face, were a pair of elegant cheekbones, eyes that had never been that large before and a pointed chin, which made her lips look as if they were stuck in a permanent pout. It wasn't like she was the Zit Queen before, but now her skin was positively glowing, even with pillow creases etched into her cheeks. Ted let her hair swing loose and the vision she'd glimpsed disappeared.

'Do you know what I'm looking at?' Ted asked Heidi. 'My early retirement fund, that's what.'

Laura stared at them both. 'I still can only get the zip up on a size-eight designer dress if I don't breathe out. All the other girls are thinner than me.'

She stepped forward and pushed up her T-shirt so she

could prod her tummy. It wasn't flat. It would never be flat, but there was a gentle slope instead of a steep downward curve. She wonderingly touched the knobs of her hipbones and then turned so she could see her back view.

There were still plenty of booty but it was all taut and toned and didn't jiggle wildly when she gave an experimental shimmy.

'Gisele,' Ted stated firmly.

Heidi shook her head. 'More like Cindy Crawford in her supermodel prime. Get on the scales.'

'But Pei-Yi says—'

'Scales. Now,' Heidi insisted firmly, whipping a tape measure out of her jacket pocket.

Laura dug the scales out from the cupboard under the sink. 'Let me just make sure it's on zero,' she prevaricated, crouching down, but Ted was bodily lifting her onboard.

'Quit stalling, sweetie.'

'You'll give yourself a hernia,' she squeaked, shutting her eyes as the needle started its vertical climb.

'That's much better,' Heidi said with grim satisfaction, already wrapping the tape measure around Laura's boobs. 'Thirty-four, that's OK.' Never had Laura been frisked so thoroughly as Heidi reached around her waist. 'Twenty-five! That's gotta be a mistake, Hang on.' She turned to Ted with a look of awe. 'She's got a twenty-five-inch waist, hips thirty-five. Jesus!'

Laura still had her eyes tightly shut. 'Good Jesus or bad Jesus?'

'I feel the dawning of a new era is upon us,' Ted pronounced dramatically. 'Curves really are back. And I have the proof right here.'

Laura opened her eyes so she could check that Ted and Heidi weren't taking the piss. 'I've already told you that I'm still not in a size eight. Maybe I can do an extra twenty minutes running a day or something.'

'Whatever you're doing, keep doing it,' Heidi advised. 'And I hope you haven't got anything on for the rest of the week because the next three days are booked solid. Go and get changed into something tight, we're due in Mayfair at ten.'

Chapter Nineteen

Go-sees had become appointments. Or meetings. Or some unspecified name to see someone who was expecting you and acted as if Laura's mere presence was a never-ending source of delight.

'I'm in love with her waist-to-hip ratio,' exclaimed one fashion editor, when Laura was coaxed into a Roland Mouret, form-fitting dress. 'I'm so sick of all these girls who just go straight up and down.'

'She has the look of a hipper, younger Angelina Jolie,' announced the head booker from Fierce's New York office. 'We'll need a digital version of her portfolio to send out.'

'Zat accent is so exotic, yes?' An Italian fashion designer, who came up to Laura's shoulder, hugged her to his chest as she tried not to flinch. 'Say something else, darlink. Anything.'

But appointments, or meetings or whatever you wanted to call them, didn't mean bookings. Laura said as much to Ted as they sat in the back of another cab. She'd been chaperoned by either him or Heidi all week and though Heidi had unbent so much that she was practically pretzel-shaped, Laura definitely preferred Ted's company. If only for the scurrilous gossip he doled out about other models and Fierce's celebrity faces, while she gaped and squeaked, 'Really? He didn't? With a Pomeranian? You're *so* making it up!'

It was late on Friday morning and they were on their way to One Aldwych to have 'a quick coffee' with . . . she couldn't remember who, just that they were really important and why she was all dolled up in TopShop's finest.

'Don't get me wrong, Ted, this week has been great and you and Heidi have been totally ace but I know how it is. On Monday morning I could be getting changed in a public loo so I can be shot by some wannabe photographer who can't work his light meter.' Laura leaned back in her seat and stared out at the neon glitter of Soho reflected in the rain puddles. 'I don't want to get my hopes up just because I've been on a few appointments.'

She sounded so *mature*. When had that happened? Ted smiled cagily; it was hard to read too much into his facial expressions, though Laura had a feeling he should try out for the World Poker Series.

'If you could do a shoot for any magazine in the country, any one, which would it be?' he asked, leaning forward to tell the driver to avoid Cambridge Circus.

Laura didn't have to think too hard. 'In an ideal world, it would be *Vogue*, like duh. And in an unideal world, where I'm being more realistic, then *Polka Dot*.'

'Can you go left here? And then cut through Seven Dials?' Ted folded his arms and fixed her with a totally smug look. 'I never figured myself for a fairy godmother but, done and done.'

That made the kind of sense that didn't make any. 'What's done?'

'I wasn't going to tell you until after our coffee thing but I can't bear the suspense any longer. You're doing a ten-page beauty story for *Polka Dot* next week and then you've been specially requested for a *Vogue* fashion shoot on new designers. They wanted an up-and-coming model and you were their unanimous choice.'

'Is this like the story you told me about that Venezuelan model and the Premiership footballers?' Laura asked crossly. "Cause I knew you were making it up? OK, not right away but eventually I figured it out.'

Ted smoothed down the lapel of his Yohji Yamamoto suit. 'Straight up. And if you let this interfere with being charming and delightful during this meeting, I will throttle you with my tie. We clear, sweetness?'

Somehow Laura managed to be charming and delightful for the time it took to daintily sip a green tea, soya milkshake and talk a whole load of drivel about Manchester United's chances this season with two more excitable Italians. Zilli and Costello were the founders of a big couture label, House of Augustine, and huge AC Milan fans. Never had Laura been more grateful for the times that she'd had to sit and watch Tom watch slo-mo replays of Premiership matches, because now she could talk knowledgeably about transfer deals and who she fancied to win Euro 2008.

She still didn't have a clue what the meeting was meant to be about or why Ted was talking in urgent whispers with Zilli, who was staring at her face like he'd never seen anyone with the full complement of lips, nose and eyes before.

There wasn't even time to grill Ted afterwards or go into a full-body freakout about *Polka Dot* and *Vogue*. *Vogue!* He had lunch reservations at The Ivy with his boyfriend and she had a train to catch.

After Knicker-gate, the only way to soothe her mother's ruffled feathers was to do it in person, with the aid of the largest bottle of her favourite perfume that Laura could find.

Manchester looked weird, Laura decided, as she caught the bus from the station. Small, grimy and damp. It was a world of corner shops and buses that weren't red and kids walking home from school. She couldn't remember the last time she'd seen anyone wear school uniform.

As she jumped off the bus and wheeled her suitcase round the corner into her street, it was as if time had been preserved in a pickling jar while Laura had been pounding the London pavements, always five minutes late for her next yoga class, or test shoot or coffee with one of her new mates. She walked past the letterbox on the green and the spot where she'd fallen off her bike that time, and there was Mrs Veeraswamy from two doors down trundling down the road with her shopping trolley. Déjà vu was alive and well and living in Didsbury.

She didn't have her keys, because they were lost somewhere in the clothes-strewn mess of her room back in Camden, so she rang the doorbell and watched through the frosted glass panel as her father slowly ambled down the hall.

He wouldn't actually let Laura over the threshold until he'd pretended to have a heart attack. 'Do we know you from somewhere?' he mock-gasped as her mother hurried from the kitchen. 'Didn't you used to be our daughter?'

'For goodness' sake, Frank, let that naughty girl in so I can slap some sense into her.'

Thankfully, slapping some sense into her translated as the world's longest, squeeziest hug and a cautionary tap on her rump.

'Don't you dare lose any more weight or I won't be able to get such a sense of satisfaction from smacking your infamous bottom,' her mother grumbled when Laura squawked in faux outrage.

Laura flexed one toned arm. 'I'm all yogacized up now. You should see my Sun Salute, it's way better than yours.'

Now it was her mother's turn to huff. 'Joking. I'm just going to wheel this to the kitchen because I have a ton of dirty laundry in here.'

'Oh, your father will do that and I'll put it in the machine, but then we'll have a cup of tea and – oh, Laura, we've missed you so much. You go and put your feet up, love.'

Alas, after five minutes of acting as if she was visiting royalty, it was back to normal and she was being told off for putting her cup down on the table without a coaster.

But it was hard to relax when she knew The Talk™ was coming. She was just amazed that her mother managed to hold off until after dinner as they loaded the dishwasher together.

'You seem different,' she ventured, rinsing a roasting dish under the tap. 'Not just the way you look. You seem different in yourself.'

'But in a good way, Mum,' Laura assured her. 'I feel like I've grown up tons in the last few weeks. And I kinda needed to.'

'You were fine the way you were,' her mother insisted tightly, as if her parental skills had been found wanting. 'You're only seventeen, Laura. No one expects you to be a fully operational adult.'

Laura took a deep breath. 'I was a brat. I was so used to getting my own way that when it didn't happen I couldn't deal. And now I can, sort of.'

Her mother's back stiffened. 'Are you saying we spoilt you?'

'I'm not saying you did, but I have two really lovely parents who had me late in life and we both know that sometimes I take shameless advantage of that.' Her mother's tension eased slightly as she acknowledged that non-newsflash. 'Plus, I'd been coasting on the whole "pretty" thing for too long. I needed to come down to earth.'

'So are you telling me that you're in it for the long haul? That you're not coming home and going back to school?' Her mother was staring at the cutlery drawer, her face set. It was exactly the same expression she wore when she was watching a documentary about sick babies and didn't want to cry.

'Mum.' Laura tugged at her arm, turning her round so she could give her a fierce hug. 'This is what I want to do. Not the oatmeal or the sitting about in draughty studios, but when I'm in front of the camera or doing a fashion show, I feel alive. Y'know, I feel *whole*. Can you understand that?'

'Well, I don't . . . that is to say . . .' Her mother ruffled her extensions, which would never feel like real hair no matter how human they claimed to be. 'I feel the same way when I'm gardening,' she claimed with a self-deprecating smile. 'I didn't imagine I'd drive you out of the family home before you were even eighteen.'

'Yeah, I became a model to get away from you and Dad

and your harsh, totalitarian regime,' Laura scoffed. 'Don't be soft! So, are you cool with this?'

'Would it make any difference if I wasn't?' her mother asked quietly, and there was nothing that Laura could say that would make the answer any easier to hear.

Cath had already told her over the phone. But even if she hadn't, Laura would have still found out when she just happened to click on Tom's MySpace page, not like she meant to or anything. There it was – a picture of him and Cassie all snuggly-wuggly and the puke-inducing comment: 'Happy 2 month anniversary to the coolest boyf in the world. Love ya, babes! XOXOXO'

'I knew there was more to it than drunken snogging,' she confessed to Cath and Jen, as they sat in Loaf on Saturday night, sipping cocktails and trying not to give the appearance that they were totally looking out for stray Man United players. Heidi had managed to get Laura on the guest list because she was currently the sweetest, nicest best-ever booker. 'And he didn't even have the decency to be a little bit broken-hearted. He must have headed straight for that troll as soon as he got back to Manchester.'

Jen grimaced. 'It did seem kinda sudden. And you know that Chandra hooked up with James? She doesn't even speak to us any more.'

'Harsh,' Laura opined, draping her arms round them. 'Sounds like things have been tough. How are you two holding up? Lots of late-night bitching fests cunningly disguised as study sessions, I'll bet.'

'See, I told you that Laura's had a complete personality transplant,' Cath said to Jen slyly, 'She keeps asking me all these questions about my well-being and she even sounds interested when I answer them.'

'I *am* interested,' Laura snapped, rising to the bait with an angry head-toss as Cath and Jen collapsed in giggles. It wasn't *that* funny. 'I'm new and improved, deal with it.'

'We liked the old you, you were just a little bit up yourself sometimes.' Jen said calmly. 'It's weird 'cause you're way prettier now but you're not so big-headed. Whatever, we're all cool, right and it's your round, supermodel. I'll have the same again.'

Mock-grumbling, just to let them know that she wasn't completely new and improved, Laura fought her way through a crowd of perma-tanned girls, each of them clutching a regulation-issue Prada clutch, only to come face to face with Tom and Cassie.

For a moment, she wasn't sure it was them. Mainly because when she imagined them together they'd sprouted matching weeping, facial pustules. So seeing them for real, all joined at the hip, Laura gave a start of recognition, like she'd just spotted a celebrity. Which, not even.

Nobody said anything, though Laura had the urge to shout, 'I'm going to be in *Vogue*, you wanker!' at the top of her voice.

Cassie couldn't talk anyway as her mouth was stretched into a smug grin, which Laura itched to wipe off her face using the medium of her fists. At least she was wearing a Marni dress, which she'd happened to 'borrow' from Hadley. Hadley wasn't there to sanction it, but Laura was sure she wouldn't mind. As it was, she could see from the way that Cassie's eyebrows raised just a fraction, that she knew that both Laura and her frock were in a different league. Maybe that's why she planted a kiss on Tom's cheek. She could have just pissed up his leg if she wanted to mark her territory.

'Laura,' Tom mumbled, looking at his cheating feet, rather than her. 'You all right?'

'I'm wonderful. How's *school*?' She put every last drop of condescension that she could into the word. Tom might have dumped her, but he was still the one who had to put up his hand and ask a teacher if he could go to the loo between the hours of nine and four.

'You slept with any boys that you don't know lately?' Cassie asked sweetly. 'Or did you manage to get a name first?'

OK, wasn't there some kind of unwritten law that you didn't spill your ex's darkest, most shameful secrets to the skank that you were currently involved with? If there wasn't, there should be. Laura racked her brains for a scathing retort and was saved from coming up empty by a tap on her shoulder.

Thank God. As she turned round to shoot a grateful smile at either Jen or Cath, she stared into the limpid dark eyes of a boy she didn't know.

'Sorry to interrupt,' he said smoothly, like he wasn't sorry at all. 'This is really embarrassing, but I've got a bet on with my friends that you're a model. You won that show, right?'

It might have been a five-out-of-ten on the lame pick-up line scale, but Laura clutched on to it as if was a lifebelt and she was drowning in rough seas. Not even metaphorically speaking. 'You're not interrupting,' she said pointedly, giving Cassie and Tom a supersized portion of cold shoulder. 'Yeah, I did win that show and I just found out that I'm going to be in *Vogue*, so I guess I can officially call myself a model.'

'Well, you have to let me buy you a drink then to celebrate.' He wasn't her type. Laura didn't have a type any more because she was done with boys. They weren't worth the heartache. Even cute ones with olive skin and Dior Homme suits. But way to leave on a high note.

'Cool,' she beamed. 'I'm here with my friends; why don't you buy a bottle of champagne and bring it over with your mates?'

Oh yeah, she'd got it going on. He was nodding dumbly. Laura had a feeling that if she asked him to whip off his jacket and lay it down on the ground because the floor was a bit sticky, he'd have happily complied.

She let him take her elbow as if she was a precious princess of a girl who couldn't possibly walk unaided, and allowed herself to give Cassie and Tom a small wave as she glided away.

'Hey, it's been real,' she called over her shoulder. 'I'll see you guys around.'

Chapter Twenty

The *Polka Dot* shoot two days later reconfirmed everything Laura had ever thought modelling would be. And not just because she got to wear a tiara on her newly shingled head, or cavort with a stunning selection of male models either.

The beauty story was a simple party make-up piece but *Polka Dot* didn't do simple. 'It's going to look very retro, very fifties prom queen,' Janka, the fiercely glamorous beauty director explained. 'We start with you getting ready, curling tongs, hairspray, blah blah – then you're at the party and you're dancing and flirting up a storm and then . . . disaster!' She clapped her hands for dramatic emphasis. 'Your boyfriend turns up with another girl and you're crying and there's mascara streaming down your face and you look totally messed up. It's going to be totally fabulous.'

It was going to be totally method, Laura thought darkly, trying to ignore the warning twinge in the tear-portion of her brain. She wouldn't have to reach very far to find her motivation. Instead she smiled and tried to look like she was raring to go.

Turned out that all Laura's hard work with the

bathroom mirror had paid off. She didn't wait for direction or get stuck on one pose any more. It just happened as naturally as breathing – she was so in the fifties prom queen headspace, that it might be time to legally change her name to Betty-Louise and move to Kansas.

But seven hours, twenty-five rolls of film, one possible cover try and six girl-group-mix CDs later, Laura was starting to flag. Her feet were killing her, the pins holding her hairpiece together were digging into her scalp and only the whoops of encouragement at the end of each shot were getting her through.

'Last one, I promise,' Janka said, as Laura wiggled into her final outfit. 'Just let me . . . keep your head still. That's it!' She stood back and admired the diamante tiara perching on top of Laura's freshly bouffanted hair. 'Now, I'll just get the tear stick.'

She disappeared in the direction of her stylist's kit and Laura realized that she hadn't thought about Tom from the moment she stepped on set. This must be what people meant when they talked about losing themselves in their work. Freaky!

'So you want me to cry, then?' she asked the photographer and Kat, who'd turned up half an hour ago.

'We don't just want you to cry,' Kat quibbled. 'We want you to bawl your eyes out. It's got be so emo that it hurts. Every girl who reads *Polka Dot* will feel every inch of your pain. Oh, and do something with the tiara so that it looks like you've been tearing your hair out. Go on, really mess it up.'

Laura plunged her hands into her hair and tried to summon her deep, aching, emo sadness. Typical! It was never there when she actually wanted it.

Janka appeared holding the tear stick aloft. Laura had had one experience on *Make Me A Model* with the micro-sized torture implement, which she wasn't keen to repeat. She winced in anticipation as Janka dabbed under her eyes, held her breath for a second, then gasped as the stinging commenced. Ah, tiny tear stick, how it burns! Laura had never had anyone rub chilli powder into her eyes but it had to feel exactly the same.

'Um, you do need your eyes open for the shot,' the photographer helpfully reminded Laura as Janka artfully smeared the leaking mascara and liquid eyeliner across her cheeks.

'Gimme a second,' Laura whimpered, scrunching her eyes tighter shut. She whirled around to face the camera and opened her eyes as wide as possible for the time it took to take three pictures before she had to close them again. 'OK, gimme another second.'

It was a painstaking process. Scrunch, squint, open. Scrunch, squint, open. All Laura could think about was less boy-related turmoil and more the magic moment when she'd hear the words, 'It's a wrap' so she could pluck out her eyes and immerse them in cold water.

'Can you give me a bit more expression, love? I'm getting pain, but not *inner* pain,' called the photographer as Laura blinked her eyes rapidly. 'I know it hurts but I need something a bit special.'

'Oh, hey, I've got this fantastic song about a Sweet Sixteen party I should play,' Kat chirruped. Her perkiness was unrelenting. 'Hang on! It will put you right in the zone.'

All day long, Laura had had to listen to equally perky sixties pop stars warbling about their crushes on lifeguards and bookish boys, so she wasn't entirely convinced that a song about a Sweet Sixteen party was going to do anything more than give her a headache. Kat was fumbling with the stereo system, so she adjusted her tiara, which was threatening to slide off her head, and gave an inward sigh as the song started with a rendition of *Happy Birthday*.

She was still stuck on the scrunch, squint, open setting as the singer started lamenting about how all her friends had gathered when the one person she wanted at her birthday party was a no-show.

'*I may look stupid to everyone but in my heart I knew you'd never come . . .*'

Yeah, she could relate, Laura thought as she stopped working her eyelid muscles and concentrated on the lyrics.

'*I open presents and I try to smile but my heart is breaking all the while.*

We had a quarrel just the night before and now you're not my baby any more,

Oh, what's so sweet about sweet sixteen?

What's so sweet about sweet sixteen?

I can do without it, what's so sweet about it, when I can't share it with you?'

She'd completely forgotten about the ouchy-inducing tear stick or the photographer clicking away, as she stood there with an ocean of liquid trickling down her face, her face quivering with barely suppressed misery. She wasn't so much relating as living every sorrowful syllable.

'That's great! Watch your bottom lip and you're slightly flaring your nostrils. Give me some movement, do something!'

Laura didn't even have to think about it, she skidded over to the pile of gaily wrapped presents perched on the side and started ripping into them, throwing shreds of brightly coloured paper into the air. Not in an aesthetically pleasing, photogenic way. More like a dark, savage way – and wouldn't it be great if this wrapping paper was actually Tom's entrails which she was stamping into the floor with her sparkly, ass-kicker shoes? For an encore, Laura kicked what was left of the present pile into the four corners of the studio and folded her arms as she watched the gifts land like ballistic missiles.

'Laura! Over here!'

She turned and gave the camera a look seething

251

with malcontent before she remembered that she was meant to be trying for something easier on the eye, but Kat clapped her hands and gave a moan that was disturbingly orgasmic. 'Oh my God, that's it! That's the money shot!'

Maybe 'money shot' was magazine speak for the exact opposite of what they wanted, but then the photographer put down his fancy-shmancy camera so he could pad over to Laura and plant a kiss on her frowning forehead.

'It's a wrap,' he shouted, propelling Laura toward the little throng who'd been watching. 'Give this darling girl a round of applause, she deserves it.'

The *Vogue* shoot was a more sedate affair with super-expensive clothes. High fashion meant posing slouchily with hunched shoulders and limbs stuck out at ungainly angles while staring at the camera wistfully. It was exhausting. Laura had never believed it when she'd read interviews with models whining about how hard they had to work. But after holding her arms above her head, in a position that they clearly weren't meant to go, for half an hour, she was fit for nothing but a long soak and an early night.

Although she loved the *Polka Dot* pictures the most, it was the *Vogue* shoot that made the fashion world remove their Chloe shades, sit up and take notice.

There were tiny ripples to begin with. Her first foreign trip to Ibiza to do a skincare story. Her first *ELLE* shoot. Her first job booked without having a go-see first. And then it became a whirlwind. Laura got bumped off the New Faces board to hang with the big girls, and lost her surname in the process.

The flat became a vague memory; somewhere that she returned to long enough to put a wash on and not have time to get it out of the machine before there'd be an impatient toot on a horn as another car arrived to whisk her off. In the end, she just bought new clothes when she got to her destination. At a rough guestimate, she currently had eleven pairs of Gap Long And Lean jeans.

There wasn't time to think about anything other than where her passport was. It was airport, hotel room, photo studio, designer's atelier, posh restaurant, airport. She learned how to follow photographer's instructions in French, Spanish, German, Italian and Portugese. And on the day she got booked for her first fashion story in *Vogue Italia* no less, after Ted had nixed all other requests because they weren't high profile enough, Fierce overnighted her own personal BlackBerry, a sure sign that she'd arrived. Or maybe that was the cover-story in the *Sunday Times Magazine* with the message across the front page:

SAY GOODBYE TO THE WAIFS AND HELLO TO THE BOMBSHELL.
Meet, Laura, the seventeen-year-old girl from Manchester, who's single-handedly putting the va-va-voom back into fashion.

And there she was across eight pages in one couture frock after another, her hair swept up in a complicated series of pin-curls as she paid homage to the stars of the silver screen.

Her mother had bought up every copy she could find to send to far-flung relatives and acquaintances. Cath and Jen came up for the weekend and wouldn't stop calling her The Bombshell, when they weren't bugging Candy to get them into the Franz Ferdinand show.

But Laura also had a gaggle of new friends, though she didn't know their surnames or where they lived. They communicated via their BlackBerries and messages on their MySpace pages so they could coordinate their schedules and meet up for breakfast in Bangkok or drinks in Dubai. Laura's new friends: Paula from Brazil, Danielle from Arkansas, Darla from Madrid, were all as homesick as her and spoke a common language: how to get upgraded to first class, which photographers were gay and which ones would try to get you to go back to their hotel rooms after a shoot to look at their contact sheets and how the Tokyo Maccy D's compared to the Moscow ones.

It was spring when she finally had some time off after a triumphant Autumn/Winter season in Paris, Milan, New York and London, where every major fashion house showed nipped-in waists and a defined silhouette. Thank you, Candy.

Three days of doing nothing but laundry and maybe

putting a dent in her bank balance, which had started bursting at the seams in the last few months, sounded like perfection. Candy was shooting an ad campaign in LA, which sucked but they'd got to hang in Milan. Irina was home even less than Laura, which just left Hadley – who fell on her with a grateful cry.

'I've been so lonely!' she exclaimed, when she found Laura curled up on the couch watching a *Laguna Beach* marathon on MTV. 'You have no idea! George is mad at me. And they want me to do a fricking Australian toilet paper commercial. Let's go out and get drunk.'

'Hadders, I'm knackered,' Laura whined, but she was already being dragged off the sofa feet-first.

Going out with Hadley was an abject lesson in the benefits of staying sober. Laura stuck to fizzy water so she could hold Hadley's handbag, run interference when she started dirty dancing with other people's boyfriends, and coax her down from tabletops before she could fall off them.

Then there was the grand finale of holding her hair and rubbing her back as she threw up in a rubbish bin on Oxford Street.

'You are out of control,' Laura said sternly, after she'd finally managed to convince a cabbie to pick them up. 'Why do you drink so much?'

Hadley's little-girl-lost face didn't mix too well with the vodka fumes. 'Old enough to drink here and you're not the boss of me,' she slurred defiantly. 'I can do anything I want.'

'Including pickling your liver,' Laura muttered, but Hadley was asleep or pretending to be asleep. Either way, Laura had to haul her up two flights of stairs only to be confronted by Irina, hands on her hips, glowering like the blackest thundercloud since meteorology was invented.

'You up for the Augustine campaign, ja?' she demanded, before they could get to the 'Hey, Laura, lovely to see you'.

Laura stared at her dumbly. 'Am I up for what? And could you take Hadder's arm? She's really heavy.'

'I'm *so* not,' Hadley protested in a tiny voice, before giving a groan and lurching past Irina in the direction of the bathroom.

'I'm going to be the Siren girl,' Irina stated emphatically, and at any other time Laura would have been sidetracked by the non-stoniness of her facial expression. She looked like she was going to vibrate out of the window, the way she was quivering with barely suppressed rage. 'Me and Zilli, we like that.'

Her entwined middle and index fingers got so close to Laura's face that she took a hasty step back. She wouldn't put it past Irina to black both her eyes. She'd heard rumours from the other girls of passports disappearing into the ether and strange rashes mysteriously breaking out after pots of make-up were tampered with. These little mishaps always happened to girls who were working with Irina. Maybe she'd have to sleep with the bread knife under her pillow or ask Heidi if the agency would expense account her a security detail.

'Well if you and Zilli are like *that*, then I'm sure you'll have nothing to worry about,' Laura shouted over the retching sounds coming from the bathroom. 'And as I don't have a bloody clue what you're talking about, I really don't care. You're up for some big campaign, right?'

'Like you don't know,' Irina sneered. 'It was down to me and some girl who tripped off runway at the Versace show. She banged up for weeks.'

It had been the talk of Milan. Everyone adored Karis because she was so perky and Texan. 'I'm high on life,' she'd beam whenever anyone asked her why she was so bloody cheerful all the time. Mind you, she hadn't been so cheerful when she was lying in agony on a stretcher while the paparazzi had snapped away. There'd even been talk that the heel had snapped off her shoe, which was a damn shame as she'd been meant to wear the wedding dress at the end of the show. Just as well that Irina had been able to step up to the plate.

'Right, well, whatever. Still don't know what you're talking about but good luck as you seem to want this campaign so much.' Just call her Mother Flaming Teresa.

But Irina wasn't down with the whole olive branch experience. 'You're not that beautiful. Pffft! If it weren't for your boobs and your big ass being in style, you'd have been sacked. Everyone knows that.' As ever, in times of great

257

emotional stress, her Russian accent faded away to just a faint base note. She stuck out her chin and turned so Laura had no choice but to gaze at her savage profile, dramatically sweeping features made even more exotic by those jutting cheekbones. 'This will never go out of style. You don't have what it takes, fat ass.'

And with that pithy reminder she swept majestically out of the hall, knocking into Laura so hard that she got far more intimate with the door jamb than she'd ever hoped to.

Chapter Twenty-One

Irina was still glaring and muttering in Russian the next morning. Laura made sure to stay out of her way and sniff the milk suspiciously before she made a cup of tea. She could understand competitiveness, but Irina was taking it to a whole 'nother level of scary.

And then the phone rang. It was Ted summoning her to Fierce even though it was her day off. Nothing unusual about that although she could still recall the days when an official summons to the inner sanctum led to nothing good.

Ted didn't look up when she knocked on the open door of his office. He waved her in and carried on chattering into his headset in voluble Italian. She'd barely had time to park herself in one of his designer chairs before he finished the call and cut right to the chase.

'Sparkle want to renew your contract, with TV as well as print, but they want to lock you in to a three-year exclusivity deal, which simply isn't acceptable,' he frowned. It sounded pretty darn acceptable to Laura.

'But that's good, right?'

'Oh darling, I forget how green you are,' Ted chuckled, wagging a playful finger at her. 'It's good but we can do so much better. And I have such exciting news – just as well you're sitting down.' He paused dramatically for effect. 'The House of Augustine want you to try out as their new face.'

So that explained Irina's implied threat to kneecap Laura at the first available opportunity. Laura couldn't help but smile, which Ted mistook for unfeigned delight.

'There's no reason why it should conflict with Sparkle, I mean they're high street and Augustine are a premium brand.'

'Ted, can you translate the fashionese, please?

'If Kate Moss can do Rimmel *and* Chanel, there's no reason why you can't appear in ads for the teen press and the fashion glossies, darling. Augustine are launching their first perfume, Siren, and if you're not fronting that campaign then there's something very wrong with the world. And, Laura, we're talking *obscene* amounts of money.'

It was vulgar to talk about money; even Laura knew that. But she couldn't help asking in a greedy little whisper: 'How obscene? Like, triple X-rated or just post-watershed?'

'Oh, definitely triple X-rated, darling,' Ted said gleefully. 'You could retire at twenty-one and still have enough money to buy a yacht.'

'Well, Heidi was saying that I should think about investing in some property.' Laura couldn't help it; she had to clap her hands in geeker joy. 'And I could buy a new pair of shoes every day, and get my dad a new car, and my mum's always wanted to go on a cruise, and—'

'Let's not count chickens, still miles to go and all that, darling.' Ted steepled his fingers and dealt what he thought was a crushing blow. 'There is one other girl they're considering.'

'Irina? Yeah, I know. She mentioned it in passing last night.' It didn't matter how vile Irina was, Laura knew that the first rule of being a model was that you didn't diss any other girl. Even if that other girl was an evil witch who totally deserved it.

'Of course, you're both with Fierce and I work closely with both of you, so officially I can't be seen to show favouritism,' Ted said carefully. 'Officially . . .'

'I see . . .' Laura really didn't. She'd worked her butt off, quite literally, and had found a sunny disposition that she didn't know she had. That should count for something.

Ted smiled. 'Oh, you really don't, sweetie. Tell you what, go and find Heidi and get her to buy you a Frappucino.'

Heidi wasn't her booker any more. And in the weirdest plot twist since the *Veronica Mars* season finale, their relationship had improved to the power of a hundred. Like, they actually had a relationship now, which was baffling. She'd even Fedexed over some Sainsbury's Red Label tea bags when Laura had been in Buenos Aires. She was waiting for Laura as she left Ted's office, and looking like she was about to pee her pants.

'Did you get the whole "officially" talk?' she demanded.

Laura nodded unhappily. 'Yeah, and about that—'

'We can't talk *here*,' Heidi hissed furtively, as if someone had bugged the Fierce offices. 'Let's go. I need caffeine like you wouldn't believe.'

Heidi's cloak and dagger routine meant that they couldn't go to the Starbucks next door but walked round the corner to Caffè Nero, with Heidi glancing behind her shoulder with every step.

Eventually they were settled on a sofa. 'So this is just off the record, but Ted has it on good authority that the Siren campaign is going to be inspired by 1940s Hollywood sex symbols,' she explained. 'So you need to do some serious research.'

'You want me to go to Hollywood?'

'Yeah, you wish,' Heidi snarled. Now that Laura didn't actively hate her, she was beginning to appreciate that Heidi's snark was about seventy-five per cent worse than her bite. 'Once we found your cheekbones, Ted and I decided you looked a lot like Ava Gardner.'

'Who? Ava Gardner? Never heard of her!'

'Yeah, well, she's never done a guest spot on *The OC*, what with her being dead and all.' Heidi pulled something from her Miu Miu tote and slammed it down on the table. 'You need to look at that.'

Laura picked up the book and stared at the woman on the cover; her head tilted back so her glossy mane of hair cascaded down her back, eyes half closed as she leaned into the shot with a seductive smile. She was beautiful in a way that people only were in old black-and-white movies. 'I look like her?' she asked sceptically, holding the cover up to her own face for comparison. 'Really? I'm not seeing it.'

'As near as damn it,' Heidi said, tilting her head so she could properly assess Laura and her silver-screen looky-likey. 'It's something in the eyes and when you don't quite smile but, like, you're thinking about it. God, the resemblance is quite startling actually. When we get back to mine, we can watch some DVDs too.'

'Back to yours?' All Laura could do was echo Heidi's sentences, which was even more annoying for her than it was for Heidi. 'You not working this afternoon then?'

Heidi squirmed uncomfortably. 'Ted and I felt that you'd be better off not staying at the flat for a while.' She lowered her voice. 'Just in case Irina gets any ideas.'

'About attacking me with a machete or a sawn-off shotgun or some other implement of imminent death?' Laura suggested wryly. 'Why are you and Ted doing this? Fierce gets their commission, whichever one of us lands the gig. And I'm only the stand-in. I mean, if Karis hadn't hurt herself, I wouldn't even be in the running.'

'Right now you have a small window of opportunity and the agency doesn't feel that Irina's ready for a big contract. The timing's off.'

'Because she doesn't just have a small window of

opportunity but a bloody great patio door?' Laura really felt the need to flounce. 'It's not fair!'

'It's got nothing to do with windows, it's to do with the fact that she's out of control at the moment. The last thing we need is her becoming the Siren girl. She needs to learn to chow down on some humble pie. And if you breathe a word of this to anyone, including Ted, I swear I'll kill you myself.'

'But she might win the contract,' Laura pointed out, wishing she hadn't had breakfast that morning because it was lodged in her small intestine like a lead weight. 'I might not get it. They might hate me. I might look shit in the clothes. Or break out in zits overnight. You can't put all this on me.'

'Don't be such a little pussy,' Heidi snapped, prodding Laura hard on the ribs. 'Just be everything Irina's not . . .'

'What? Like friendly . . .'

'And don't lose your focus. Think Ava Gardner, think sexy without being slutty and, if you're staying at mine, don't even think about borrowing my clothes.' Heidi zipped up her jacket with a flourish. 'You can do this, Laura.'

Chapter Twenty-Two

Laura had Ava bloody Gardner on the brain after repeated showings of *The Barefoot Contessa, The Snows Of Kilimanjaro, The Sun Also Rises* and *On The Beach*, and fell asleep the night before the Siren test shoot, with Ms Gardner husking, 'Life, every now and then, behaves as though it had seen too many bad movies, when everything fits too well – the beginning, the middle, the end – from fade-in to fade-out,' through her head.

It was just as well she had an eleven a.m. call time as the photographer, an old school English aristo called Snowy, who'd been snapping debutantes since the fifties, didn't like to shoot before lunchtime, 'It takes *hours* for ladies' faces to settle,' he'd confided to Laura on the one other occasion she'd worked with him. 'Otherwise they turn up with pillow creases on their skin and really, it's too distressing.'

He was perched elegantly on a director's chair when she got to the location: an old-fashioned Mayfair nightclub with the original art deco fittings. 'I remember you, you ravishing thing,' he cried extravagantly.

Laura carefully leaned in to kiss Snowy on the cheek. Yeah, he seemed like a sweet little old man but he could reduce the fiercest model to tears if she didn't follow his direction. '*Courage, mon ange,*' he whispered in her ear, then he straightened up and tapped his cane on the floor. 'Now get yourself in make-up, we're on a very tight schedule. They told you about the screen-test too, didn't they? Really, it's ridiculous trying to cram everything into one day.'

Nope, no one had thought to tell her that they'd be filming too. At least *Make Me A Model* had given her some camera experience. Apparently top models didn't giggle when they were trying to deliver their lines. Or talk in Mancunian accents.

As soon she was ushered into the dressing room, a script was thrust into Laura's hands.

'You need to memorize that,' someone grunted at her. 'We're not running an autocue.'

Deep breaths, Laura told herself. *I am calm. I am poised. I'm not going to throw up my breakfast.* The inner pep-talk worked and by the time two stylists were putting rollers in her hair she was staring dumbfounded at the twenty-six-word script.

Like, what*ever*! Was there some law that people always had to spout some pretentious drivel in perfume ads? It wasn't Laura's problem – she just had to act like she meant it. And yeah, she could so do that.

Cool, collected Laura seemed to rub off on everyone and when Ted appeared there was a contented little hush as clothes were steamed, coffee was drunk and Laura sat perfectly still as the last coat of scarlet lipstick was applied.

'You look very serene, sweetie,' Ted said quietly, peering at Laura's face. 'Oh yes, very *Barefoot Contessa*.'

Laura wiggled her toes obligingly and tried not to think about the jewel-festooned, skyscraper-high heels lined up in rows by the clothes rails. 'I'm channelling my inner Ava,' she whispered.

'I'll leave you to it,' Ted murmured, looking around. 'Isn't Irina here yet? Call time was over an hour ago!'

The Moscow Mule was nowhere to be seen. Laura hoped that she'd self-combusted over night into a heap of ashes and charcoal.

As Laura walked through her shots and tried not to panic that two of them involved a sweeping, ornate staircase, which she was meant to glide down gracefully, Irina burst in, looking windswept and glamorous with a black scarf wound round her hair and a cigarette clenched between her lips.

'You're two hours late, Miss Kerchenko.' Snowy banged his cane on the floor. 'It's inexcusable.'

Laura waited for the inevitable tantrum but Irina hung her head. 'I'm sorry,' she simpered. 'I was so nervous.' And then she bent down so she could place a kiss on top of Snowy's bald head. 'Say you forgive me, I be heartbroken if you hate me.'

No way was Snowy going to buy her bullshit, Laura thought smugly, but he was pinking up and made a great show of gently rapping Irina's knuckles with his cane. 'You really are a dreadful girl but I find it impossible to be mad at you,' he purred. 'Go and get yourself made up, though how they'll improve on perfection, I really don't know.'

Cool, calm and collected fled the building. Without their support, Laura was just a scared girl with knees knocking together as she teetered at the top of the stairs. 'Oh, rats!'

'Are you still up there?' Snowy enquired querulously. 'Do come down. I *told* you we had a lot to get through.'

Irina had spread herself out over three stools and the entire counter. Her eyes flashed as Laura walked into the dressing room and hurried over to the clothes rail, with her name pinned on it.

'You stupid girl!' Irina suddenly shrieked, snatching a brush out of the make-up artist's hands. 'I don't like it! Take it off!'

The sound of Irina's staccato growl was the equivalent of someone running their nails down a blackboard. Laura flinched as she waited for the stylist to unzip her dress from the garment bag. But it wasn't a dress. It was a gown. Because gowns were elegant and sophisticated and made your breath hitch at the thought that you were actually allowed to wear them.

'It's couture,' the stylist noted, stroking the black lace and satin carefully as Laura undid the belt of her robe. 'It cost five thousand pounds, so don't even *look* at food while you're wearing it.' The girl gave a dreamy sigh. 'Hand-stitched lace and the hem's weighted down with an eighteen-carat gold chain. I'd kill for a dress like this. Actually I'd maim, torture and kill.'

Laura forgot everything – her nerves, Irina bitching behind her, the shoot – everything but the gown, which was ceremonially lowered over her head. If it didn't fit, then she'd bc floating belly up in the water before she'd even got in front of the camera, but as the stylist carefully inched up the hidden side zip, she let out about one quarter of the breath she'd been holding.

Laura looked up and gasped. She was another girl in another time. A girl with sloping, sloe-like eyes and a perfect cupid's bow of a mouth. A girl poured into a gown that cinched her, hugged her, caressed her and transformed her into a vampy creature whose breasts looked like two scoops of fluffy white ice cream as they emerged from the austere black lace. A girl who should have spoken with an impossibly husky voice and said things like, 'Fasten your seatbelts, boys, it's going to be a bumpy night'. Not a girl who had to suffer the indignity of a stylist scooping both hands into her bodice so she could rearrange her boobs . . .

'I should wear that dress. Take it off!'

Irina jumped off the stool and prowled towards Laura.

'I wear it. Take it off!'

She totally knew Irina's game. She thought if she said her batshit demands loudly and frequently and menacingly enough, everyone would bend to her will. Her mum used to try exactly the same trick when Laura was stalling over bedtime. It hadn't worked then either.

Making sure that the stylist was positioned between her and Irina, Laura stood her ground. 'I'm sorry you feel like that but you'd better take it up with the Augustine peeps. They're out there now with Ted.'

'Your dress is just as lovely,' the stylist cajoled. 'Lovelier,' she added, without a hint of anything approaching tact.

'I don't care. I want that one.' Irina jabbed a belligerent finger in Laura's direction. 'You look like shit anyway.'

She didn't. She *so* knew that she didn't, but a little seed of doubt was trying to burrow its way through the boning and into her ribcage. *I'm calm. I'm cool. I'm an ice cube. I'm a freezer full of ice cubes.*

It was very hard to meditate cool thoughts with Irina now sandwiching the stylist between the two of them, as she tried to swipe at Laura, who took a cautious step back and tried not to trip over her train. If the gown got damaged, well, she didn't even want to think about the gigantic load of wrong that would be.

'Stop it! What is the matter with you?' she snapped in the coolest manner she could muster. It was barely below zero. 'Just listen to yourself. I want. I want. It's not your dress so back the hell off!'

'You not talk to me like that!' Irina demanded, and right now she resembled nothing more than a card-carrying crazy lady with her hair in curlers and one false lash hanging precariously from her eyelid. 'I get booked far more than you!'

It was rapidly descending into a playground fight and Laura wondered if she was going to have to play the 'well, my dad's bigger than your dad' card, when there was a pointed cough from the door, where Snowy was leaning on his cane.

'Now, now, dear,' he admonished, wagging a playful finger at Irina, who melted into girlish giggles in less time than it took to blink. 'You and your Russian temperament. You really are a little empress, aren't you?'

'I just want to be beautiful for you, Snowy,' she cooed.

Laura just wanted a sick bag to throw up in. 'And is our North Country flower ready for her close-up?'

Irina got the royal treatment and she was a flower? Something was not right with that analogy. 'I just need to put my shoes on,' she said sweetly.

'*Charmant*, my dear,' Snowy exclaimed, coming into the room. 'Give me a twirl.'

A girl didn't twirl in a frock like this one. So Laura did a full 360° at a glacial speed, aware of Irina's dagger-like eyes cutting interesting patterns into her back.

'Breathtaking,' Snowy decided. 'Irina, get back to your stool. I quite fear for my life when you're glaring like that.'

And once Laura was smiling through the pain of a pair of £700 shoes that nipped her feet in exquisite agony,

Snowy offered her his arm and led her out of the dressing room as if she was a debutante on her way to her first cotillion.

'I do so like a little drama behind the scenes,' Snowy confided with a sly smile. 'These shoots can get dreadfully dull otherwise.'

Thankfully they did the staircase shots first. Laura had to lean backwards over a gilt-adorned balustrade, arms stretched wide as her body arched into a shape that suggested she had scoliosis of the spine. And look sultry too.

Then she had to sit on the railing and act like her hands weren't clenched tight around the cream-painted wood, so she didn't plunge to her death.

I'm calm. I'm cool. I'm an ice cube, she repeated like a mantra over Snowy's constant stream of instructions. Behind him she could see Zilli and Costello plus assorted minions, clustered together like some mythical five-headed beast as they conferred in low, lyrical murmurs. She had to shut it all out and focus. Not that she knew the woman personally, but Laura had a feeling that Ava Gardner would have delivered the goods even if a spaceship had suddenly crash-landed on the roof.

After one last shot where she had to sweep down the stairs like 'you're making an entrance, darling – you're the most beautiful girl in the room . . .' Laura was allowed a five-minute break to sip carefully at a bottle of water through a straw so she didn't spill any. That didn't stop the make-up artist primping her hair and puffing imaginary specks away with a brush that made her want to sneeze.

There was a loud crack of static from the PA system, which nearly sent her popping out of her dress, before the haunting strains of a plaintive horn section and a smoky-voiced woman rasping, '*Southern trees bear strange fruit, Blood on the leaves and blood at the root . . .*' crackled out from the PA system.

'On the dance floor, Laura, let's have a little movement in these next ones,' Snowy called, and Laura moved toward the 'X' that had been taped to the parquet, trying not to wince as her feet protested. She swayed gently to the rhythm and tried to make sure that her arms didn't hang like planks of wood. Snowy seemed pleased enough until Irina arrived on set in a gown so identical to Laura's that neither Zilli or Costello would have been able to pick them out of a police line-up.

Not putting her heel through her hem and keeping her eyes half closed but wide open (it didn't make a lick of sense), weren't that high on Laura's list of priorities. Not when Irina was laughing up a storm with the lighting techs and shooting triumphant little smirks each time Laura moved into her line of vision. Ava Gardner would probably have got Frank Sinatra and his boys to sort Irina out, but there was never a fifties crooner with Mafia connections around when you needed one.

It wasn't until the last shot, where she was artfully draped on top of the bar, that Irina's off-set antics reached a fever pitch. Out of the corner of her eye, she saw Irina point at her then puff out her cheeks and affect a waddling motion. Why the hell wasn't anyone ejecting Irina from the set?

'Please give me some sign of life,' Snowy called peevishly from behind the camera. 'You're the belle of the ball, not a dead fish on a slab.'

Irina's smile reached new depths of malice and it was just the motivation that Laura needed to get her shit well and truly together.

'Sorry,' she said quietly and Snowy, delightful and devious as he was, was just going to have to wait for her to get her model on. She thought back to that night with Tom and how she'd woken up to see him staring down at her so tenderly, his hand stroking the hair back from her face and then . . .

'I'm mad for that little half-smile of yours,' Snowy exclaimed excitedly. 'Half close your eyes but keep them wide open, and turn to me a smidge of an inch . . .'

They'd kissed for hours, until the sun started a slow ascent and the darkness had turned smudgy around them. She could remember it perfectly. And even though Tom hadn't said. 'I love you,' Laura knew that he'd felt it.

She smiled at the memory, not even seeing the blinding glare of the lights or the camera flash, but Tom's face.

'It's a wrap! Five minutes, people, and then we'll do it all over again. Laura, we'll have you back in two hours to shoot your screen-test.'

Giving Irina the widest berth she could, Laura ran for the dressing room. Or actually walked really fast. As she gently toed off the shoes, she almost reached for her phone. Even after months without him, it was still a reflex action to call Tom so he could talk her down from whichever ledge she was clinging to. She could imagine how that might go down: 'Hi sweetie. No, we haven't spoken in ages because I slept with someone else and you're dating a moose, but I'm at a shoot that might actually catapult me into the supermodel league and I need some advice on how to handle my arch nemesis.' No, it really wasn't going to happen.

Part of her wanted to lurk in the shadowy corners of the ballroom so she could see Irina in action, but it would either send her into a inferiority spiral or Irina would fix it in some master-villain way that Laura would get into trouble for distracting *her*.

Her iPod was her salvation. Laura randomly selected a playlist and gave a start when she realized it was her *Make Me A Model* mix. She'd listened to these songs in constant rotation when she was in that Docklands flat. She'd dance in front of the mirror, blowing herself kisses and loving her reflection like the deluded, narcissistic minx she'd been then. God, if she could summon up, like, a fraction of that self-belief now . . .

Time to get back in the game. 'I want this,' she said under her breath. 'I want this more than anything I've ever wanted. And I always – well, most of the time – I always get what I want. Irina is history.' Repeat to fade.

When Ted finally emerged from wherever he'd been hiding to collect Laura, she shot him a beatific smile and glided back on to the set.

There was a lot more fussing over the lights this time. One of Snowy's assistants kept clicking his light meter in front of Laura's face so often that she thought she might go permanently cross-eyed. She arranged her skirts over the pink velvet of the banquette she was sitting on and relaxed her muscles by pulling stupid faces. Actually it helped to relieve some of the tension, especially as Irina wasn't even bothering to lower her voice as she told Ted how fantastic she'd been.

'Snowy loves me. He say the camera loves me. I get all my shots right first time.'

She deserved to choke on humble pie and have no one around to perform the Heimlich manoeuvre, Laura thought as one of the Augustine flunkies told her what she had to do. Mostly it involved speaking to the camera like it was her long-lost lover, then holding the bottle of Siren in shot for the last line. There wasn't any perfume in the bottle as it was under twenty-four hour guard in a warehouse just outside Naples, which slightly destroyed the illusion.

'What does it smell like?' she asked, then wished she hadn't as the woman kissed her fingers and proceeded to have a wordgasm right there. 'A top note of rose for a deep burgeoning sensuality,' she exclaimed. 'Balanced by the fresh modernity of the peony flower, while the tart sweetness of blackcurrant adds vibrancy. It's carnal and savage but contained within a quiet, inner strength. Also, the bottle is adorable. I love it! It's so vintage!'

Laura hadn't been allowed to touch the bottle yet in case she got fingerprints on it. Yet another minion, wearing protective gloves, would push it into shot at the right moment. 'It's very pretty,' she said enthusiastically. 'Rose, peony, blackcurrant, carnal . . .' She stopped. If she got sidetracked with perfume ingredients, she'd totally forget her lines.

Gradually the fussing and the different conversations faded down and it was a surprise when she heard the words: 'Take one'.

For a second she couldn't think of a damn thing except that she was meant to be talking and nothing was happening. Her mind was as blank and empty as a . . . she couldn't even think of a suitable analogy. What was the first line?

'For a moment,' she heard herself say and the words were flooding back as if they'd just been hiding round the corner. 'For an eternity. For ever . . .'

She was doing so well, even remembering to talk sexy-posh because her accent became thicker when she got nervous.

'For a day . . .'

CRASH! There was a shattering explosion in the still of the room and then, 'Sorry, is not my fault,' from Irina as she stared in bemusement at the broken glass at her feet as if she couldn't quite believe how it got there.

'Mop it up, someone!' shouted Snowy. 'Before Christmas would be wonderful.'

Laura hid her shaking hands under the folds of her dress and tried to focus, but her head was a whirling mess of for evers and roses and eternities and blackcurrants.

She completely fluffed the second take by forgetting her lines.

On the third take she remembered the words, but was stopped by Snowy who icily reminded her that she had to sound as if she was 'from Capri, darling, not Cheadle Hulme'.

By the fourth take, she'd developed a stammer.

On the fifth take, she stumbled through her lines, and almost dropped the perfume bottle as it was handed to her. Only a split-second save from the gloved minion averted catastrophe.

'Laura, take a minute to pull yourself together,' Snowy told her curtly. And Irina smiled like the cat who'd got the cream and the multi-million pound contract too. Irina was behaving atrociously and not one person was acting as if it was anything out of the ordinary. It was almost as if everyone not only expected it, but was cool with it.

What was *that* about? Like, if Laura acted all diva-y, then would she get away with stuff too? There was only one way to find out.

'Excuse me,' she said falteringly, her heart pounding. 'I'd like everyone who isn't needed off the set, please.'

No one was more surprised than she was. Not even Irina, who was slack-jawed with disbelief.

'It's just this could be the actual advert and there's all these people and it's distracting and I want to do this properly and put my soul into it . . .'

'Clear the set,' Snowy cut right through her garbled explanation, shooting an amused smile at Laura that she couldn't decipher. 'And yes, Irina, I think that specifically means you, though Miss Parker is far too polite to come straight out with it. I, on the other hand, am not. Leave. Now.' He settled himself back behind the camera as Irina swept out of the room, back swaying like an angry cat. 'Congratulations, my dear, you're finally starting to act like a supermodel and not one of the rank and file. Positions everyone and – take six.'

Take six was so perfect that it deserved to be gift-wrapped and tied with a pretty bow. Take seven was just to be on the safe side, and there was no take eight because Laura was beaming and not even attempting to be modest as she got the round of applause she so richly deserved.

Half an hour later, she was de-Sirenned and packing up the last of her things, but she couldn't resist sneaking back on to the set and hiding behind a pillar to see Irina's screen-test. She delivered her lines in beautifully modulated English, like she'd attended the world's finest finishing school, and never had her almost alien beauty been more apparent. The image of Irina being played back on the monitor was even more alluring than the flesh and blood version. The camera didn't just love her, it wanted to take her home and have its babies.

Irina didn't have to pretend to be anything, she just *was*. Too bad she was also the biggest bitch since for ever. Who else could have submerged Laura's iPod in a large Styrofoam cup of coffee?

Chapter Twenty-Three

Laura was a little vague on the finer details, but her phone should have been ringing with Siren news pretty much instantaneously.

But fashion worked on its own peculiar time scale, where nothing ever happened when it should. Five minutes meant five hours, especially when she was feeling homesick in a foreign city and waiting, waiting, waiting for her itinerary to arrive for the next week or for the photographer's assistant to stop faffing about with the lights or for the call that said she was the Siren girl and not just another jobbing model.

But the call refused to come and life went back to normal. Or Laura's version of normal, which was watching her father sign her new Sparkle Cosmetics contract and watching his hand tremble ever so slightly when he saw the number of noughts at the end of her fee.

'I'm buggered if I know what to get you for your birthday now,' he'd half joked as they'd celebrated with a quick cup of tea before he drove back to Manchester. 'It doesn't matter if you don't get the other job, love. You're set up for life – if you don't go mad buying handbags.'

But it did matter. It mattered a hell of a lot. Not just the money, though the money was of the seriously good, but the knowing that she'd made it. That all the running around Regent's Park boating lake and forswearing Snickers bars had been worth it. That taking a chance on her career, rather than what her heart had really wanted had been worth it. That *she* was worth it. Irina obviously felt the same way because she now started every sentence with the words, 'When I become the Siren girl . . . I will move out of this flat. I will never wear the same thing twice. I will employ a personal assistant. *I will still be a stark, raving bitch.*' Even Hadley joined in the game and would whisper to Laura, 'When I become the Siren girl, I will open a chain of stinky sausage shops.'

Ted would just shake his head and smile blankly when Laura asked him if he'd heard anything. Heidi was even less forthcoming: 'If you mention it again, I'm going to rip your head off.'

So, all in all, flying to New York, which was smelly and hot and just as magical as it always was, was something of a relief for everyone. Laura knew that the plan was to keep her busy so she could stop making sad puppy faces at her BlackBerry. Busy was all right. Busy took her mind off the Siren campaign for three whole seconds at a time. There was her Sparkle print campaign to shoot, as well as ads for a trendy clothing company's autumn catalogue. And Candy was in town so they could hang out.

Hanging out was a really loose description for Candy

riding shotgun on Laura's catalogue shoot and nearly getting herself thrown out of the studio after she picked up a corduroy dress and declared loudly, 'Oh my God, I can actually feel myself becoming fashion backwards just by touching this.'

'Shut up,' Laura suggested through clenched teeth and didn't unclench them until Candy sailed out of the studio with an airy wave.

'There's no need to be so touchy,' she called over her shoulder. 'I'll meet you at Balthazar later.'

Balthazar was the famous French bistro where the likes of Kate Moss chowed down on – well, Laura was pretty sure that Kate Moss didn't chow down on anything – but she made do with steak and salad, while she rubbernecked for celebs.

'You could at least look at me when I'm talking to you,' Candy sighed eventually. 'There are no famous people in here tonight. Apart from me,' she added with smug satisfaction.

Laura speared a stray piece of raddichio with her fork. 'I'm a little distracted is all. Like, I'd have thought that Ted would have rung by now. I mean, how long does it take to look at two screen tests and decide that I was better? Or Irina was better and I sucked like nobody has ever sucked before in the history of sucking.'

Candy listened sympathetically for all of a nanosecond, which was her absolute empathy threshold. 'If Irina beats you to it, then I'm emigrating to the moon,' she spat. 'She's an unbearable witch as it is. If she gets the gig, then actually her head might get so big that it explodes, which would be good.'

It would be good and then they'd have to give the job to Laura instead. 'Not that anyone's head has ever exploded from sheer conceit.' She allowed herself to slump on to the tabletop. 'Sorry, I know that I'm lame company but when I try not to think about it, then I think about it even more.'

'Well, snap out of it,' Candy demanded, waving her hand at the waiter. 'Let's get out of here and go to Club Gotham, they never check for ID.'

Candy and her ADD never liked to stay in one place too long, so Laura let herself be chivvied out of the restaurant and into the back of a cab. Before she knew it she was disconsolately sipping cranberry juice in a club that was just like all the other clubs that Candy ever dragged her to.

A DJ was spinning sounds that actually made her ears hurt while lots of dieted-to-the-bone girls milled about wearing not much in the way of clothes and striking a pose for the guy who was ambling about with a camera. New York clubbers were a whole bunch of seriously scary, including the multitudes of boys with regulation stubble and baseball caps, that Candy insisted were meant to be ironic.

'No one in Manchester would ever wear a baseball cap, ironic or not,' Laura pouted. As well as angsting about the Siren campaign, her cute-boy radar had seriously malfunctioned. That was a side effect of being cruelly dumped that none of the agony aunts ever told you about. Not like she was in the market for another boy to crush her half-mended heart beneath his Converse-clad feet, but the faintest stirrings of lust at the sight of a foxy man-child would have been nice.

Laura sighed again, then wished she hadn't as Candy rolled her eyes and clicked her teeth. 'Are you still pining for Mr Manchester after all these months? You have to get back on the horse soon, Laura.'

'Yeah, because that worked out so well last time,' Laura reminded her sourly.

'Look, my friend Crispin is over there,' Candy continued, like Laura's words were of absolutely no interest to her. 'He's in this band that think they're the new Strokes, which they're so not. Shall I get him to come over?'

Laura peered at a particularly dimly lit corner of the club, where a guy with long, messy hair and a suit and tie was trying to subtly gaze at himself in the mirrored wall. 'God, what a poseur!' she snorted, digging out her BlackBerry for the gazillionth time. 'Why hasn't Ted rung?'

'Pick a new tune!' Candy went into a full body spasm of irritation, which involved flopping down on the seat with great force and flailing all her limbs. 'You're being boring, Laura and I can't be seen with boring people. It's bad for my image.'

At least the one thing guaranteed to cheer Laura up was the thought of Candy having a hissy-fit. They were always entertaining, now that she'd got used to them. She grinned to herself and then sat up and gave an excited yelp as she saw a woman teetering toward them on six-inch heels. 'Um, Cands, isn't that, like your *Mum*?'

Candy followed Laura's gaze and gave a stricken groan. 'Oh, shit! Who let *her* in?'

'There's my little Candy Cane,' a voice cooed and Laura scooted back just in time for Bette Careless to plonk herself down on their banquette and cover her furiously squirming daughter's face with kisses.

'Get the fuck off me!' could be heard over the excruciating ear-wormy music and yeah, this was definitely better than moping about boys and waiting for the phone to not ring.

Bette Careless was exactly like the character she played on TV. And she didn't seem to come with an off-button either. But what she didn't know about fashion . . . Correction. There wasn't anything she didn't know about fashion. She whipped out a Sidekick and within ten minutes, Laura had a full day of appointments booked with people that even Ted couldn't get her in to see.

'Just tell Marc that Bette sent you,' she ordered in her breathy, girlish voice. 'And that he still owes me a dress from his last collection. Do you think I should get my tits done?'

Only the greatest effort of will stopped Laura from

snorting cranberry juice out of her nostrils but Candy just finished chewing on an ice cube before replying. 'You could probably use a little work. Especially round the eyes.'

Bette didn't even blink. 'Bitch.'

'Whore.'

'Brat.'

'Groupie.'

It was horrifying and fascinating in equal measure. And time Laura made her excuses and left before things got really ugly.

Laura was star-fished on her hotel bed a couple of hours later. After two days of God knows how many shots for the American Outfitters catalogue, the bone-weariness was taking hold. Plus, she couldn't remember what it was like not to have jet lag. She'd got as far as smothering her face with cold cream and dragging on her rattiest pyjamas, but stretching out her hand so she could grab the phone and order a wake-up call was unthinkable.

When there was a sharp rap at the door, Laura groaned and rolled over. If it was the Swedish businessman in the room next to hers asking if she wanted to share a bottle of wine *again*, she was going to bop him over the head with it. As long it didn't require her to actually move.

Laura rolled off the bed, marched over to the door and pulled it open.

'Look, I've already told you . . . Oh, hey, Ted. What are you doing here?'

Ted was standing there in his favourite Paul Smith suit and a sombre expression. She remembered then; Irina was in NYC too, staying across town. He must have gone to her hotel first to deliver the good news. 'Siren?' Laura asked him in a voice that only wavered slightly. 'You've heard?'

He opened his mouth to destroy all her dreams. She knew it. Maybe that's why she was clamping her hand over his mouth before he could actually start ripping her life into itty-bitty pieces.

'Make it quick,' she begged, deciding it was best to let Ted breathe freely as she took her hand away and stepped aside to let him in. 'Don't tell me that there'll be other chances or that it was a really close call. Just get it over and done with.'

'Well, if you're sure, darling,' Ted said, placing his Louis Vuitton briefcase down on the coffee table. 'Don't you want to sit down first, instead of hovering by the bathroom?'

'I'm going in here to have a cry, right after you've given me the thanks, but no thanks,' Laura explained and Ted tilted his head in an understanding manner.

'It was a really close call,' he began, even though she'd just told him to forget about the platitudes. He could be such a pig sometimes. 'And there will be other chances . . .'

'*Ted . . .*'

'For Irina. Not for you, darling. You're the face of Siren, Laura. Congratulations, my newest, little supermodel, you.'

'Is this a joke? It's a joke, right?' She caught sight of herself in the mirror, white gunk smeared all over her cheeks. Her PJs had fairy cakes on them, for goodness' sake. She didn't look like the face of anything.

Ted patted the seat next to him. 'Come over here,' he coaxed and Laura flung herself down on the sofa. 'They loved you. They loved how you wanted to know about the perfume. They loved how you dealt with the problems on set and they just about wet themselves when they saw the advert. They want to reshoot the print stuff as the lighting wasn't everything it could be, but they're going to sign you to a three-year exclusive contract.'

'Three years? So, like, I won't be able to model for anyone else?' Laura frowned.

'Well, you won't be able to front any other high-end fragrance campaigns, but they're going to pay handsomely for the privilege.'

'How handsomely?' Laura sounded as if her vocal chords were underwater. Maybe she was coming down with a cold.

Ted reached behind him to grope for the complimentary hotel stationery. Then he scribbled something down on the notepad. Something that looked a lot like £1,000,000. 'Is that handsome enough?' he enquired archly. 'Of course, it's spread over three years and your agency fees and our commission will be deducted but it's still not too shabby.'

Laura pushed the notepad off her lap so it landed on the deep plush carpet with a dull thud. Now all of her felt like it was underwater. She seemed to be having trouble making her limbs do stuff that they normally took for granted.

'Are you all right, darling? Any time you want to actually speak, would be good.'

Laura got up on shaky legs. 'Bathroom,' she mumbled indistinctly. And once she was in there with the door safely locked behind she, she went with her first scenario and burst into tears.

Chapter Twenty-Four

There had been more tears. From Ted actually, once he'd worked out what his own commission would be. After the tears came the hysterical laughter as Laura paced up and down. 'I don't believe it. I don't fucking believe it. Yes I do! Hey, have you told Irina yet? Can I tell Irina? Is that mean of me? I don't care! I'm the Siren girl!'

Then Ted had started jumping up and down on her bed. With his shoes on. 'Oh my God, Laura. We've done it! We've bloody well gone and done it! Get up here now!

And she'd imagined this moment for so long, played it over and over again in her head. But she'd never dreamed that she'd celebrate it by holding hands with her senior booker as they bounced up and down on a $500 a night bed, until the Swedish businessman in the room next door called Security because their screaming was cutting in to his shut-eye time.

'. . . So that's how I heard the news,' she finished up. Daisy Bloom chuckled politely, as she turned back to the camera.

'Hi, welcome back to a very special edition of the show

where last year's winner, Laura Parker, will be telling us how she went from *Make Me A Model* to supermodel.'

Laura could feel her mouth stretching into the same goofy smile that she'd worn at judging panel.

'Laura's joined by her senior booker, Ted Curtis from Fierce Model Management, who's one of our new judges on this season of the show. Ted, when Laura won *Make Me A Model*, did you recognize her star quality right away?'

Ted shot Laura a wicked grin, which she knew wasn't a sign of anything good. 'When Laura first turned up at Fierce, we knew that we had our work cut out for us. I'm sure she won't mind me telling you that her nickname at the agency was the Didsbury Diva.'

Yes, she did mind him blurting that out. Quite a bit, actually. Which was why she surreptitiously gave his thigh a warning pinch while smiling serenely. And he said that *she* needed a media handler.

'But actually we didn't do any work. Laura did. Five months ago, she couldn't get any bookings, was overweight and had to take time out to make some tough decisions about her future. So she went away and modelled for anyone who'd give her a free picture for her book, yogacized herself down a dress size and learned more about the fashion industry in six weeks, than some models learn in a lifetime.'

Yeah, the glowing praise was a lot more like it. But she and Ted were still going to have a little chat about how he was never to use the D word and her name in the same conversation.

'But Laura didn't simply get two huge cosmetics contracts because she put in the hours. She got here because she wanted it so badly, that she made it happen. So what I'll be looking for this year on the show isn't just the most beautiful girl, but someone who's got the guts and determination to make it in a really tough industry.'

The camera pulled back to scan the nervous faces of the twelve *Make Me A Model* finalists who were arranged on the two sofas opposite them. Laura had never been under such intense scrutiny, not from Heidi or casting directors and supercilious fashionistas, as she was from twelve pairs of envious eyes scanning her to see if she was prettier, thinner, cooler and more deserving than they were.

'Laura, what's your secret for making it in a such a competitive field?'

She focused her attention back on Daisy and tried not to scrunch her face up in thought. 'Well, I won the show and I thought the competition was over,' she admitted. 'But actually it hadn't even started. Trying to get booked for jobs with other girls who'd been doing it for longer than me was when the real competition started. I learned really quickly that I didn't know everything and that I had a lousy attitude. No matter how tough and ruthless modelling can be, it still pays to be polite. I turn up on time, I say please and thank you, I remember people's names and even if I hate the clothes and I'm PMS-ing, I just have to get on with it.'

Daisy was nodding in agreement, not that she'd ever given Laura the lowdown on these tips when she was on the show. 'You see, girls, it's not just about looking fierce, you have to *be* fierce. So, who wants to ask Laura a question?'

'How did you get around the fact that you're way bigger than most models?' demanded an aggressive-looking girl with a stomach that actually went *in*. Laura made a mental note to get Ted to bring her down a peg or forty when he had the obnoxious little brat in front of him at the judging panel.

'I'm a small size ten or a large size eight, which is another way of saying that I have more booty than the average model.' She made her rueful face as the audience politely laughed. 'I got lucky. Last season's collections were all about nipped-in waists and I was in the right place at the right time.'

'Laura didn't just get lucky,' Daisy chimed in. 'Good models are able to follow the trends, but top models like Laura set them.'

One of the girls bit her lip anxiously. 'So do you eat chocolate 'cause I don't think I could give up Twixes? Or Maltesers. Or KitKats . . .' She tailed off and gave Laura a tremulous smile.

'I wish I was one of those girls that can eat my

bodyweight in chocolate and not put on an ounce. My weakness is chips and crisps and all the things that models aren't supposed to eat so I try not to eat them and if I do then I have to run a lot. Like, really a lot. Some things you have to give up.'

'What else did you have to give up and was it worth it?'

Now it was Ted's turn to give Laura a warning pinch, probably because he'd had to stroke her hair far too many times when she'd been working late, got overtired and started weeping on his shoulder.

She looked at the girl who'd just asked the question. It was hard to see anything but the bright-pink hair and the eyebrow rings, but if you like, *really* looked at her, there was something about her that made it impossible not to keep staring. Ted was equally transfixed and Laura could feel him trembling with the need to whip out a pen and force the girl to sign a contract there and then.

'I'm going to lay it on the line,' Laura told her. 'I've lost friends because they couldn't handle my new life and I split up with my boyfriend. It's been hard to keep myself in the game when loads of negative stuff is happening. But I take all those mixed feelings with me to photo shoots and use it in my work. If you want to be one half of a couple, then you can't be a good model too. You have to think only about yourself.'

'Oh, Laura, you're going to meet some cute little popsy and he'll heal your hurting heart,' Daisy exclaimed with a wink. 'It can get lonely at the top, girl. Everyone needs some boy-loving.'

Daisy should know. She was on her third marriage and she wasn't even thirty.

Laura shook her head firmly. 'The only thing I'm focusing on is the camera. Relationships just get in the way. Like, you can be alone without being lonely.' She was travelling at her own speed now and she didn't need anyone slowing her down.

There was a deathly silence as the entire audience contemplated Laura's embittered state of spinsterdom, while she lifted her chin defiantly and smiled. They could pity her if they liked but hey, she was the one with a £1,000,000 modelling contract to keep her warm at night.

'Well, let's see just how in love with the camera, Laura is,' Daisy said hastily. 'We've got a little surprise.'

The curtain behind the girls swooshed back to reveal a large TV screen. If this was the video of her doing karaoke to well, *anything*, there was going to be a full-blown massacre. Then the Siren logo flashed up and Laura let herself breathe out.

'This is a world exclusive of Laura's first TV spot for the new fragrance from House of Augustine, Siren . . .' Daisy lowered her voice in keeping with the solemnity of the occasion.

The screen went black. And then all there was, was Laura – gliding down that sweeping staircase, in a froth of black

296

lace couture, her skin glowing pearly-white in contrast, her hair a glossy cloud of curls.

In the next shot she was arranged langorously on the pink velvet chaise longe as if she was in some post-orgasmic bliss and not worrying that her breasts were about to pop free of the bodice. She smiled a secret smile as if the camera was her one true soulmate, before quirking her eyebrow knowingly.

'For a moment,' she husked, the slight twang of her Mancunian accent truly sounding exotic for the first and probably the last time. 'For an eternity. For ever. For a day. For time itself was held captive in her spell.'

There was a pause while the camera lovingly caressed her face. 'Siren, the first fragrance from House Of Augustine.'

The last shot had her rubbing her cheek coquettishly against the Siren bottle as if the minute they stopped filming, she was going to do unmentionably rude things to it. Then the screen faded to black again, apart from the stark, silver Siren logo spinning slowly around in the centre.

There was another silence, an exquisite silence. Laura glanced over at her parents in the audience, who looked stupefied; as if someone had slapped them both in the face with a wet fish. Ted was smiling proudly. Candy was 'wooh wooh'-ing at top volume and Daisy Bloom might have been looking just the teeniest bit envious.

'Wow, Laura,' she breathed. 'You really got it going on. I didn't know you were that sexy.'

Laura shrugged helplessly. 'Nope, neither did I.'

There were a few isolated handclaps from different corners of the room, rising in a crescendo until it was impossible to hear anything else but the gunshot scatter of palms smacking together and the sound of her name being shouted.

Applause. And it was all for her. Because she had symmetrical features and when the products were piled on and the lighting was good, she stopped being a pretty girl from Manchester and was transformed into a beautiful dream. Somebody that only existed in the moment.

That was fine. As long as when the moment passed, and the photos faded into blurry, yellowed images, she was still the same Laura that she used to be. But with a lot less attitude.

Daisy was wrapping things up now and the moment the end credits began to roll on the monitor, Laura got to her feet. Her mum was waving at her frantically, Ted was murmuring in her ear something about a photo-call but she was staring at that spot on the stage where her entire life had changed.

She could see the ghost of that other Laura biting her lip and squirming anxiously.

'Laura, really, you need to go and press the flesh and also

get the phone number of that girl with the pink hair,' Ted murmured urgently in her ear.

Ghost Laura looked up and for a second their eyes met, past and present collided, and the future lay just ahead, just in reach.

Fashionista Glossary

What the Heck Does All that Fashion Speak Actually Mean?

Agency

A company, which finds, promotes and gets work for models in exchange for a commission on their earnings. Good agencies will look after their models, put them up in special 'model' flats and generally act as surrogate parents.

Agent

The person at the agency who masterminds a model's career, who talks her up to clients, negotiates her contracts and fees and is super connected in the fashion world.

Beauty Shot

One of the trickiest of all shots, because it's usually a close-up of a model's face (for a beauty story) so every blemish, feature and stray eyebrow is visible. Not all models are used for beauty stories because their features aren't up to it.

Booker

Someone from the agency who looks after a model's day-to-day affairs from booking jobs to being a shoulder to cry on.

Booking-out

If a model wants to take some time off – say, two weeks – she is 'booking out for a fortnight'. Its a posh way of saying she's going on holiday.

Callback

The follow-up meeting with a prospective client after the first casting. A callback is a good thing because it usually means that the model has been short-listed for a job.

Casting

An interview or audition where a model meets with clients for a shoot or a show. They might be asked to walk up and down, have their photograph taken and be asked a few questions to get an idea of their personality.

Casting Director

The person in charge of choosing models for a big job, like an advertising campaign or a music video.

Cattle Call
A huge casting where models are shunted in and out super-fast and given a quick once-over by the casting director.

Catwalk
Another term for the runway used in fashion shows.

Check-in
Each day a model has to contact their agency or 'check in' to find out if there are any castings, go-sees or bookings.

Colourama
This is a huge roll of paper, which can be just about any colour in the world and which is unfurled and used as a backdrop (and even floor covering) on photo shoots. Photographers go mental if anyone puts marks on it!

Commercial
The sniffy description given to models who have a girl next-door quality and shoot catalogues and mainstream fashion.

Commission
The cut from a model's fee that the agency takes for their work.

Comp Card (also known as composite or zed card)

A model's calling card; it features her name, vital statistics (including shoe size) and a selection of her three or four best pictures. He or she will keep them in her book to leave behind on go-sees and the agency also sends out comp cards to clients, casting directors, fashion editors, etc. when they have a new model on their books.

Directional

Just a high-falutin way of saying that something or someone is 'fashion forwards' or wearing the trends before they happen.

Editorial

If a model has a good editorial look it means that she can do the edgy, high fashion that's needed for serious fashion magazines or catwalk shows. Most really successful models can do editorial and commercial.

Fit Model

Not just a really cute girl! Most designers make and tweak their clothes on a model whose measurements they consider ideal, so they can get the fit just right.

Glossy

An 8×10 black and white photograph, usually a head shot. Particularly used by actors that are sent out to casting directors.

Go-see

Literally to go see a client who's looking to cast models or simply to get your face known. Usually, a model will pop along to their office with their comp card and portfolio for a chat and, if they're lucky, will be kept in mind for any future work.

Haute Couture

French for high fashion. This is the collective term for the bonkers outfits you see on the catwalk that showcase a designer's talent and creativity but aren't practical for every-day wear.

Head Shot

A close-up (tight) shot of just the model's head and shoulders.

Jolie Laide

French for, quite literally pretty–ugly. Jolie laide is a good description for those girls who have strange faces that shouldn't be beautiful but are.

Layout

Technical term for all the bits that make up a printed page like the photos, words, logos and other bits and bobs.

Look Book

All designers have this. Basically it is a swank catalogue with pictures of all the clothes from their collection to send out to buyers and fashion directors.

New Face

A young model who's just signed with an agency – most models spend a little while on the 'new faces' board working for teen magazines and the like until they get a higher profile.

On Stay

This is a long stint that a model does away from home for another agency, so that he or she can get a lot of experience. Tokyo and Milan are popular 'on stay' locations.

On Trend

Just a really fashion way of saying that a designer's collection or a piece of clothing is very of the moment because it's working some of the season's biggest trends, like colour or cut.

Option

This is a tentative booking a client makes on a model, subject to confirmation. It's not unusual for a client to have first, second or third options on a particular model, depending on the kind of shoot they're doing or if the model has other requests for the same date.

Portfolio

A photo album with pictures of all the model's best work in it and that shows all her different looks, like beauty, editorial and commercial shots. The model will take her portfolio with her to castings and go-sees, and the agency will also send it out to clients.

Prêt-à-porter

French for 'Ready to wear'! Unlike the *haute couture* shows, *prêt-a-porter* collections are what influence the fashion we buy on the high street.

Residuals

Extra money a model gets if she appears in, say, a popular ad campaign which runs for a long time in lots of different territories.

Runway (See also Catwalk)

The long stage where models strut their stuff at a fashion show. Though it doesn't have to be a stage; it could be stairs, a walkway, a floating platform, anything, but the models still have to walk it – usually in very high heels.

Sample Size
A lot of clothes used in fashion shoots are samples sent by a designer, before they hit the shops. They're usually in a size to fit models rather than real girls. Sadly, sample size is usually a UK size 8 (US 4-6) and most models have to get into sample size otherwise the clothes they're modelling won't fit.

Scout
Agencies employ 'scouts' to find new models anywhere and everywhere – from browsing clothes in TopShop to the streets of Eastern Europe where a lot of the newer models have been discovered.

Season
Designer fashion collections run in seasons, autumn/ winter and spring/summer.

Talent Division
This is the part of an agency that would deal with celebrities who've been signed up as models, as well as representing actors and singers and helping their own models break into the world of entertainment, such as acting, singing or dancing.

Tearsheets (also called tears)

Instead of using pictures, portfolios can also contain tearsheets which are the actual pages from a magazine that show a model's shoots. This is proof that the model has experience and the more fancy the magazine, the better!

Test Shoots

Lots of people starting out in the fashion industry – models, photographers, stylists, etc. – will get together to do test shoots so they can all gain experience and have pictures to put in their portfolios – even if none of them are getting paid!

Can't get enough of the

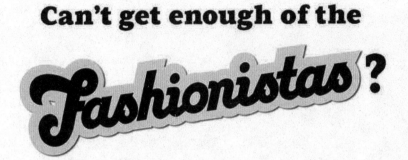

Fashionistas?

Then turn over for a sneak preview of Hadley's story...

Prologue

. . . It wasn't until the car pulled up by the Virgin check-in desk at LAX that Amber spoke again.

'You're really not going to get much modelling work, sweetie,' she advised casually. 'You have a short bottom lip and your arms have no definition. I'd aim for TV, if I were you.'

'Thanks, Mom.' Hadley slid out of the car, shades on in preparation for the paparazzi – but they seemed to have got lost en route from the courthouse. 'I know it will work out. You gotta have a dream in order for it to come true, right?'

'Yup, that's the spirit,' Amber drawled in a monotone. 'Shut the door, you're letting the heat in.'

The door slammed in Hadley's face and she stared at the two cases that the driver had just hauled out of the boot. What was she meant to do with them? Where was the studio lackey to carry them for her?

Newsflash; there wasn't one. She was going to have to do it for herself. She was going to have to do a lot of things for herself that she'd never done before. Like, check in her luggage and not lose her passport.

But how difficult could it be? Normal people managed to do it all the time.

Hadley grabbed the suitcase handles and started dragging them towards the entrance. It was just as well that she worked out so much.

'Miss? Excuse me, miss?'

She turned round to find two overweight women in matching 'California Dreamin'' T-shirts, staring at her. At least she could still rustle up a couple of fans, even if they were middle-aged and had bad dye jobs.

'Hi,' she said brightly, turning on her Hadley smile. 'How you guys doing?'

'Miss, you might find it easier if you roll your case on its wheels.'

Suitcases had wheels? Since when? Hadley shoved her sunglasses further up her nose and smiled at them. 'Oh, I know, but I prefer to drag them so I can work on my upper arms,' she lied. 'Gotta keep toned.'

Now they were both staring her, getting that glazed look that never led to anything good. She could predict the next words out of their mouths. Something along the lines of, 'You used to be so cute/It's such a shame you had to grow up/When are you going to make another movie?' (delete where applicable).

'Oh! My! God!' one of them squealed and Hadley braced herself for the inevitable.

'It's Hadley Harlow! We thought you were dead!'